PHILIP KIMBALL grew up working on his family's farm in Oklahoma. A graduate of the University of Kansas, he was a Woodrow Wilson Fellow as we'' ˌ Fulbright Scholar at the University of Heidelberg. Mr. Ki'' author of two novels, *Harvesting Ballads* and *Liar's M* York Public Library as one o 2000." He lives in Kansas.

ALSO BY PHILIP KIMBALL

Harvesting Ballads

Liar's Moon

Liar's Moon

A Long Story

PHILIP KIMBALL

A PLUME BOOK

PLUME
Published by the Penguin Group
Penguin Putnam Inc., 375 Hudson Street, New York, New York 10014, U.S.A.
Penguin Books Ltd, 27 Wrights Lane, London W8 5TZ, England
Penguin Books Australia Ltd, Ringwood, Victoria, Australia
Penguin Books Canada Ltd, 10 Alcorn Avenue, Toronto, Ontario,
Canada M4V 3B2
Penguin Books (N.Z.) Ltd, 182–190 Wairau Road, Auckland 10, New Zealand

Penguin Books Ltd, Registered Offices: Harmondsworth, Middlesex, England

Published by Plume, a member of Penguin Putnam Inc. This is an authorized
reprint of a hardcover edition published by Henry Holt & Company, LLC. For
information address Henry Holt & Company, LLC, 115 West 18th Street, New
York, New York 10011.

First Plume Printing, August 2000
10 9 8 7 6 5 4 3 2 1

A section of "Coyote in Hand" originally appeared, in slightly different form,
in *Green Mountains Review*.

 REGISTERED TRADEMARK—MARCA REGISTRADA

The Library of Congress has catalogued the Henry Holt & Company
edition as follows:
Kimball, Philip.
Liar's moon: a long story / Philip Kimball. —1st ed.
   p.   cm.
"A Marian Wood book"
ISBN 0-8050-6148-7 (hc.)
    0-452-28183-0 (pbk.)
   I. Title.
PS3561.I4165L52   1999   99-27191
813'.54—dc21   CIP

Printed in the United States of America
Original hardcover design by Michelle McMillian

PUBLISHER'S NOTE
This is a work of fiction. Names, characters, places, and incidents are either the
product of the author's imagination or are used fictitiously, and any resemblance
to actual persons, living or dead, business establishments, events, or locales is
entirely coincidental.

BOOKS ARE AVAILABLE AT QUANTITY DISCOUNTS WHEN USED TO PROMOTE PRODUCTS
OR SERVICES. FOR INFORMATION PLEASE WRITE TO PREMIUM MARKETING DIVISION,
PENGUIN PUTNAM INC., 375 HUDSON STREET, NEW YORK, NEW YORK 10014.

For Jennifer Brown,
who says she's still glad
she came

Thanks to Marian Wood for editing, to Christopher Schelling for webmeistering and representation, to George Garrett, Breon and Lynda Mitchell, and to Tony and Suzanne Whedon, just for being around.

Frederick Jackson Turner, in a paper, "The Significance of the Frontier in American History," delivered in 1893, said this:

> For a moment, at the frontier, the bonds of custom are broken and unrestraint is triumphant. This is not *tabula rasa*. The stubborn American environment is there with its imperious summons to accept its conditions; the inherited ways of doing things are also there; and yet, in spite of environment, and in spite of custom, each frontier did indeed furnish a new field of opportunity, a gate of escape from the bondage of the past; and freshness, and confidence, and scorn of older society, impatience of its restraints and its ideas, and indifference to its lessons, have accompanied the frontier.

Liar's Moon

The River Crossing

Most people in these parts thought it was ghosts. A hard-luck fur trapper walking his line on Good Gal Creek at the Ninnescah River was the first to see them, early in the morning, thick fog hanging over the water so he couldn't be sure. He'd heard the crows bickering over some dead meat or other, started working his way downwind, see if he could bag him a coyote. When he got to where he could make out the two of them tugging one on each end of a stretch of small intestine, he must have let out a gasp. They dropped the steaming entrails, heads up looking right at the trapper, hard to be sure, haze shot through with low dawn sunlight, but he swears by his guardian brother, the red-tailed hawk, their ears perked, lips curled back from large yellow teeth, greenish eyes glowing, hair tangled and snarled—one's

Brother

long and red, twisted all round the body, the other's woolly, black and matted—they were demon faces, not coyote, wildcat, or wolf. They let out a yip-yowl and disappeared, running low on all fours or just the hind legs, forepaws slapping the ground now and then, for balance it looked like, scattering crows into the mist.

By the time I came into the district, riding circuit for the Church in those days, rumors thick as mosquitoes in springtime along the river. Llorona, looking for her abandoned baby, some said, ancestors, come back to drive ever goddam one of us off the land. Others thought the McMillen twins, froze in last winter's blue norther—temperature dropped so fast drove the fence post where the thermometer was an inch and a half into the ground—died so quick they didn't even know they were dead yet. Somebody had to go out and assure them everything's all right, the turkey vultures that ate them been caught and buried in the cemetery along with what scraps and bones were found. The schoolmarm said it was witches, stole away a gypsy girl camped over on Bad Trouble Creek, the local exhorter believed the Antichrist, a plague of locusts and wormwood to follow. Saloonkeeper reckoned succubus, seduce you in your sleep, tempt young women out to lie down with the animals. Fathered the Widow Neary's miscarried child. *Los chupacabras*. Seen them dancing around dead cows on the slough grass bottoms, killed all the chickens in Huhnerman's coop, drank the blood, heavy smell of sulfur clinging to the carcasses. Hear them at night singing with the coyotes and the wolves.

Lying in my bedroll inside the sisal rope loop laid down to keep the rattlesnakes off, beneath a giant lightning-struck cottonwood, stockman's moon, not a breath of wind, I heard them for the first time: two foreign voices joining the group howl rising all around me, slowly waxing, dominant, to my overwrought ears, everywhere and nowhere, gargling and laughing, a pagan mournful plea and baleful menace bound up in one haunting plaint. It all came back to me, and I was afraid—the tattoo on my wrist in dying ember light, coyotes everywhere surrounding me, guilt, the memory of my lost baby brother, the Ole Woman's favorite, the one she called the chap of infinite possibilities, and of little Sojourner, the African's youngest child. All of us searching in the pale bleak river dawn, rage and despair, trembling against the stench of freshet mud. I remembered the Ole Woman, what had happened a lifetime, a scant thirteen years, before.

Restless. She'd never confess it, always claimed to be a hardworking, God-fearing drudge, but it was clear to the whole family, to all of us fourteen children, the Ole Woman was at heart an adventurer. It was what always got her into trouble. The Ole Man a little bad to drink, footloose, what to a young strapling fifteen-year-old girl slopping hogs in Indiana would look dashing and chivalrous, an escape from the dreary farm and the claustrophobic small town, a heroic struggle to make a home in the Kansas Territory with the land warrant the Ole Man got as bounty for his service in the Mexican War, but what to a strong-willed woman, one of the first to try to break the plains, digging in on the Great Bend Prairie to keep herself and her fourteen kids from blowing away, would be clearly recognized worthlessness.

Left her for months at a time to fend for herself. The only childhood memory I have of him in the flesh: a trip into town, I must have been nine or ten, he wanted to do a little horse-trading. We'd stop off at every shack and dugout along the way to see if there was anything we could bring back from the general store, and every place we'd stop the man, if he was around, but more often than not the woman, would come out to meet us, first living thing other than the skinny cow and a goat or two she'd seen in over a month sometimes, offer a dram, a road-shortener, a belly-warmer, antidote to bilious fever or to snakebite. Trip that should have taken two days there and back lasted seems like a week. Started out with a buckboard and a team of Morgans, returned on foot leading a pissel-tailed mule. When I worried, the Ole Man would tell me the reason we came out west was to escape suffocating social restriction and unreasonable regulation, but some rules necessary to avoid the slippery slope into barbarity, and one of the most essential is: never refuse a drink. Even at the last supper Jesus served up wine. Can't hold it against the man, Kentucky sour mash wasn't available. But think how much more impressive it would have been, instead of this is my blood, he holds up a gleaming amber shot: this is my *spirit*!

He was no-account. Said the prairie was wild and woolly and full of fleas, and a man to get by had to be the same. Only more so. While the Ole Woman and us kids were keeping the homestead from total ruin, he was out speculating, either with our livestock or with the Preemption Act. Carried a little log cabin carved out of blackjack oak just for the purpose, twelve inches by fourteen, could put it together in a few minutes, had an old army-issue latrine shovel, from his days in the Mexican War, to dig a well with. They never did ask at the land office how deep or if he'd actually struck water, just if he dug a well, and the promise of a little snort in town got him a witness to come along and testify to the nifty twelve-by-fourteen cabin he'd erected. Sometimes he'd just split a stick, wedge a piece of glass in it, drag in an old two-by-twelve, cover it with a blanket to sleep under, next day claim he'd built a house with glass windows and a plank floor and he's off to the old states to collect the family. Get a half section for sixty to eighty cents an acre, sell it at a hundred and fifty. But don't think he was exploiting the territory, like a parasite sapping the economic strength of the prairie. He was actually doing a lot of good, to hear the Ole Woman tell it. Keeping the assets liquid, so to speak. No sooner close a deal than he'd head to the nearest ridgepole, hay-thatched goat-house saloon, set himself down, not rise again till he'd put his entire profit back into local circulation. Amiable, hell of a good storyteller, and, from the evidence, at least adequate in his conjugal duties. But, no two ways about it, a good-for-nothing ne'er-do-well.

And the Ole Woman got restless. That's when the trouble began. Found out another family turning sod thirty-five miles downstream, said it was time to move on, damn country getting so crowded can hardly turn around, next thing you know we'll all be trying to shit through the same hole.

One night a bunch of men came to the sod dugout to ask for some water from our well. The Ole Woman stood at the door, her nose wrinkled against the smell of cheap whiskey and randy smiles.

"Where you men from?"

Their horses uneasy behind them, a bois d'arc bow and quiver of arrows, a gunnysack jiggling and bouncing, whining and whimpering, hung from the pommel strings. "Missouri, ma'am."

"What's your business?"

"Could we speak with your husband, ma'am?"

Her knuckles whiten on the broom handle she's carrying. "He's not . . ."

Creaking leather, the men look from her to each other. "Not home, ma'am? We were just wanting a little water for our saddle stock and permission to pitch our blankets down on the creek out of the wind."

"What's your business?"

Points to the gunnysack. "Hunting coyotes, got a bunch of pups out of a den to sell."

"Don't look like trappers to me. What else you doing?"

Pushes his hat back on his head with his thumb, narrow eyes scanning the place, shrugs. "There's a runaway slave family may of come through here. We aim to bring them back to their rightful owner. Just need water and a place to sleep." Big grin. "Down by the creek we were thinking." Rubs the chin whiskers, her feed-sack cotton dress blown taut against hip and thigh. "But since your old man's not here, maybe there'd be room, you know—"

"Slave catchers, huh. Bounty hunters."

"Just trying to make an honest living, ma'am." Takes a step toward her, scratches the left ear, looking back at his companions. "Now we sure are ready for some rest—"

"You can rest in hell! We came out to this country to escape the dark evil poisoning the heart of the nation." Raises the broom. "If you all aren't off this place by the time I count to three, I'm going to start to swinging. And when I stop there won't be nobody left standing but me. One . . ."

They all laugh. "Ma'am, I like a filly with spirit."

"Two . . ."

Another step forward reaching out for her, a roundhouse *swish*, broomcorn and ash catches him solid upside the head, showering a broad spiral of sweat, the others flinch. He touches his fingertips to his temple, looks at them, big grin, turns, legs gone rubbery, wobbles once, and crumples to the ground. The Ole Woman strides over him, axlike stroke square on top of the next man's hat, driving it down over his nose and ears. The others back away, turn, and scramble for the horses snorting wild-eyed at their tethers—*god damn shit, ma'am*—two of them return, arms held above their heads to ward off raining broomsticks—*Jesus*—retrieve their fallen buddies—*fucking hell*—and hightail it off toward the creek.

"Three."

The Ole Woman was riled, the last straw that broke the camel's back. We started packing all our personal and house-hold effects: an iron hog-rending kettle, the one they hid little Will under to protect him from the mosquitoes, a squirrel rifle, and a chopping ax. She lined all fourteen of us up, got out her needles and dyestuffs, indigo, goldenrod, and cochineal, tattooed a blue-yellow-and-red jayhawk on each of our left wrists. Just in case we got lost, she said, kidnapped or carried off by child merchants, she'd always be able to recognize us if she ever ran across us again.

At dawn we hitched up Spot and Buck to the broken-down wagon, nailed a note for the Ole Man on the dugout door: *gone west, maybe you can catch us.* We'd eaten all the poultry except for two hens and the tall Shanghai rooster, tied the cow and her calf on behind, the spotted hog we called the sweet-potato pig, and moved out across humid gray-green and blue prairie tilted and heaved on every side, old yaller hound dog running along beside nipping at the wheels.

We hadn't traveled a mile when Old Yaller took off, bounding high above the bluestem, back arched, head and ears cocked, forelegs tucked to the breast, hovering, then dropping from sight, sparrows swirling from the grass in front and settling in her wake. Atta girl, gonna have jackrabbit for supper tonight. But when she returned all she had was a raveled wool shawl. Put it on the ground by the front wagon wheel and dashed back in the direction she had come, stopped ten paces off looking at us, head cocked sideways, waiting for somebody to follow. She led us to a buffalo wallow where a black woman and five kids huddled asleep. Old Yaller barked, the woman started awake, on her feet in one motion, legs spread before the children, brandishing an old enameled soup ladle gleaming dull gray light.

The Ole Woman stepped back and smiled. "Sleeping on that cold wet ground sure put you in a churlish mood."

Eyes dart from the Ole Woman, to Yaller, to all of us rimming the wallow. "That's not the half of it."

"I reckon not. I ran a mean-looking bunch of slave-catching cur off my former place last night."

"Your former place?"

"We're headed west. Where you going?"

A long anguished pause. "Anywhere but here."

Laughs. "Looks like we both need some help, and the only people round I see to give it is you and me."

Perplexed, quick glances at the five children bunched together under a shawl the same weave as the one Yaller brought, sucks her top front teeth.

The Ole Woman sweeps both arms up and over the empty plains. "Who else you got to trust?"

"You run them off, huh?"

"Yep."

Slowly sticks the ladle back in her skirts. "West sounds good to me."

"Then let's get to jumping, woman."

She stands there awhile, looks all around her, the endless land and sky, big cautious smile for the first time, maybe a hungry, acquiescent, and exhausted grimace. "I'm much obliged."

"My fourteen and your five make nineteen kids, divided by two leaves nine and a half each. Looks to me like I'm the one four and a half ahead."

The spring had been halfway rainy upstream, had to bump and jumble along the banks of the Ninnescah until we found a flat wide shallow place to ford. Mighty crowded in the wagon, nineteen of us kids when we were all in, which wasn't too often, and I was in charge. Nineteen, I thought, until we made camp that night downwind of a creek bluff, kindled a fire of deadfall and buffalo chips, nineteen of us should be, until I took a head count, two or three times, and only came up with seventeen. Little baby brother Will and the African's youngest child, Sojourner, both unaccounted for. We thought and thought, no one could remember seeing them since we crossed the Ninnescah. We called and circled, voices swirled and lost out across the grasslands, answered by the yip-yowls and screams of the coyotes. Backtracked all night long as best we could find our way in the cold white moon, spread out earshot from one another, until we arrived hoarse, cold, and shivering at the river as the sun rose, found indentations in the mud between the wagon ruts where they'd bounced out below the cutbank where we'd crossed. Handprints and footprints along the brake, coyote tracks, one, then two, then lost among too many to count.

Thirteen years gone by. And I'm come along the Ninnescah again, to chase ghosts, creatures, haunting these desolate plains. The embers of my campfire now gone to gray ash, the blue-yellow-red jayhawk on my left wrist luminous in ghostly light, my horse snorts and cocks her ears. The coyotes stop their singing, the two strange voices continue a wavering duet, each modulating to discordant harmony at the other's changes, an exuberant, heathen celebration, the shimmering prairie broken beneath the moon. I clutch my Bible. Devil's work. Somebody has to get them. And it looks like, as a man of the cloth, it falls to me.

I didn't know where to start, not sure what I wanted to find. Read the Bible and prayed, didn't help. Finally decided to look for the trapper who'd been the first to see them. I asked around at the taverns, the general stores and post offices, nobody knew where the man was, an outsider nobody ever had much to do with, not sure he's still in the country. Best thing to do, head out along the Ninnescah up toward Mad Woman Creek. Since there was a family at Blackstrups Mill needed a funeral said, that's what I did.

It had turned cold and wet, a penetrating drizzle from dense blanket clouds overspreading the land, distant crumpled thunder, my horse carefully picking her way over the muddy gumbo along the river. We stopped at every shanty and hut, asking about the trapper. On the third day out a young woman sitting on a rocking chair under a wagon sheet strung from the cabin to a locust tree, a cowbell suspended from the eaves slowly clunking in the wind, buckskin dress, her hair the color of winter bluestem, braided, slick with animal fat, nostrils corroded at the edges as if by fire, a rough-carved soapstone pipe held between her teeth, quillwork across her knees, leans back and laughs at my inquiry.

"What are you after that reprobate for? I gave up looking for him long time ago, and the only reason I wanted him was he run off with a couple of my best steel traps."

"I need to talk to him about something of considerable interest to me."

She looks at my horse and then at me. "Take my word on it, you don't want him. You're the god-speaker, aren't you, been asking about the spirits people say spooking about. You don't want *him*. But I know what you *do* want."

"What's that?"

"A coyote den about three mile up the creek in a dry draw behind a chinaberry thicket."

"What will I find there?"

"The creatures. Unless they've already packed up and left."

"Left?"

"Coyote's a mighty wily animal, God's own dog. They'll change their lair ever couple of weeks, usually have three or four to choose from roundabouts. They think something's sniffed out where they are, they're gone. But the last time I was up that way I saw Old Red, that's the head bitch of the pack, saw her hunting mice up on the rise, been six–seven days ago. Good chance they're still there."

"You mean the creatures?"

"They seem to be part of the pack."

13

"You've seen them?"

She pounds the soapstone pipe in the palm of her hand, spits, blows in the bowl to clear the stem, fishes a deerhide pouch from between her breasts. "There're nine or ten in the pack: Long Tooth the head man, Gimp helps with the pups, she may be Long Tooth's sister, I'm not sure, and Tore Ear takes his turn at the den, brings in his share of mice and ground squirrels. There's only three pups this season—and then there's the other two."

"The creatures?"

"Yes."

"You've seen them?"

Finishes tamping tobacco with the thumb. "Heard them, caught glimpses of what might of been them. Coyote a wily rascal, and those two the wiliest of the bunch. The spring after we settled on the creek, I was alone, late at night, must have been first choir practice with that year's younglings, found out later it was Gimp had them out. She'd crooned a simple short song, kind of a *here we are, anyone else around*, and the pups were trying to squawk the same thing after her." She stops to light the pipe, blows puffs of smoke about her, offers it to me. I decline. She looks at me, studying me, it seems. I look away. She's young, peculiar, takes another draft from the pipe, lets the smoke roll slowly from the nostrils and the mouth. "There's a stool inside the door, why don't you fetch it out and sit. Probably a cup of hully gully left in the pot on the stove."

It's dark inside, have to stand crouched beneath the low ceiling awhile to let the eyes adjust. Heavy sweet aroma, damp strings of wild garlic, a haunch of cured venison slung from the rafter beams, steel traps hanging from pegs driven into the walls, the cot in the corner made of sycamore branches, twisted straw, and army-issue wool blankets, a tin cup standing beside a sterling silver mill, a bowl and plate, an old carbon-steel butcher knife on top of an oaken dresser by the cast-iron potbelly stove. The fire is out, drizzle sounds stronger on the canvas roof. I sniff the oily, bitter decoction in the pot and decide against it, take the stool outside. We sit watching rain fall on the Ninnescah.

"You were telling me about the creatures and the coyotes."

She slaps a mosquito on her forehead. "Damn wet weather." Picks up the quillwork. "I heard nine pups putting up a garble. Pretty good for the first lesson, and Gimp thought it was time for an embellishment, *I'm here and feeling pretty damn good my own self, how about you?* All of a sudden these two hoarse howls like no dog you'd ever heard in your life. I near jumped out of my skin, it come as such a surprise, didn't know what it was, a wouzer come to devour the coyotes, sasquatch or something. But when Gimp started right back up as if nothing more than a sour note, and the two strange voices jump on in, even though far from the pitch, I decided I just had to find out what was going on.

"Next evening right at sundown I sneak up to a bunch of sand plums on a rise an easy bow shot beyond the plain where I figure they did their rehearsing, waited for the moon to rise. When it was three hands high a coyote comes limping up from the creek. That was Gimp, first I'd seen her. I thought just a goathead sticker in her left forepaw at the time, but turns out she's crippled. I've seen her since with Tore Ear or Long Tooth hunting together. They run the mouse into the burrow and start digging while Gimp lurks at the rear door for the mouse to panic and jump out the hole right into her mouth. Doesn't need that no-good forepaw at all. Most times two coyotes trade off digging and ambushing until they both get their fill, but Gimp can't dig, so she stays at the escape hatch gobbling mice beyond her share, to belch up for the pups or for Old Red to eat. She does her part watching the den too, so everybody else can go out to hunt and she gives music lessons, which is what I was telling you about.

"She came up from the creek and sat down in the middle of the open prairie and here come the pups, jumping, tumbling, biting faces and scruffs, jaw-wrestling, chins on each other's shoulders, hopping up on backs, rolling on the ground belly up, finally gathering around Gimp in the moonlight. She started out like the night before with a simple *this is where we live*, and the pups listened and then gave it their best. The moon two days past full, I could see them plain from the sand-plum bushes. This went on for two or three more songs, nothing unusual, the nine pups doing their damnedest cater-wauling away at the moon, none of the uncoyote howling I'd heard from the cabin. I was ready to give up and leave when a scream right behind me set every hair on my body straight up on end like I'd been struck by lightning. I jumped and turned, spooking Gimp and the whole choir after her to the creek. A thrashing through the sand plums, something knocked me down—all I saw for sure was that there were two of them, lop-ing along all fours, ass end up in the air, hightailing it after Gimp and the other pups. And the ripest stench you'll ever want to get wind of. I scrambled downstream to the cabin and barred the door. Sat up till dawn with my butcher knife in the bed beside me.

"Next night they were out again, but when I got up the nerve to go looking they were nowhere to be seen, packed up and moved after finding me in the bushes. I've been hearing them ever since, now and then catch sight of something strange dashing through the big bluestem the other side of the river or disappearing in a clump of sunflowers. Sometimes along the creek bottom that stench hangs in the air and I'm overcome by secret eyes watching.

"That's all I know about them. Except I saw Old Red come out of that chinaberry thicket I was telling about, must have been six days ago, to greet Long Tooth and beg food from him, and I suspect that's where the whole clan is holed up still."

She stops, rubs the side of her nose with the hand holding the pipe, looking askance at me, knocks the ashes out, puts it in the patch pocket of her outfit. Rain trickles off the canvas roof into a puddle seeping around the legs of my stool, clatters through the leaves of the trees along the river, the land expands into the mist. I shiver, a mosquito whining about my ear. A man of the cloth, looks like it falls to me. "You think you could lead me to the den?"

Stares right at me, what looks like surprise that this is where it's been heading lingers in her face. She finally squints into the low clouds. "I expect it'll clear up by morning. I got a pot of fatback and beans inside. That floor is damp, weather like this, but it beats sleeping in a hollowed-out log."

The next morning is clear, hot and muggy but a strong wind from the south. We lie in tall bluestem on a knoll about ten rods from the den, stay there all day without seeing a thing. Beginning to think they've moved again, or the woman telling me a tale, a twisted joke, some kind of a snipe hunt or other. At sundown she taps me on the shoulder and points to the next rise up-channel. I can't see anything at first in the thick low slant light, then a brown animal slides down the grassless slope into the creek, trots out on the floodplain, stops, looks right at where we are, a lop-eared coyote. *That's Tore Ear*. After an instant of rigid attention, the good ear cocked forward, he turns toward the chinaberry thicket, croons *woo-oo-wow*, a gray coyote limps out—*Gimp*—tail wagging, spine arched, head down, ears laid back, licks his muzzle, drops the forelegs flat on the ground, hindquarters raised, tail wagging, hops side to side, then up licking his muzzle again, right paw raised. Something in the bushes, can't see what. Tore Ear moves closer, regurgitates, I can barely make it out in the evening sun, red, tangled red hair, something, an animal, lapping up the half-digested mice.

"Old Red?"

"No. That's one of them."

When we got back to the cabin I told her I wanted to capture them. Her face went blank, the eyes widened, a sudden intake of air. Sat silently staring at me, reluctant, angry it looked like, as if remembering something painful, I thought, even, she was going to run me out. Finally turned to her bed and didn't speak the rest of the evening.

I lay awake all night, excited, maybe by more than the thought of the creatures out there and who or what they might be. I could hear the woman breathe in the darkness, toss and turn in the sycamore cot, could tell she was also unable to sleep. In the middle of the night she rose and came to me. She would do it.

"We'll wait for them to enter the den, then dig them out, but we need help. No one around here would want to go near them, too many wild rumors. You ride on upstream, we'll need shovels, pickaxes, ropes and nets or something, see if you can find anyone doesn't know anything or care."

"Are you afraid?"

She looks at me, hardly make her out in the lunar light filtering in through the oilpaper window, a chuckle deep in her throat. "I been living alone on these plains for a long time."

I brought back three drifters from Missouri I found sitting around a table in a run-down roadhouse, playing cards and swapping lies. Said they knew all about raiding coyote dens, willing to come along for a steel ax each. We coiled our ropes around us, picks and shovels across our shoulders, and began the tedious walk up the creek channel: a hot night, not much wind to blow our stink away, a feeding frenzy of mosquitoes floating along with each one of us, the slightest slap or curse maybe enough to give us away, quivering howls and barks spectering up around us, which side, how far? And then the alien moan joining in the coyote song, or setting itself off from it, surrounded, stark, an anguished loneliness relieved against the welling accompaniment, shivering down the spine.

We settled among the sand-plum bushes on the rise above the floodplain of the creek and waited. My palms sweated, heartbeat never slowed, even after an hour or more crouched low to the ground trying to pierce the dark shadows of heavy clouds flowing across the expanse of grass separating us from the entrance to the den. The howling stopped. The wind rose and blew the clouds away. The sky turned blue and green at the horizon, then white and violet red. We waited. The man next to me set an arrow in his bois d'arc bow, I reached out to stop him, shook my head: *no shooting*. Suddenly the chinaberry shook, Gimp out to greet Old Red, Long Tooth and

Tore Ear trotting down the steep path from the west bluff. Then one quick revelation, a face, the eyes seemed to reflect hard yellow light all the way across the distance, then two of them, red and tangled, black and woolly, barely visible above the bluestem, behind the leaves at the mouth of the den, and gone!

We spread out and start forward, the man beside me unquivers his arrow again, Long Tooth and Tore Ear see us, take out over the plain, Gimp growls and woofs, bares her teeth, ears laid back against her head, tail thrashing side to side, finally turns and hobbles away a few dozen paces downstream, stops to watch us, barking and whining all the while. The rest of them must be inside the den. We begin to chop away the chinaberry, the sun high enough now to light the entrance through the mangled bushes.

"Here we go, boys. Start to digging, a tunnel probably two–three feet long, down into the chamber. We got them trapped for sure."

We hadn't gone six inches before Old Red leapt out at us, we stumble back, she snarls and huffs, saliva and snot flying, the man with the bow draws an arrow—*don't shoot!*—pierces the breast below the throat, she yelps a sharp cry of alarm, twisting in the air, snapping at the flights at the end of the shaft, rolls down the foot of the bluff to the edge of the creek, the woman slams the bow from the man's hand with the handle of her spade. For no good reason now. Old Red lies trembling by the water, Gimp crawling closer on her belly, whimpering, a stream of blood diluting out across the limestone bed.

"Asshole."

"There's a bounty on prairie wolves."

The man stands there holding his wrist, the hand beginning to swell. The woman stands, tears welling in her eyes. The rest of us slowly get back to work.

We approached the chamber shovelful at a time, could hear the pups inside, but nothing from the devilish creatures we were after. Right before we broke in, the woman picked up her spade, motioned the rest of us away, climbed up the bank, leaned down close, and sniffed the cold air rolling from the opening.

"They're in there."

The helpers smell the foul odor, move down the slope to the creek. "What the hell's that. I thought we were after coyote pups."

"Let's get back to digging, we're almost in."

"What are we digging for?"

The woman rises up from her knees, brushes them off. "I can't say."

"Never smelled no coyote ever stunk like that before."

"What do you mean, you can't say?"

The woman looks at me, I shrug. "We don't know what's in that den with those coyote pups."

The two stand there staring at us, look at each other, throw down their shovels. "I don't like the sound or the smell of this. Let's get out of here."

They jump the creek, walk away a few steps, one stops, jumps back, pulls a knife and hacks off Old Red's ears, then takes after the other across the floodplain to the third, sitting on the rise in front of the sand-plum thicket still holding his swollen hand. They confer, make their way down the channel toward the river, a mournful howl rises from both sides of the creek as they disappear around the bend. I look at the woman squinting against the sun at where they've gone. She doesn't look at me, turns directly to her spade, and chops away at the hole. I raise my pick and join in.

We broke into the chamber. The three pups cowering in the farthest end rolled on their backs, feet up and paws curled down, pissed when we picked them up and stuck them in a gunnysack. But no sign of anything else, except the thick stench.

"They've got to be here, there couldn't be another way out, not in this bluff."

"Maybe they didn't come in."

"Use your nose."

My eyes grow used to the dark, the dust settling out of the shaft of sunlight pouring in through the hole we've chopped. The chamber clean and dry, smooth walls and floor, no droppings, bones, just the powerful odor: human sweat? and sulfur? Then I can see, off to the side, the other passageway. Just room to stick my head in, the stink, a sudden growl and swipe at my face, jam my head against the ceiling, rock back on my heels, the woman laughs.

"They're here, what did I tell you."

"But what are they?"

"One way to find out."

It's rough digging in the narrow confines of the chamber, end up using my jackknife and fingers, the woman behind me, totally committed to the task now, it looks like, throwing out the clods and rocks I dislodge. The closer I get the quieter the two creatures become. I'm too weary to think much about

22

what I'm doing, why I'm feverishly pawing at the hard-packed earth, sweat filling the eye sockets, fingernails bleeding, don't notice the constant barking and howling of coyotes, the caw-ing calls of crows outside, nor know anymore what I expect to find. Ghosts? Devils? Haven't looked at my Bible for a week now, not preached a word, a cadaver upstream at Blackstrups Mill still awaiting my ministrations to be returned to the dust. I stop to rest my aching arms. Some vague surge of guilt, the Ole Woman and the African, alone on the high-plains claims staked out west between Ladder and White Woman Creek above the Cimarron. I look down at the jayhawk tattoo obscured beneath the sweat and dirt, blasphemy, I *must* be mad, and begin to dig again.

I break into the second chamber, the eyes adjust to the deeper darkness, takes a while to recognize matted and tangled hair, arms and legs balled together. Trembling, I slowly reach out. Black Woolly pounces, a growl, teeth flashing, a slash at my arm, I scramble backwards on all fours. The woman gives me a blanket to pitch onto them, I strike, finally wrestle the two apart, bundle up the red one, kicking, biting, and spitting, piss splattering over me and the earthen walls, squirm back to the first chamber where there's room enough for the woman to tie the blanket. We pull it out, crashing down through the saplings to the creek. Before I can get back to the mouth of the den, Black Woolly leaps out and scampers upstream over the west bluff: damnation! A chorus of yip-yowling and barking rises all around us.

We got the red one to the cabin and released him from the blanket. He is hideous. Naked and burnt brown by the sun, callosities on the knuckles, the heels of the hands and knees, scars and cockleburs, hunkered in the corner, snarling at us, cutting sulfurous farts. I stare, drenched in sweat, aching, lacerated and bleeding, can see beneath the grime on the left wrist—it has to be my brother's—the one I lost, the favorite child, the chap of infinite possibilities—Will's jayhawk tattoo.

We spent the next two days searching the draws and coulees for Sojourner. The woman no longer spoke to me, fixed me when we'd return, exhausted, frustrated to the cabin, with an angry stare and loathing I couldn't fathom. A growing, aimless revulsion eating away at me, cold fear—could this animal that clawed at the warped boards of the walls when we were gone, scratched and chewed the sides of the wooden crate we had to put it in to prevent escape until paws and muzzle were bloody, that snapped at us and ground its teeth when we approached, that sat in the corner, still covered with the dirt and fleas of the coyote den, silently rocking back and forth, abject, alone, gazing at the moon blurred in the oilpaper window, stared at the wavering surface of the water pan put before it—fear turned to terror torn from fitful sleep in the middle of that chaotic first night, savage howls, every coyote alive on the vast dark prairie all now seemed to prowl and sniff close by this dank, fragile hut, the raucous calls dissolving the human, sacred constructs of the world, my very mind and soul, into absolute wildness—could this animal that paced the dirt floor just beyond my sight, whimpering, anguished sweat and farts constricting the air, could he ever have been, ever be my brother again?

The morning we left I took my Bible down to the Ninnescah and tried to pray. Blue-black clouds clotted above the tall grasses of the floodplain, the flat, meandering river. Thunder rumbled. Pressed down upon me, mosquitoes swarmed, I could not speak. The book heavy in my hand began to shiver. I cursed and heaved it out into the shallow muddy water, a flight of cranes startled, rose from the opposite shore.

Coyote in Hand

Autumn Tallgrass | She needs to seek a vision of the sky. It is Texas, it is the Brazos River, that much has been told her by the soldier uncle and some decrepit god-speaker taking her back. It has happened before, abducted by horsemen many summers ago when she was a little girl. Slowly, tediously, it comes back to her as the flat miles pass. It's the morning clouds that lie on the horizon beyond the trees, the heat. Texas! That complicated world the folk all talk about of wooden structures and dusty streets, stores and churches, saloons where firewater spirits possess the idle hunters and long-knife soldiers, bizarrely painted women fuck for greenbacks instead of pleasure. They say the men bugger goats and cattle, bluster and gun each other down just to settle bets how long before the blowflies cluster. Have to roll their prick up to get their tight dungarees on, the women quiet and meek to look at, warm and tenacious as river-bottom mud in the summertime. And she used to be one of them.

She remembers. A truck garden along the river, warm air from Mexico slowly flowing up the valley. She is six or seven winters old, a woman thirty paces up the slope is planting a row of sweet corn. Grackles rise suddenly cawing from the cottonwood canopy, the woman stands where she'd hunkered, it's her other mother! A gunnysack of seed, low crystal sunlight on the cotton-print bonnet, the fold of her dress, the shadow thrown long and blue across rough-tilled grooves in the soil, the last vision of her, her call, a name she couldn't grasp garbled up in the unshod pounding of hooves. Screaming. She turns to see a squat brown buffalo-horned rider and a pinto pony, she's hit from somewhere, grabbed, legs and feet whirling in the air, yanked down hard to the gray bony wet rump of a horse. Breath knocked loose, they course through locust and mesquite, jump and splash the creek up the steep bank and gone across the floodplain on the other side. The only thing to do is press against the pain, the sweat and dust, hold on, and ride.

Three horsemen, running a herd of eight or ten animals, stop beneath a hillock in a copse of redbud trees. Laugh and joke, stubby fingers hold out jerky. She does not eat. They push on.

Days and nights pass like this, tied to the pony, piss running down the leg mingling with the grime of the trail. Hot. A constant wind blowing, a lifetime like this, eroded away till nothing more to miss, faulty memory lingers and disintegrates, the mother, a father, sisters, just numbness and fear.

The three riders leave off bantering, grow sullen, cling to the ponies. Days and nights cycle and repeat, sun rises on the right behind her, sets on the left in her eyes, a constant wind, hungry, exhausted delirium. Then the riders perk up, sit higher on the blankets, begin to grin and shout. She starts from a rhythmic trance of muscle contractions, eyes stuck shut, dull aching in the joints, chafed thighs, rawhide burns, blisters, wrists and knuckles stiff from grasping. The lead rider points: morning sunshine collected in smoke rising beyond the domed horizon, the encampment below the crowns of newly leaved sycamore and elm, crows against a low and threatening sky. They file down the steep trail, tipis strung out along the river as far as she can see. A dense mist lies close on the water, thunder, dogs bark and whine, boys and girls run, prance, chase, swarm around, women cling, pull her from the horse, spit, beat her knees and elbows, kick, taunt, and jeer, then shove her to a fire. Numb, not really aware of tears streaming down the face, the pinches and the blows. Burning sticks appear, flourish, and poke. A scream grows somewhere distant. That screaming, she realizes after a moment of wonder, is her.

She wakes. Lost and alone. Pain pushing consciousness out, all memory burned away of who she is, the center of the face shriveled, crusted over. Terror. Grief. A brutal black embrace. Blinks the eyes unstuck, a tipi top, stars glisten, a twisted grass mat, buffalo fell, an enormous flat, dark face floats, blocks out the moon. A large woman, whispering a concatenation of stark, senseless noise, gently applies strong-smelling lard to the burn. Singing, an unintelligible croon, hardly separable from the wind caught above in the smoke hole, the thrum and loft of taut buffalo hide, the changes in the air. She turns, stares, listens. Becomes convinced, the salve, the soft, warm hand on the forehead, she understands what the woman means: *I will save your life*. And is overcome, desire, relief, unbounded gratitude, hard to tell from love.

New Mother called her Girl-with-Hair-like-Tallgrass-in-Autumn. She was dependent on her, afraid to leave the tipi. Finally New Mother forced her out, alone, lonely, her face scabbed and painful, the foreign children crowding around her, dogs yipping and snapping at her feet as she walked. One evening she ventured along the riverbank, heard something, a rhythmic stomping, like the drumming of prairie chickens, singing perhaps, saw it, a creature, a spirit, a man dancing among the trees. She stopped, afraid to stay, afraid to leave. He came to rest a few paces from her, his back glistening, heaving with each breath. Then motionless. He slowly turned, the face painted yellow and red, saw her standing in the dusk at the edge of the woods, suddenly fell to his haunches, spread out his arms like eagle wings. Looked at her darkly. She wanted to run, but where to? The entire world destroyed but for this one spot where she stood, terrified. He rose and cautiously moved toward her, held out a hand, with the other described a fleet, dancing flourish across the air, repeated it, inviting her, she realized, into the very middle of the clearing. He helped her across. They danced.

His name was Coyote Dropping. From that time on she followed him around, even traveled with him to other encampments scattered up and down the river. They watched meadowlark, turkey vulture, grasshopper, butterfly, harvester ant, rattlesnake, possum, prairie dog, antelope, deer. They

imitated every creature they saw, captured their spirit in movement. She would watch when ceremonies formed around him,
unexpected at first, spontaneous gatherings, it seemed to her,
heathen magic out on the high plains when the enormous flat
moon rose golden red, the night stayed stifling hot, and the
wind continued to blow, when the drummers chanted, the fire
boss stacked on seven sacred woods, and all the folk danced
until dust, then rising sun, obscured the stars. She was slowly
pulled into the circle by New Mother, by Coyote Dropping,
but there was distance there—he seemed by choice to cultivate
it between himself and the folk, what attracted her to him in
the first place—which she could not avoid. She could not give
up those fractured images she knew were her Texas family and
home.

Coyote Dropping began to teach her to speak and what
there was to talk about, what she had to understand to get
along. He knew more about the folk, and what the ancestors
had done before them, than anybody else around, observed
everything as closely as he did the animals, and he also knew
there was a world beyond the Llano Estacado, wanted her to
teach him to palaver in her tongue, asked all about her time
with the Texans, the only one who ever did. She realized when
she finally tried to tell him what she remembered, what
remained after the brutal pony ride and her life among the
folk, the key to that lost world was words. Sounds she had
thought all-encompassing, as bound up with things as green
on leaf, she was learning now were specific, grafted by a particular people on a particular place, and were in danger of
being pushed from her mind by the oddly structured tongue
New Mother and Coyote Dropping spoke, the plains they

wandered with wolves and crows, following the migrating buffalo.

Her Texas language became useful to the elders among the folk, forced more and more to deal with agencies and armies contending with them for life on the prairie. These dog-faced, crooked-footed, flop-eared, laughable incompetents, whatever else you could say about them, were stubborn, persistent as river-bottom mosquitoes in the summertime, magpies at a pronghorn kill. Some of them even smart enough to pick up the ways of the folk at war, damn nuisance nipping at your heels clear out on the high plains where no other generation of their kind had ever dared set foot. And what those damn Texans and their Colt revolvers couldn't accomplish, the sickness they brought with them did. Bad medicine to suffer them close to you, the grasslands beginning to teem with them, locusts in a dry year. As the winters came and passed, Autumn Tallgrass had plenty of opportunity to palaver in her former tongue.

One early spring a delegation came with the long-knife soldiers and an old man claiming to speak for some mean-tempered spirit they called Father or Lord or God. Had to be quite a windbag live like he does, they say suspended above the clouds. Reminded her of something, the old home she still held in her mind, distorted with time, some cantankerous relative maybe, but she was not allowed to find out. Hidden away by New Mother in a tipi far removed from the council instead of being called to talk.

Autumn Tallgrass was worried, normally a central figure in these complicated exchanges, and when, after many hours of oratory she could not understand at this distance, she heard New Mother moaning and cursing, casting aspersions on several big men's grandparents, an insult to their dogs, when she heard the scuffle right in front of the tipi, she realized what was going on: they are going to send *her* with these people back to Texas!

She jumped back from the entrance, began tearing at the staked-down buffalo-hide skirt of the tipi. New Mother burst in, grabbed her and refused to let go, Woman's Heart and Kills-by-Stealth close behind, they pulled, tumbled, and rolled over grass bedding and dead embers, tangled in the rawhide thong holding the lodgepole-pine poles down. They dragged Autumn Tallgrass, still clinging to New Mother, through the camp to the council fire. Finally separated New Mother, her wailing heard all along the river, stood Autumn Tallgrass in front of the god-speaker and an old gray-goat-bearded soldier.

They looked at her, the buckskin clothing, long hair greased and braided. The soldier took a step toward her, eyes glistening, held out a palsied hand. "Do you remember me?" She was trembling, the soldier cautiously moved closer. "You have your dear slain mother's visage, unmistakable despite the scarification, the savage costume."

She pretended ignorance.

"Mary Ellen."

That was it! Those fragmented sounds echoing around her head all these years, clear and precise in tormented dreams, dissolved to nothingness when she woke, the debris she could not stitch together with the sunstruck bonnet in the truck garden, the dispersion of light and voice. She pounded her breast. "*I* am Mary Ellen!"

New Mother cried from the river. "Autumn Tallgrass!"

They carried her off. Another abduction, this time riding alone on a fine Spanish saddle, trying to make sense of it.

Going back with the man who said he was her uncle, brother to her mother killed in a raid soon after Mary Ellen's capture, an excitement underlying confusion and fear: going to Texas!

The house they came to was beyond anything she could have imagined when she said the word, seemed to jut from the prairie, see it miles away, late evening glow, a final, flat light lying over the land, gables and chimneys touching the clouds, windows stacked three high, absurd, brilliant yellow-red. Desultory shouts dispersed across the plains as they approached, coaches on the circle drive, horses stamping impatiently nose the oats in their feedbags, shadowy figures rise from the chairs on the porch, tall wide-brimmed hats, long coats, dresses dragging the floor. The large double doors, faceted glass, brass handles, fling open spilling internal illumination, no sound other than the restlessnesses of the wind, the clouds overspreading the sky. She stares through a corridor of people up the wide wooden steps at a towering silver-haired woman and a large hunched man leaning on a stick, bearded, like the soldier uncle bringing her. They're glowering, a hostile curiosity, uncertain fear, hate, funneled down between those she has to pass, whispering, stepping back as she climbs the stoop. Thick unstable humidity, skitterish sheet lightning, rolling thunder rattle behind the house, the wind quickens. She wants to stop. The soldier uncle grabs her shoulder and forces her on, speaking in a low, rasping voice as they near the two aged giants who wait, seem to grow larger with each step, at the top of the porch: *do not be afraid. These are your grandmother and grandfather, senator of the Lone Star State, your kin before the savages stole you away.*

Before the old woman, taller than any person she has ever seen, can utter what her thin, painted lips prepare to speak, a thunderclap, a rush of heavy, damp air hurling dust and tumbleweeds, large globules of cold rain, whips the old woman's dress into her face, presses her nose and mouth, but the eyes, large and green, an abrupt, dissident intensity in the puckered, powdered folds of weathered skin around them, still fix Autumn Tallgrass where she stands in turbulent dusk. Yells and shouts, hail scatters about them, she is grabbed, gives herself up to terror, blind ecstasy, is dragged into the unknown house.

The only smell she can identify in the dense musk enveloping her is roasting meat. Something to cling to, the last vestige of the world from which she'd been suddenly snatched. And the thunder and the rain pounding the walls containing this absolutely alien place. Angular, straight-edged, intensely lit, oily heat from many small fires in glass globes bright as the sun within the dark storm outside. Patterned, exact. Saturated red, purple, yellow, intricate woven carpets on polished, parallel wooden planks, black walnut scrollwork table, plush chairs, cut-glass crystals, decanters, bowls, silver, brocade hanging from the windows, shelves of leather-bound books. The men and women, the children, come again to some order ringed about her, gold and diamonds, sharply pressed trousers, starched collars, pleated gowns, plumes, bracelets, gorgets, diadems, the words for all of this missing from the inadequate morsel of language she'd been able to salvage and succor from her past life among these strangers, her decaying memories of it now irretrievably crumbled by the total, palpable unworldliness of these rooms.

Everybody grows quiet. The man with the walking stick sits in a rocking chair in the corner, the tall woman approaches her, painted rouge cheeks and black borders around the eyes distorted by thick streaks and blotches of rainwater, the green pupils as keen as a hawk. Stands there, not so overwhelming on level floor, but clearly head and shoulders above her, the lips moving, words stuck to the palate, an itch inside the nose, a black run trickles down the face: tears. The long fingers of her bony hands work, the right slowly rises to the mouth, hesitates there. She finally breaks off the gaze, a disconsolate, futile gesture, looks back at Autumn Tallgrass, urgent, imploring green eyes clouded over, then walks away.

Two black-skinned buffalo women, who'd suddenly appeared in the room, now took Autumn Tallgrass to the back of the place, through the kitchen where more buffalo people, men and women, worked over large iron stoves. She had never seen buffalo women before, just a few of the men who came to the folk, run away, they said, from masters who live in wooden houses and plow the earth. The women laughed, large teeth flashing uneven light from the wood fires, thunder and lightning through the windows, set her at a small table and brought plates of meat and other things Autumn Tallgrass didn't recognize, silver knives and spoons and forks. Everyone laughed again when she tied into the roast with both hands, not even slowing down to sniff the beans and rice.

A large cast-iron tub sat on iron claws on the enclosed back porch, the women poured it full of steaming water from copper kettles, stood, sleeves rolled up, looking at Autumn Tallgrass cowering in the corner. The younger woman took her by the hand to the tub.

"Can you speak English, honey?"

She wasn't sure if she could anymore.

"¿Español?"

Remained silent, more out of exhaustion than anything.

"Well, honey, we gonna give you a bath. Understand? Get in the water and wash, you ever do that before?" The other woman laughs. "No, guess you haven't from the looks of you, you hear what I'm saying, just nod your head if you do, save yourself a lot of trouble, you go in peaceful like. Now come on, I hear tell you can talk."

Hadn't realized how weary and sore she was, slowly nods.

"That's the time. Now let's take off these nasty buckskins and hop in the tub. Make you feel real good, I can tell you that."

After the bath they rubbed her with fragrant oil, so pungent it almost turned her stomach, dressed her in a soft robe, took her upstairs to a small garret, a bed with a large oak head and baseboard, carved twining vines and flowers, told her to sleep well and not to worry. She heard the key turn in the latch when they left, jumped to the door, pushed, felt for something to pull, found the handle, she was trapped. The window solid too, considered smashing it with a chair but could see how high up she was, the storm past, vague moonlight filtering through the clouds on the wet shingles of the roof. Where would she go, naked except for this flimsy gown. Best to wait, see what was going to happen. The smell of the sheets and blankets on the bed was so intense she was afraid to get in. Spent the night curled in the corner on the floor.

At dawn a plaintive cry from somewhere under the roof, a howling song with the coyotes who seemed to surround the house.

She lost track of the seasons, shut up indoors. Got brief glimpses of the sun in the south, or followed patches of light across the carpets when left alone in the big room downstairs, absorbed in intricate designs, could see the moon wax and wane from the garret where they kept her locked at night. Trying to teach her to be like them! Long sessions with her grandmother, who sat in the rocking chair leaned over close to her needlepoint, weak, cold radiances on the sill, north wind and sometimes snow and sleet against the pane, repeating a complex and tedious story of ancestors traveling in wooden boats across endless expanses of monster-infested salt waters, trekking through dense grim forests where the sun never touched the ground and the earth buckled and thrust up to the sky. Ghastly tales of starvation, sickness, injury, and death, the whim of some despicable, malignant spirit's will.

Autumn Tallgrass refused to speak at first, had lost all confidence in her ability anyway, best to learn by listening and watching the god-speaker and the tsk-tsking women, many claiming to be her kin, who came to stare, to smile at her wrapped up tight in the uncomfortable dresses, which at first they had to force her into. Endured the silent pity, the disdain, couldn't reconcile what she saw and heard with the shattered memory of her other mother working in the field, confused somehow now with New Mother, could really believe that Texas women's vulvas run east and west. She rarely saw the men but overheard them from the back porch talk and laugh through their beards: *meat tainted by all the bucks and warriors spread those legs, wrap them around your buttock, buck supple and hungry like the wild thing she is.*

It never occurred to her again that she was one of them. Vowed not to yield, to wait for her chance, to find a way to escape this barbarous folk.

She slowly began to talk. When she was grinding coffee in the silver mill she was so fond of, her job in the kitchen, or bathing on the back porch, talk and listen and laugh with the buffalo people, who, she found out, were captives in the house just like her but had no place to run off to, and even at that, now and then they'd all gather at the stove, in the laundry shed, or the stables, whisper stories of somebody made a dash for it. The *it* they spoke of a little vague: follow the drinking gourd, they said, what's that, she asked, the stars that point toward the star that always sits at the top of the sky—the way out of here, the north star to freedom. She knew that star and, like them, she knew it was the direction out of here. She also learned from the buffalo people the tools necessary to get out of here, watched them move about the house carrying an iron ring with iron tokens they called skeletons jangling on it, representing, maybe, bones of some guardian animal possessing special medicine, the keys that opened doors and cabinets, saw where they hung them on a nail by the kitchen stove, asked them which was hers, which one for the larder. They grinned and winked when they pointed them out.

She also knew the north star led over vast reaches of flat, desolate, dry, inhospitable land. Began to steal bits of jerky, dried apples, and sand plums for the journey, hid them away under her bed, listened to the buffalo men talk about the horses, learned which were gentle, tough, got along without water, those who didn't need oats, could live on prairie grass. She was ready. All she needed now was opportunity.

Spring finally came again and her grandmother took her out of the house for the first time, a long blustery ride across the grasslands turning green, beginning to bloom, stirring an urgency in her to get on the move. She knew the folk would be cracking jokes, packing up the travois, running down the horses, the refuse of the winter camp beginning to stink as the sun climbs higher in the sky, thunderstorms rumbling all around, the wind blowing in from Mexico, the season to wander. Autumn Tallgrass sat impatiently beside the old woman, who seemed to be shrinking with the passing of time, no longer the giant she was that first day, withering here on the leather upholstery of the buckboard bouncing over the rutted trail, it was all Autumn Tallgrass could do to suppress a joyous whelp: they're easing their vigil, her door left unlocked the last few nights, and now this outing.

The old woman looked over, wrapped the shawl tighter about her broad but now frail shoulders, though the day was coming on warm, the green eyes shining from the wrinkled face collapsed around them like a plum too long on the bush, a gaze that caused Autumn Tallgrass to catch her breath. The haughty pity was gone, as if the old woman was seeing her for the first time in good light, the weather-beaten hardness melted away, the narrow red mouth again chewing on difficult words. The blotched hand, the bony wrist startling in its thinness, slowly worked its way from beneath the carriage blanket across her lap, hesitated, then settled on Autumn Tallgrass's knee. The cold touch, even through the long dress and petticoats, made her flinch. The old woman let the hand rest, slight movement with the trotting of the horse, her voice dry and transparent in the turning of the wheels.

"It must be difficult for you, Mary Ellen. Lord knows I understand the terrifying loneliness of this godforsaken place."

Autumn Tallgrass watches her eyes turn away to search the horizon for some unknown sign. "It is time, Grandmother, to follow the animals."

They were going to church. The congregation watched them enter the naked, narrow white clapboard building in silence, whispered behind their hymnals when they passed down the aisle, they sang out frightening songs, strange harmonies and plodding rhythms, the god-speaker droned on. Autumn Tallgrass squirmed in the constricting clothes on the hard oaken pew, watched a yellow-jacket wasp meander among the rafters, through shafts of light and dust slanting across the contained space from high slender stained-glass windows that creaked and banged in the south wind outside. The children in the Sunday school taunted her when the instructor turned her back, pulled her hair, splattered her dress with ink from the pots in the desks, but she did not fight or run, did not want to lose this new trust and freedom: the time was near, she could feel it in the air, see the waxing of the new-grass moon, the turning of the season, sense it in the blood.

They returned to the house. She went to the kitchen and saw the preparations, heard the buffalo women talking. She knew the time was at hand: a big celebration tonight and the sky is clear. They would eat lots of beef, pork, prairie chickens, and pheasant, drink living water, use monstrous amounts of tobacco, flaunt the spirits, a belligerent confrontation, it seemed, and late in the evening no one would wonder where she was. Seen these ceremonies before, the spirits eventually take over, men lose their reason, shout and laugh, fire gunshots at the moon from the porch. Even the women, though more discreet, give themselves up, giggle flushed in their chairs, dance and sing around the piano, fiddles, guitars, harmonicas, a complex and dense music could easily take possession of your soul. During this possession she would slip into the kitchen for the skeletons, gather the supplies from under the roof, the larder, the horse from the stable, would follow the drinking gourd home.

No trouble slipping down the back stairs and out to the stables, found the gray mare she'd chosen, tied the gunnysacks of provisions and two canteens of water across the shoulders, leading it out of the stall when the barn door creaked open. She crouched, pushed the horse back. Footsteps, slow and hesitant, more than one person, stopped now right beyond the stall. Whispers.

"Mary Ellen." The horse starts, snorts, and shakes her head, a hand falls across the top of the door. "Mary Ellen, we know you out here, saw those keys missing, what you think you doing, trying to leave out of here without you say good-bye. Come on, girl, we got to get back to the big house before they miss us, got something to help you on your way."

She stands up, barely visible in the darkness. The buffalo women from the kitchen hug her, hand her a bag of biscuits, a butcher knife, and the silver coffee mill.

"Take this to remember us by, be careful, and God ride with you."

She moved with the south wind, carried by excitement the first few hours, all senses alive after months of dull confinement, bubbling over, a constant jabbering to herself, to her mount, about what had happened, nobody needs to frighten her with bogeyman tales anymore to try to convince her Texans an evil lot if ever there was one.

41

The moon was one day past full. She fell silent, grasped the horse's mane in the monstrous light, watched the ears for sounds she could not hear, a desperate determination, the unsettling realization the world is large, flat, and featureless, danger lurking all round, deep shadows, gorges, quicksand in the river bottoms, and she is alone. Nothing to guide her but her immature, untutored will and the glimmering star in the northern sky.

The second day she begins to feel weak and nauseous, her head throbbing with every step of the horse, she thinks it's the stale, dry biscuits and salty jerked beef, the flat, warm water, the sun beginning to blister down. The morning of the third day she clings heavy to the horse, dull aching along her spine, her abdomen clenched tight about her bowels, which seem to squish and mix, the stomach, lungs, and liver dissolve and churn within her. Then she sees the blood-smeared horsehair beneath her thighs. Rubbed raw she thinks at first, but her belly cramps, her nipples harden and hurt. Dying, she thinks, no one to help. Then it comes to her in a wave of panic: she is a woman. No one to guide her, no yellow pollen, no buckskin bag to gather it in, New Mother's ancient aunt not here to instruct, to lead her. She is lost.

She hangs on to the mare's neck, fighting off confusion, indifference, tears, the monotonous concentration of the ride, lips cracked and dusty. The horse snorts, trots on. She looks over her shoulder, cottonwoods still clattering new leaves in the wind along the creek she's following, tule cattails, new spring sprouts and old dry blown heads. She looks west, the yellow sorrel blossoms among the grasses, north, white thunderheads, then east, a distant black stand of buffalo, distorted, shimmering like giants in the heat of the morning sun already rippling from the ground, and south, the sky dusty blue to clear. The black blood oozes from her vulva pressed hard on Old Gray's back. She will have to invent her own rite of passage, stumble blind across the divide, through all the savage powers disposed to swallow her up.

She turned down to the creek, stopped in the shade along the cracked bank, water small and muddy, dismounted, and tied Old Gray to a sapling. No sign of Texans on her trail.

She didn't know what to do, only two biscuits left. Stood listening to the wind, the tule cattails tossing back and forth, the world eaten away, her very being with it, bloated and strange. She began to shake, eyes filled with tears, menstrual blood trickling down her leg, the raw stench of rotting mud. A great blue heron a hundred paces downstream slow-stepping through the water, head cocked sideways. The tears stop, she must do it alone. Removes her clothes and washes them in the creek, lays them out on sumac bushes, finds a spot of warm, quiet water to settle in, her Texas grandmother thought it important to bathe. The abdomen relaxes. She thinks, there must be something to hold on to, New Mother, a flowered bonnet in the Texas morning. Something. Coyote Dropping, he helped her across. That's it! He led you to the very middle of the middle of the world. A song, a dance.

She tries to chant, prattling whatever words waver through the mind, the blood of the lamb, the sun and moon to come, mother heron and her fish. Looks for pollen among the tule, not enough to paint her body yellow, a dab for her forehead, cheeks, the pubic mound, inside the thighs, the desultory song degenerating into mumbling now and then but still giving structure, the winding course of the creek, south wind in the new green leaves of the trees, grasses rising up the slope to the rolling hills on either side. A coyote stands at the ridge looking down on her, she laughs and does a little dance along the smooth bleached trunk of a fallen elm into the sun to dry, a blue-heron-and-a-coyote dance. The light intensifies around her lean and wiry naked body, catches and surges through the mind. She is a woman now.

By the time the flow stopped she was trembling and weak, huddled in the nested grass beneath the lean-to she'd made below the cutbank, hadn't eaten in how many days. She bathed again, chanting the song now settled into intricate patterns, daubed the last of the pollen facing to the east, the west, north, and south, dressed, struggled up on Old Gray, and started out. But grew dizzy and fell.

Hungry. Strips bark off an old gnarled cottonwood to get at the sweet white sap beneath, Old Gray snorts behind her. She looks back at the butcher knife the buffalo women had given her, the piece of bark held between her knees, waves away the flies swirling around it. She will have to do what the folk have to do on the long trail, during the moon when the children cry.

Picks up the butcher knife, holds it behind her back, and slowly approaches the horse. With her free hand she grabs the rope halter, looks her in the eye.

"Thank you, Old Gray."

New Mother was out from camp picking up firewood along the draw when she saw something emerging from a liquid pool of blue light trembling on the high plains beyond the thicket. She thought it a strange place for a tree at first, but it was moving, a buffalo strayed from the herd maybe, crazed by early spring heat and dry weather. She laid down her bundle and watched, uneasy. She'd been unusually skitterish since they snatched Autumn Tallgrass from her, but she held her ground, somebody on foot, not a threat, somebody in trouble. Close at hand she could see she was young, sunburned, chapped cracked lips, coated with white alkali dust, a Texas child. She rushed forward, took the butcher knife from the girl's limp grasp, the bag from her shoulder. Looked at her a long time, the gnarled, eaten nose, the apathetic green eyes showed little recognition, she struggled with memory, uncertainty, a mind too willing to trick her susceptible spirit, it's been a full cycle of the sun. She seemed the right age. It *was* Autumn Tallgrass!

"Daughter?"

Her breathing was shallow, rapid, skin flaccid on the bones of her face, mouth twitched, parted, then closed, could only sign: *very tired, Mother, many suns without drink.*

Autumn Tallgrass, another tedious journey winding her dreams to consciousness, awoke. All very familiar and strange at the same time, the conjunction of lodgepoles, sun glaring on buffalo hide through the smoke hole, New Mother sitting by her on the twisted-grass pallet. How many times do you have to go through all this.

"Mother. I'm a woman now."

Slow to comprehend. "The world will weary you down. The hailstorm ceases, to allow the whirlwind to come."

"What do you mean?"

Looking at her, the spreading hips and swelling breasts, no doubt about it, she speaks the truth. "One trouble after another:

now you're a woman I can no longer put off Blue Leggings, been wanting you since you first came."

Also slow to comprehend. "But I don't want him."

"He will bring horses."

"He is the ugliest, evil-temperedest man of all the folk on the prairie. I want to live with Coyote Dropping."

"What? Why that good-for-nothing-but-story-and-dance?"

"He used to play with me."

New Mother throws her hands up. "You've been with the Texans too long."

Autumn Tallgrass rested, walked about the camp. The children who followed her, the people she stopped to talk to, even Woman's Heart and Kills-by-Stealth, who'd sent her back to Texas, marveled at the escape, the long journey over the plains, the killing of the mare to eat, the moccasins she was still wearing, made of Old Gray's hide. One morning there were horses hobbled outside, no question about it, Blue Leggings's stock.

"I told you, New Mother, I will not go with him, been carried from place to place against my will often enough."

"But he's been waiting for you to ripen."

"No. He can kill me right here in this tipi if he wants to but I won't go, rather be killed. The man has to sneak up on a creek just to get a drink of water."

The commotion attracted the attention of most of the settlement, people from up and down the river standing around looking at Blue Leggings squatted by his horses outside the tipi. They give advice: if Autumn Tallgrass spreads out her sleeping mat next to your fire, better redesign your medicine bag to fit a cunt instead of a dick because you're sure not going to be the one wearing it. You'd better keep those animals, they do lot more cooking for you than Autumn Tallgrass ever will, she's Texas blood, you know, won't be long that mare of yours start looking mighty good.

New Mother comes out and throws up her hands. "She wants to live with Coyote Dropping, is he around?"

A pack of barking dogs and little children sent off to fetch him, still half asleep. Normally takes till the sun in the middle of the sky before he knows if he's going to live or die, rubbing his eyes and scratching, wants to know what's so pressing it couldn't wait, new-kindled campfire smoke still clinging to the ground along the riverbank. New Mother calls Autumn Tallgrass out, stands her in front of the two men. They look at her, she at them, they at each other, the whole population staring at New Mother.

"Coyote Dropping, I want you to tell this hardheaded daughter of Texans to go with Blue Leggings."

"Why should *I* tell her that?"

"She's decided she wants to sleep in your tipi."

Autumn Tallgrass thrusts out the butcher knife she brought from Texas. "Here, take this. You might as well strike me dead on the spot as tell me to travel with him. I won't go."

Coyote Dropping smiles, looks at Autumn Tallgrass, last danced with her when she was still a girl, hadn't seen her up close since she got back, become a woman. Laughs, waves the knife off. "New Mother, this is a very fine bunch of horses. I can understand your desire to husband them. Blue Leggings bound to hold it against them if he's rejected, see bad medicine every time he throws a riding blanket on, blame them whenever his arrows fall short. Soon be so uncertain, his eyes so blurry, bow tremble in his hand thinking about the unprovoked evil sure to befall him, would rather slaughter them for jerky as climb up on their backs, and no other father or mother on all the flat rolling earth would accept them in fair barter for even an ugly, sharp-tongued daughter whose breasts beginning to sag. But don't you think Autumn Tallgrass should have time to recover from her recent ordeal?"

New Mother looks at her, still holding the butcher knife for anybody wants to plunge it through her heart. Motions the two men over behind the tipi away from the folk pressing around offering all manner of irreverent advice, enjoying this more than anything happened since Hears-the-Moon-Come-Up decided she'd had enough of Antelope Prong's grass pallet and Kills-by-Stealth suggested his might be more to her liking. "Doesn't anybody have hides to tan or buffalo to jerk around here?"

They sit for a while, glancing back over their shoulders at Autumn Tallgrass now and again. Finally Coyote Dropping stands.

"Tell me, Blue Leggings, what would you want for your claim on her?"

Watching harvester ants along a trail from their den. "I've been waiting a long time for her."

"I can understand. She is becoming a fine woman. But what good is she to you if she doesn't want to stay? One night you return from the hunt and find poison ivy in your bed, or she's off in some young boy's spindly tipi teaching him what his penis is for. Be gone in a few months and you've traded those fine horses for nothing but a good story the folk will tell loafing around the Hard Stick Canyon fire."

Blue Leggings looks over at Autumn Tallgrass glowering back at them from around the tipi, scratches his ear, scans the treetops along the river. "I guess if you could come up with three silver agency dollars and a crowing chicken, she'd be all yours."

It is so.

Coyote in the Brush

Cannonball It was the whiskey made me do it. Had a taste for it ever since I was nine, hiding out in the tobacco shed back on the plantation in David-son County, Tennessee, saw my mother bury something in the sweet potato patch, turned out to be a crockery jug of the Master's best distilled spirits she'd pilfered from the big house cellar. Righteous stuff, sisters and brothers. Kindled a raucous warm well-being, a longing for some essence of freedom, enough to get you to thinking there may be a God existing somewhere beyond the Sunday camp meeting after all, how else account for such power sequestered in the lowly barley-corn.

I didn't think there was enough bad whiskey in all of Dodge City to get me drunk. Me and the boys just delivered a herd of

two thousand long yearlings and were out to cut the alkali
water we'd been drinking all summer, they couldn't make it as
fast as we could drink it, take a bookkeeper to have kept check
on what we consumed, drank until it didn't taste right, and on
our way back to camp we passed Fort Dodge. I saw the soldiers on the grounds, and the notion came to me, a kind of
inspired desire, to rope a cannon. Take it back to Texas with us
to help fight the barbarians. A bright idea, brothers and sisters.
But a damn fool one, just the same.

I canter up to the open gate, the sentry pacing back and
forth, his white gauntlets like two doves in tethered flight here
and there through dusty gray light. I don't pay any more attention to him than I would an empty bottle, a big smile showing
off my gold tooth, the one with the star cut in it representing
the Lone Star State of Texas. Let the guard know it's a successful man he's dealing with. I wait, *hut-two, hut-two*, till he's at
the far end of his foot-worn trough, spur my horse, and dash
into the yard. Sentry's mouth falls open, a curse, calls *halt*, I'm
full speed for the cannon, let my lariat fly, turn, spur, rope
snaps taut on the pommel, bout knocks the horse down, damn
cannon won't budge a hair. Somebody blowing a bugle by
now, boots and saddles, dust swirling up across the parade
ground, I'd coppered the play to win, but don't even have time
to retrieve my rope, beat a hasty retreat for the gate. The sentry jumps out in front, got a good look at the quality of his
rifling, but my luck's not all bad, he doesn't pull the trigger and
I'm out on the prairie, whooping and a-hollering like a wild
man, the cavalry on me like stink on buffalo shit. Those soldiers' ponies couldn't cut a sick cow out of the shadow of a
tree, but when it comes to a straight run, I had to admit their

advantage. Whether I admitted it or not, they were soon clasping wrist irons on me, bedding me down in the Fort Dodge guardhouse. Yeah, sisters and brothers, a damn fool idea.

I'm a man that doesn't like constraints. When I was a young boy planting tobacco after all us slaves had been freed, according to everything you heard, out gathering piles of brush and wood to burn the weeds out of the field, spading and raking, sowing, transplanting, pulling off suckers and tobacco worms, all day picking blackberries, walnuts, hickory nuts, chestnuts, shirley bark nuts, dragging that old homemade sled with the big box nailed on it from tree to tree to get enough to haul to market, dollar a bushel for chestnuts, fifty cents for the rest, a few cucumbers from Mama's kitchen garden thrown in, at it from can-see to can't, I couldn't tell much damn difference between this and what we were supposed to have been freed from. Just couldn't shake the feeling after all these years of slaving it was supposed to be more, there was something else out there, down the road, over the hill, across the river. Freedom. It wasn't proclaimed, it had to be found, and it was anywhere but here, overcome with a delicious, constant sweet lust to wander.

I always was good with livestock. Me and the son and daughter of old Master, who rented us our land, used to sneak into the barn when he was off the place and ride the horses. He had a particularly mean stallion that nobody'd been able to break, and the boy and girl bet me twenty-five cents I couldn't handle him. We drive him into the barn one Sunday morning, get him into a stall, full of himself, snorting, rearing and kicking at the planks, I'm talking to him, *come on boy, nice and easy*, clamber up beside him, trying to get on, and all of a sudden he stops struggling, stares up over his shoulder at me, a keen look in his eyes, like he's saying, *come on. You want a ride, I'll give you a ride, we'll you and me take a little turn, climb right on if you think you man enough.*

The son and the daughter swing the stall door open, that horse bails out straight for the barnyard, I got my knees dug in, two fistfuls of mane, soon as we hit sunlight he does a high-twisting kick, got two fists and one mouthful of mane now and that's all, looks like I'm doing a handstand when we land, a quick cut, a mincing string of sharp hops, I'm flopping like a circus pennant in a high wind. Finally get my legs back down around him, tries to rub me off on the fence rails, no luck, damn this bucking, a spirited spine-shivering whinny and he clears the corral gate hell-bent for election beeline though the henhouses and kennels, chickens flapping, track hounds yapping and baying after us across fields, over stone walls, stampeding pasturing mares and colts, through hedgerows and creeks, all the neighbors mounting up to give chase. By the time we slowed to an easy gallop and everybody else caught us up, we'd covered a good twenty miles and had collected an entourage any dog-and-pony show would be proud of. That stallion was mine, and I just kept on going, on my way to the land of old John Brown, the free state of Kansas.

Now here I am all these years later, broke out of the Fort Dodge stockade, walked, hitched, on the run back to Texas, a fugitive. One of the best cowpunchers ever to ride herd up the Goodnight Loving and the Abilene trails, and I had to shuck hides in the tallow factory at Quintara to get by. Kindle hell-fires to try out the tallow, skid the carcasses down the chutes into the Brazos River—so many damn cattle in south Texas, brothers and sisters, don't even need to save the meat, not worth the effort, can't find a market for it. The catfish growing monstrous, thrashing and oozing in the muddy putrid water gorging themselves, sharks wriggling their way upstream from the Gulf to cut out their share of the carnage. I had to scrape and squirrel enough money together to buy me a stake: two horses, a sorrel and a thick-barreled grulla, a bag of cornmeal and dried beef, a couple of piggin strings, and a length of good three-eighths-inch rope. Head into the bleak and rough god-forsaken blackwaxy hogwallow gulf country to try to scratch out a living till things blow over, hustling mossy-horned coastal brush cows. And that's where I first met him, the one the vaqueros call *el coyote*. At least I thought it was him.

One chilly, drizzling morning, rained pitchforks the whole night through, I was awakened by the strong smell of coffee. Near as I could tell it was almost dawn, gathered up the horse blanket I'd thrown over a pile of sticks to bed down on along-side the muddy cattle run, got my orientation by the piggin string I'd left pointing the direction I was traveling the night before. No question about it: coffee, and somewhere close by. The thicket so dense couldn't see more than a few yards any way you look, find your way by ear and nose, and with the coffee it wasn't hard to do. Hadn't gone fifteen feet when I saw the smoldering dab of embers in a narrow wallow, more smoke than anything, mixed with mist hanging in the coral bean and pistache, somebody hunkering the other side, a tin cup huddled close to the chest. A slim, slight man, wearing a red flannel shirt, what looked like a coyote pelt vest, and an old worn pair of dungarees, but barefoot. Appeared to be doz-ing till I took one step his way and the head snapped up, eyes wide open, yellow green luminescences in a face darker than a stack of black cats. A noise I chose to interpret as greeting instead of growl. His ears flattened against the matted, woolly hair, the lips drawn back, not sure if it's a smile or a simple baring of the teeth, a very young boy is all. I get a cup from my chuck bag hanging on a pommel string, reach for the coffeepot, slowly. He doesn't react, pour half a cup before the dregs come, so strong I may have to drink it with a spoon. Take a quick sip. *Ooweee!* Knock the sleepy right on out, about one-third chili juice, make a man want to cut a step right there by the wallow. He flinches, lowers, sets his tin cup down, raises the right arm out as if to shake hands, but I'm too far away for that, low trembling howl or whine, definite grin across his mouth. I take another slurp, cut another step since he seemed to enjoy the first one so much, gather a few sticks, see if I can't get what's left of the fire to flame up. Pass the time of day.

"Looks like the sun might burn through this fog shortly."

Nothing. But looking at me real close.

"*¿Hablas inglés?*"

Nada.

Well, a man don't have nothing to say, can't hold that against him. Finish off my coffee and chili juice, got to see if I can run down a steer sometime soon some kind of way, get me by till spring when I know lots of outfits going to be looking for men to take a herd north. The unpleasantness with the cavalry cannon sure to have been forgotten, nobody giving the black book too close a reading, a good trailhand more important than any legal technicality. I thank the boy for his brew, wish him luck, and push on through the thicket.

Must have been past noon when I heard something behind me. Couldn't smell no steer, but wind not real favorable and I was getting desperate. I'd hoped the direction I'd been going all morning was leading to open country, where it's a little easier to spot stock and to run them down, but the brush was heavier than ever. Don't see how I could circle back without giving myself away, not much hope of success anyhow, chasing a longhorn through this tangle of briar, but I carefully turn my horse, and there he is: *el coyote*, standing in the run behind me, downcast eyes and that shit-eating grin. I wave, he tries to cut a step like the one I'd done before, don't quite know what to make of it, not too sure I want this young kid following along spooking any prey I might come across. I move on. Every time I glance back he's there, on foot near as I can tell, break into as much of a canter as I can manage under the circumstances, look over my shoulder when I pass through the small clearings, and sure enough, he's still trotting behind, rocking from side to side as he comes, leaning forward the faster he runs, not even breathing hard. This goes on about an hour and I finally give up, damn if it don't look like I got myself a sidekick.

I decided he was deaf and dumb at first, palaver away at him and if he wasn't looking right at me when I started he wouldn't react to a thing I said, English or Spanish, and the only sounds I ever heard him utter were dull murmurs, guttural grunts, and an occasional *woo-oo-wow* when I'd cut a few steps for him, which for some reason sure tickled him to see. But one night I was ripped from the sound sleep of the just by the godawfulest caterwaul you'd ever want to hear, thought for sure all the demons of hell and some from south Texas set loose to collect my piddling soul, jumped up with my bowie knife ready to by God go down fighting, and there he was: howling away at the big old hunger moon just risen into the clear black sky above the fog-bound thicket, ever coyote along the gulf coast joining in the chorus.

And I found out he could hear all right too, if it was something he thought was worth his time to listen to. I'd scared up a mess of pecans, loafing around the fire getting ready to eat a few, he was about thirty feet away, over by the horses, sitting like he did, rocking slightly to and fro, left and right, head held up high, chin forward, his eyes fixed on something far off that I for the life of me couldn't make out, like a bird dog on a prairie chicken. Now and then a slight spasm start around his mouth and nostrils, shiver over his entire face, and tremble down his spine. I could've fired off a round or two from a Colt pistol and he wouldn't even have flinched, but I took two of those pecans in my palm, and at the first, faintest crack he spun and loped on all fours over to me. If he'd have had a tail he would've been wagging it, half expected him to start licking my face, begging for some of that nut.

His eating habits were the most peculiar I'd ever seen. All he had with him when I come upon him was a dull butcher knife, that coffeepot, a sterling silver mill, a tin cup, and a jar of chili juice. Making coffee was quite a ritual. Sometimes he'd disappear all day long, think I was rid of him, but never failed, right before sunup I'd hear him scavenging sticks for the fire. He'd set out the mill to the right, the chili juice jar to the left, pot, cup, and coffee sack a triangle in the very middle, then he'd select the beans from the sack, sniffing them one at a time, drop them in the grinder, pour water into the pot, put it on the fire behind him, start to grind, staring blankly at where the sun was beginning to rise through the undergrowth and trees until the water boiled. He'd shake the ground coffee in, remove the cork stopper from the chili juice, sniff it, dump a slug in the pot, let it steep for a while, fill the cup, gather it up to his chest in both hands, and squat down over the embers to sip and sleep.

I don't know what else he ate before I met him, lived off the land, I guess. I used to run across fresh-killed longhorns, look like something large, a cougar or a wouzer maybe, had done it, took the tongue and left the rest for wild dogs and crows. The vaqueros always said it was *el coyote* did it. Hard to believe. Slight as he is, have to be hell-for-stout to bring down a steer on foot in this briar patch with nothing but a blunt butcher knife. About all he did now was look for wild grapes, honey, nuts and seeds, beetles, and grubs, whatever he came upon he'd sniff at, and if he liked what he smelled he'd eat it. Anything left over he'd bury somewhere. Wouldn't touch my corn bread at first, eventually acquired a taste for it, but any jerky you'd offer him he'd take with one hand, steal what was left in your lap with the other. Devour any kind of meat, cooked or raw, even chase the buzzards off a dead jackrabbit and bring it into camp for me to roast. I didn't think too much of it, just goes to show you what this damn desolate coast country and these bad-tempered longhorned cows will do to a man.

From the looks of him he'd led a pretty rough life. Covered with scars, most of them pretty small, some looked like burns, but some bad cuts on the right eyebrow, middle of the right cheek, and chin. The nastiest ran from below the left ear down across the throat to the Adam's apple, wasn't done by a locust thorn either. Made you think it had something to do with his lack of talk. But still, he wasn't a bad looker in his way, a little slew-footed, a bunch of purple blotches across his cheek, teeth gone yellowish at the base, gums curling back, but long lashes and a pleasant smile. Very handy with his fingers, most flexible digits I've ever seen, thumbs almost as long as the others, he could bend them back nearly to touch the wrists, and the largest, strongest set of nails you'll find this side of a cinnamon bear.

Queer-acting, but couldn't help taking a liking to him. I figured if he's going to be my sidekick I better commence to teaching him something about herding cows, and I wasn't too sure how to go about that with somebody who either couldn't or didn't want to talk. By this time we'd worked out a pretty good sign language—I was fluent at it, once lived among prairie nomads for almost a year—and I decided the first place to start was with the horses. He got along with them just fine, think he liked the grulla better than he did me, spent most of his time huddled close when he wasn't off in the brush, but it was clear he'd never been on top of one in his life. I'd point and give the sign for horse, drawl it out long and slow: *horse!* Have him bring them over to me or tie them to the picket pin. After a while I could just say the words and he'd jump to it, and I began to work on things like halter, chuck bag, rope, thinking sometimes he was doing real well, and others I was the dumbest nigger in the state of Texas wasting my time with a foundling clearly no brighter than a moldy cow pie, ought to ride off in the middle of the night and be shut of him. Then he'd come up to me and murmur something sounded for all the world like *horse* and point. By God, one would be loose and he'd smile at me and trot off after it. He'd bring the animal back, calmed if it was spooked, not even holding the picket line, the horse nuzzling him like a hungry foal her mother. The way he could navigate the underbrush I wouldn't be able to lose him anyhow.

Before long, using pecans, roasted potatoes, and horehound candy for a prod, I had him packing and unpacking, and he was catching on how to hunt longhorns. Getting damn good at it, on foot, maybe better than I ever was to begin with, and it was him teaching me. He could sniff them out. Most of us beating the brush can smell a steer, but he could latch on to them a good minute or two before I could, fog, freezing rain, it didn't matter, he'd not only whiff out where they were but what they were thinking, know where they were planning on going next. Sign language not worth a shit in a thicket, he must be able to smell what *I'm* feeling and thinking too, which direction I'm going to turn, and I swear he usually got to the steers before me. Stare them down, sometimes jump them, clench their lower lip in his teeth, and hold them until I could get my lariat around their necks.

Not much a man can do on a cattle drive, though, without he has to rest his ass on the back of a horse and to toss a lasso. The last thing I had to do, and the hardest, was teach him to ride and rope. I could get him to hobble, curry, shoe, sleep with the horse, but when I'd try to get his foot in a stirrup he'd fall into complete terror, scratch and kick, bolt off into the brush, not see him again till dawn. This went on for about a week, and I noticed he not only refused to mount up but had never put the saddle on the horse, was staying clear of it even when it was laid out on the ground, and it finally sunk in: that's what he didn't like. Wasn't so much afraid of getting on the horse's back as he was of that damn piece of metal and worked leather. And it made some sense: the boy is half wild, wilder than any nomad I ever knew, and they never use saddles. It wouldn't hurt to give it a try. So I signal for him to bring the grulla over, and sure enough, the first thing he does is give that old worthless saddle a quick fearful glance. I laugh, pick up a horse blanket, throw it back down, don't even need that, walk up to him, grab hold of the collar of his shirt and the seat of his pants and pitch him up onto the horse. His eyes get real big, ears laid back, hunched down like a barnyard dog caught in the middle of a corral full of short yearlings turned in to be branded, holding on to the mane with both fists. The grulla just stands there, slight shiver up and down the withers, and snorts. I go to the fire and start making hoecakes. The horse idles around the clearing, grazing what she can find, his grip relaxes, knuckles regain some color, starts to breathe a little slower, finally a big grin. Prouder than an egg-sucking hound.

After that I couldn't get him off the damn animal. He wasn't really riding, just up there, go anywhere the grulla took him, even sleep there, beat anything I'd ever seen. I put a rope halter on, looped it around the horse's neck, just left it hanging, and before long he'd pick it up and hold it, sit upright, chest swelled up, shoulders thrown back, looking from a distance like the Big Auger himself, expected any day he'd be wanting to smoke cigars and spout out wisdom.

The next step was the saddle. One morning when he'd fallen asleep over his cup of coffee and chili juice sitting by the fire, I put it on his horse, then moved off a ways, leaned against a tree acting like I was taking a snooze, one eye squinted under the brim of my hat to see what would happen. He woke, yawned, down on all fours, stretched one limb at a time, hadn't noticed anything out of the ordinary, went off into the bushes, came back, finished the coffee in his cup, and that's when he saw the saddle. Let out a little yelp, ran up to the horse, tugged at the surcingle, backed off, circled the animal, then ran to me, pawed at my boot, I swear he said *horse* and *saddle*, but I lay there like a pile of fresh-dropped manure. He whimpered, sulked about the clearing kind of hangdog—I was starting to feel sorry for him—walked around the horse again, laying hands on rump and withers, looked like he was trying to find a hold, a way up without he had to touch the saddle, moaning and growling over at me. Finally, kind of a desperate act, he sprung up on the contraption, hanging on to the horn with both hands, sitting on his heels at first, then slid his legs down. Didn't put his feet in the stirrups, but you can't have everything all at once, he was mounted.

It was about this time he began to acting a little peculiar, that is to say stranger than he normally would. We always did horse around a lot, cutting steps and grinning, even wrestle a little and tickle. He loved it, roll over on his back, hands and feet limp in the air, let me scratch and rub his soft belly like some big old pup, laugh and grab my hand to keep me doing it. But lately his tickles started slowing down, he'd cuddle up beside me at the fire instead of sleeping with the horses, reach out those long slender fingers and tickle me, kind of a slow caress, gently pinch my hand, arm, and knees, then suddenly throw a hissy fit. Push away, even bit me once, burst into tears, and kissed the knuckle he'd bitten, crying and laughing at the same time, fling his arms around my neck, sigh, push away again, pull my hand to his hips to tickle. He's putting on a little flesh there, my hand rests on it, don't know what to think or do. Like the song says, *you don't know what lonesome is till you go to herding cows*. At it long enough the younger heifers and the mares in the remuda, even the horse wrangler, start to look pretty good, and it had been a long, dank winter, brothers and sisters, in this damn coastal brush.

I was powerful glad when April rolled around, time to head inland for the general roundup. Figured the drier air and open sky of the prairie, the company of other human beings, do us both a lot of good. He wasn't yet the best man handling a horse I'd ever seen. Not that he couldn't ride—he and that grulla got along like next of kin, especially without a saddle the way he was most of the time—it wasn't that he couldn't cover territory, I just had my doubts it would ever occur to him or his mount to take the trouble to break up a mill, turn a stampede, or cut out an angry steer, unless he was hungry and figured it was something he could eat. And lessons with the lariat hadn't gotten past a mumble that no one else on the vast windy plains beyond me would ever recognize was *rope*. But I figured this time of year with every outfit getting ready for a trail drive and hard up for a crew, and everybody knowing what a first-rate hand I was—hell, if it wasn't for my previous condition of servitude, as they call it, I'd already have been the Segundo, maybe even the boss, the Big Auger, of a trail drive— somebody ought to sign us both on somewhere just to get me in the bargain.

West of the Brazos we come upon a bunch of cowboys sitting around the chuck wagon, a small group of Africans off to one side. I recognize Bronco Jim and Big Mouth Henry, think

I'd better question them a little about how things are looking. I dismount, motion Coyote to stay a ways off, walk to where the men are down on their haunches going at their tin plates of side meat and beans, passing a can of tomatoes around.

"Big Mouth! I didn't ever reckon on seeing you, thought I heard you drowned fording the Red River at Doan's Crossing last spring's flood."

"Naw, that wasn't me, no river mean enough to drag me under."

"Sure glad to hear it. If it was you in that river, all the trail herds have to look somewhere else for water, keep from poisoning the cows."

"What about yourself, Cannonball? Didn't think I'd see you down here, understood you was taking up artillery with the cavalry at Fort Dodge."

"No, brother, not for me. I did try it awhile, but it was altogether too sedentary an occupation to suit my taste."

"Too sedentary, huh. I did hear when you took up the slack in your rope on that cannon, knocked you and your horse flat on your ass."

"You heard right. But when I told them Bat Masterson a good friend of mine, they apologized for the inconvenience. Most those pony soldiers freedmen from Kentucky and Tennessee anyway. Long as I bought a round of drinks they saw no reason I couldn't be on my way."

"Glad you told me that, cause that's not the way I heard it." Points with his knife. "Who's your partner?"

"You may not believe this, but you heard tell of the man the vaqueros on the gulf coast call *el coyote*. Well, that's him."

"You don't say. I always figured him to cut a more impressive figure. You been hanging out in the coastal brush, huh."

"Yep."

"I thought I recognized that waxy mud clinging to your clothes."

"How about you, Big Mouth, you still charm a herd of longhorns with your singing?"

"Hell yes. Sing a song for you now if I thought it'd do you any good. Go get yourself a plate of beans and tell us some more lies."

After we finished our chuck, Coyote sitting off to the side rocking back and forth, eyes fixed on something distant at the horizon, I went to talk to the Big Auger and the Segundo. They needed some mustangers right now. If we could bring in some horses he'd probably be able to use us on the drive. I told them to get their corral ready, in a month we'd be back with all the horseflesh they could handle.

I didn't know what I was getting myself in for, but at least I had one more month to see if I could make a hand out of Coyote. Going to be hard, if not downright impossible for us—meaning, I thought, me—to bring in a *manada* of mustangs. Usually takes fifteen–twenty men working shifts, they surround them, keep them moving for two or three weeks, wear them down, and starve them into submission. I don't have a notion in hell how we're going to manage it. Riding into the falling sun, fresh south wind rolling over the Llano Estacado, nighthawks and killdeer pivot and dip about our heads, I don't know why I didn't leave him in the coastal thicket, why I don't just spur my horse and abandon him now. Look at him ten yards behind, up in the saddle Bronco Jim give us, more like a dog on the back of his master's horse than any cowhand you've ever seen. An animal smile, calm rapture caught in honey light, the rhythmic trotting of the horses swirling dust

PHILIP KIMBALL

over the long slow rise of grassland, fitful heat lightning flickering across the dark line of the sky. When the moon rises, a group howl chortles up far around us. His eyes gleam and he throws back his head and joins in the mournful cry.

When I made clear to him we were going after mustangs he got downright excited, never seen him like that before, his eyes shone, actually looked like he was thinking something, paced up and down by the campfire instead of sitting and rocking and staring at the reflection of the moon on the coffee in his cup. By the time we saw a herd, he was fit to be tied. Come up over a ridge in New Mexico near Yellow Fox Canyon, following a cloud of dust for two days, can see twenty miles across the valley floor, flat, new green to the trees marking the streambed, must have been thirty or forty grazing in the harem. The stallion, off a ways sniffing the air, catches wind of us and calls out. When Coyote sees them gallop off, leap and splash through the water, he takes off too, gone loco for sure, no doubt in my mind now he knows how to handle a horse, all I can do to keep from falling too far behind. He's going to chase them clean out of the valley, get them so riled up it'll take another week to maneuver in close. But he stops when he reaches the river, jumps from the horse, starts tugging at the surcingle trying to get his saddle off. Finally has it on the ground, I don't know what to do but watch, a cinch I can't stop him, hopping around pointing, grunting, and mouthing what sure is *saddle*, until I remove mine. He grabs the chuck bag, his grinder, coffee beans, and chili juice, hangs them all in a tree, then commences trying to heave the saddles up there too. I begin to laugh, it sure seems like some kind of breakthrough to me, I mean to tell you the boy has a plan and it has something to do with wild mustangs. And that's a damn sight more than I have.

When we had our mounts stripped down to nothing but rope halters he moved across the river, lying on his belly, arms and legs draped over the grulla's rib cage, cheek on the withers, so he could see the tracks the mustangs made. We followed the rest of that day, never getting closer than two or three miles, then circled back to the trees where our gear was hung, but he wouldn't let me build a fire. Ate cold biscuits, no coffee or chili juice, slept huddled together without blankets, started out before dawn to rejoin the herd. He could tell the trail from other horses that crossed in the night, recognize the droppings, at least it looked that way to me. I'm beginning to take very seriously what at first had been a desperate bluff.

After a few days sleeping on the ground, eating nothing but raw cornmeal, we'd moved within half a mile and the mustangs didn't seem to be paying us any mind at all. It dawned on me what Coyote was up to: we were becoming a part of the herd. Couple of days more and we were sleeping on the backs of our horses right in the middle of them, basking in the spring sun all day long while the animals grazed, only difference between us and them, we didn't eat grass and they didn't have the long, long thoughts that humans have to wile away the enormous, dreamy time.

But I wasn't so sure about Coyote. Look over at him across the alkali flats on the other side of the herd, grazing closer and closer to the stallion, shimmering in the afternoon heat rising from buffalo grass and prickly pears, his eyes as opaque and indifferent as any of the mustangs. Not so sure any more's going on in his head than in theirs, wonder sometimes if he knows even as much as a clever dog. What was I doing following him and the herd in this random drift from stream to wild sorrel patch and back again, bound to the cycles of sun and moon and water and grass. As much a slave in a way as I ever was with old Master down in Tennessee.

I'm lying back on the rump watching thunderheads boil up into the radiant slant of evening when a sharp, soul-rending cry tears me from my reverie, my horse jumps and turns, I almost fall to the ground. The stallion rears, prances on his hind legs, hooves pawing at the air, lips pulled back, baring teeth, ears cocked—goddam, sisters and brothers, if it didn't look like Coyote was challenging for the harem. Uncertain light fraught with electrical charge, the condensing, unknowable dark where spirits scatter like skitterish sparrows before the shadows of low tumbling clouds, breath before the wind. Coyote and his horse have the stallion confused, turned blinded into the sun, an enormous fireball lying eye-level above the horizon, no match for them, more than horse and rider, an extension, a specter of horse–coyote growling, bark-howling rapid expulsions of air, spit, and snot, no match for this unexpected challenge from his own herd, panic ruptures across the stallion's eyes, he stumbles backwards away from the sun, the relentless attack, breaks and runs. God damn! Never seen anything like it. Coyote chases along after him, the grulla nipping at the stallion's tail, until he crosses the river. Coyote comes back to the nervous horses, circles, reassuring snorts and whickerings, gathers them up on the ridge together where all can see, he sniffs for danger. Then, when everybody's settled down, leads us all to the water to drink and to the nighttime grazing ground. The horses are his.

The next morning, after running off the stallion still lingering around the herd about a mile distant, we slowly started
drifting back toward Texas. Nothing to it. When we get within
a day's drive of the ranch I'll ride on ahead and have the boys
open up the corrals, all we'll have to do is break into a short
run right before we get there and the horses will follow. Close
the gate behind us and we'll have a *manada* fresh as the day we
first come across them, not half starved, worn to a frazzle, and
on the verge of an emotional bust-down of some kind the way
they usually are when mustangers bring them in. Brothers and
sisters, I had me a horse wrangler. And trouble I'd never in my
twisted life ever figured on.

When we got to the Pecos I decided it was time to build a
fire and make up some hoecakes, kind of a celebration, our
return to normal after weeks of being horses. Maybe even get
out the coffee grinder and chili juice, the flask of whiskey I
keep in my chuck bag for special ceremonies. The harem was
well in our control now, a few human peculiarities on our part
shouldn't spook them. A warm evening, Coyote didn't seem to
go for the whiskey, looks like I had to kill it myself, sitting
there after supper by the smoldering embers, explaining as best
I could how proud of him I was. He scooted over close, put his
hand on my arm and stroked, pulled on the hairs and pinched,
snuggled his head on my shoulder, hip and leg pressed against
my thigh. I don't know. I'm a man, been one all my life. When
my nature comes down, it comes down. I suppose it's an ordinary thing to feel affection for your pupil—I mean, I was teaching him—but suddenly the whole vast prairie, the screaming
frogs up and down the river, a series of herald barks and a lone
howl in the distance, jumbled red-green-blue stars, alcohol

washing the moss and dust of a long winter in the coastal brush, endless days living on the back of a horse eating raw cornmeal and drinking muddy water, night pressing in, thicker than the walls of the Fort Dodge guardhouse. He snorts, pushes me away, pouting and laughing at the same time, I jump up. Got to do something, hot sultry evening, hadn't bathed, been out of my clothes for weeks, go jump in the river, that's it, cool down some, clear my suddenly worried mind.

I remove my breeches and shirt, he's hunkered off a ways on the shore, wade out into the current, realize what a mistake this is, damn, brothers and sisters, standing here butt-naked now, my member bobbing in the breeze like a log caught in high water, bare feet sinking, slow warm suction of sand and mud. Hear him close behind me, a soft whimpering, the horses lining up along the bank to watch. I turn, he's naked black against the sickle moon, splashes out to me, there's nothing I can do, the body against me, warm and soft, tears flushing down the cheeks and lips, biting my nose and ears, my confusion is complete. Soft full buttock, hips, swelling buds of breasts. Tangled pubic hair and mound of Venus open and wet, pressing on me hard. I laugh. What else can I do.

Coyote is a woman child.

Going to Kansas

Spartacus He knew, when they cut off Brother-in-law's hands, it was time to leave. Brother-in-law had gone to Kansas, early on, before the exodus fever had hit and spread along the Mississippi, Vidalia, Natchez-under-the-Hill, Buttonwood Bayou, before the roads filled with poor folk carrying what they could, what they didn't want to leave behind with the burden of their past lives, scant little to show, when you get right down to it, for generations of slaving and then the freedom to sharecrop on old Master's place: rent the land with cotton, five bales for twenty-five acres, one bale for a mule, one for mule feed, another one for tools, had to mortgage the harvest to buy your supplies on credit from the company store, pay two dollars a bushel for seventy-five cents' worth of cornmeal, thirty dollars a barrel for fifteen-dollar pork, and old Master himself gin and market the crop for you, keep all the books. No matter what the weather, what the taxes or the price of cotton, year after year, come January, same old story: looks like you owe about a hundred dollars, Uncle, looks like you better sign up for next year, get that debt paid off. No matter what you do, never gonna get that debt paid off.

Brother-in-law, hardworking man that he was, had figured he could get a better deal ginning and selling somewhere else. The next night there was a knock on the cabin door, old Master's foreman and a couple of his henchmen come around to make a sales pitch. Brother-in-law a hard man to best in a fair fight, and even outnumbered four or five to one, which he was, he could inflict some serious pain. A catalog of the damage—busted lip and two cracked ribs versus a bitten ear, black eye, a bloodied nose, broken jaw, and a sprained ankle—could lead you to the conclusion that right had triumphed. Unfortunately, Brother-in-law's beating was not spread over six or seven bodies but condensed on his own aching self. And nothing angered the foreman, his henchmen, and his boss more than somebody willing to fight for free enterprise. Brother-in-law knew he was a marked man.

Notions of an open marketplace not the only thing get you in trouble either. An equally dangerous proposition to vote. On top of everything else, Brother-in-law was a Republican. The local Democrats had their minds set on redemption, and politics were simply an extension of war by other means. The bull-dozers, terrorists in white sheets, had already broken up a rally at the African Methodist Episcopal Church, beat the reverend senseless, and burned the building down. Every community had a similar story to tell, reconstruction on its last legs, Rutherford B. Hayes letting it be known if he's elected he did not intend to intervene in the South on behalf of freed people. Rumors spreading the country like sticky in the molasses shed: the South shall rise again and slavery be reinstituted, every African leader who dares to think otherwise is going to be killed.

It was the Fourth of July, a hundred years since the Declaration of Independence, everybody sitting around Brother-in-law's place rubbing their bellies and swapping lies, fried chicken, corn on the cob, yams, poke salad, and collard greens, nobody remembers where it came from, somebody had brought a circular advertising land for freed people: a four-color lithograph, a family seated at an oak table, enamel cookstove, apple and sweet-potato pies, woman in a bright flowered calico dress serving roast beef, new red potatoes, and carrots from a silver tray, scrolled wallpaper, portraits of ancestors, out the window through lace curtains a split-rail fence, cows grazing by the stone barn and waist-high wheat ripening in the wind. Come to Kansas, the land of old John Brown.

People here and there started talking about it, and after the election of '76, the Compromise of '77, the drop in the price of cotton from $84.37 a bale just three years before to $52.00, Brother-in-law did more than talk. He packed up, bid Sis and the kids goodbye, be back to collect them when the first crop was in, took off on foot through a cold spring drizzle headed west to find for himself the promise land.

Spartacus had had his doubts. Thought they'd heard the last of Brother-in-law, seen it happen before, not to better men than him but to just as good: the orneriness of the world get too much for you, the inexorable gnawing away at the spirit. Do your best to provide for family and friends, laugh and cut a step in the face of evil, devil coming to collect your troubled soul remind you of a story, bighearted, hard-working, good-timing until you crack. Usually a piddling thing, broken wagon spoke, damn mule come up lame, the toothy smile of some sapid young woman, just enough to stir up the notion from the turbid sediments of the mind: freedom. To live by mother wit, without restraint, without past or future, out on the open road. And house and church and wife and children left clicking their tongues wondering how long that train been gone.

It was a crying shame that Spartacus had been wrong.

A miserable dark, raining March evening when Brother-in-law come back, almost two years since he left, and the way his eyes flashed, that big booming laugh rattle the dishes on the buffet, the way he swept Sis up and carried her off to the barn leaving Spartacus to tend the children, the tales he told, passing the crockery jug of corn from hand to hand, the wide dry prairies of Kansas, the Solomon River valley, the unexpected joy of his return made the heart leap.

Spartacus realized for the first time *everybody* talking about going to Kansas now, everywhere he went, the church social, the barbershop, sitting around the town square on benches Saturday afternoon: free transportation, free land. People lined up on the banks of the Mississippi to catch the packets to St. Louis, a train of steamboats supposed to be churning upstream to Kansas City, fifteenth of the month, the *City of Vicksburg*, the *Gold Dust*, *Grand Tower*, the old *Joe Kinney*, don't need no ticket, children, just get on board, good

74

God Almighty, General William Tecumseh Sherman himself back in Atlanta marshaling the veterans of the Army of the Cumberland, ready to march north to Leavenworth. Don't know where it is, what kind of land, want to get there, that's all. Every woman and man their very own Moses now.

Spartacus didn't know what to make of it, a confusion of old memories and desire held in check all these years, he was too old for this, but they kept coming back. He didn't want to quit Mississippi, why should he have to abandon the land where he was born and come into manhood, they've already stolen everything else, labor, mother tongue, but they will not get this black earth, this dirt. His woman been gone so long she's no more than a haunt in the unguarded realms of the mind, a spirit of dwindling dawns and dusks, but a ghost Spartacus has remained true to in his way all these years all the same, now come back to unexpected life. She might be in Kansas. Should have been with her, wanted to leave back then before the war, but that's not the way things sort out. He had slipped from the quarters to meet her and their five children at the four corners, their trysting spot, between the two plantations. She'd hoarded food from the big house kitchen where she cooked, but the clouds they'd counted on to conceal them turned violent, tore the woods, wind, rain, and pitch darkness. Spartacus lost his way and when at first light he finally crouched soaked and shivering in the flooded ditch the only thing he saw was bloodhounds and overseers sniffing for a washed-out trail. Maybe, some said, just maybe she got through Tennessee, Arkansas, and Missouri, hard to imagine, a woman and five children, but some who tried weren't caught. If she were captured, if she were drowned crossing some rain-swollen creek, the bodies found, some news, surely, would have whispered down. Just maybe she made it through all God's dangers to the great plains beyond.

Kansas! Encysted all these years just beyond consciousness, and now a fever sweeping the river bottom, salvation, the answer to three hundred years of prayer. Large meetings being held in the churches, if anybody tried to talk against the idea, mentioned stories of drought, hail the size of a squirrel's head, tornadoes lift entire families from their scant meal of wormy hoecakes and hickory nuts, anybody make reference to grasshopper infestations, hundred-degree days and nights, the incessant howling wind and lonely reaches of brittle sun-brown grass, if anybody had the audacity to suggest this was a plot by railroad representatives, land speculators, and dastardly politicians, they were hooted down for a fool or more likely an agent of the landowners, lucky to escape the hall with no more than a knot or two slapped upside their head. Going to the promise land and don't want to hear none of this negatory jabber.

People were leaving, and the landowners were beginning to take notice, getting a little nervous about the cotton crop, who the hell going to chop it. Convinced the constable to start hauling folks from the Mississippi landings to jail, breach of contract, lock them up for the bill they owe at the company store, got the packet boats to refuse to put in to shore, the merchants wouldn't sell food or supplies to anybody looked like they were even thinking about heading down to the river.

Spartacus didn't want to leave. He was doing all right, had his team of mules for hire, the only thing he'd managed to salvage from the chaos of the war and the turmoil that followed, and he would have to take care of Sis and Brother-in-law's farm, couldn't leave, but still found himself one day wandering toward the river landing, March given way to a hot, humid April. He found himself standing among men, women, children, even, dogs and a few chickens, lean-tos and tents, drawn by curiosity, the voices, the shuffle and rumble, argument and song, some deep compulsion of the soul.

A packet churning upstream puts in toward the landing. Everybody suddenly surges toward the bank, the garbled voices swell, the boat, billowing black smoke into the thick air lying on the water, veers abruptly away from the dock, gathers steam back out into the channel, the captain shouts through cupped hands: *no more niggers for St. Louis.* A communal cry, woman next to Spartacus falls to the ground beating her breasts and pulling fistfuls of hair. He pushes forward to get a better look, can't hear what they're saying, commotion at the rear of the crowd. County health officers! They're forcing their horses stamping and prancing into the crowd: *break it up, a danger of yellow fever, everybody get back to the fields. Going to have to put some of you-all under quarantine.*

Spartacus watches them drag people away, mostly younger men, good working age. A gnarled old man, red face, blue veins netted across the cheeks, white hair, white linen suit, seems to have picked him out, works his way toward him through the milling, shouting tumult.

"Looking bad, boy, don't reckon any you-all going to make it past Memphis."

Spartacus smiles and nods, sees other agents working the crowd.

"Why you-all want to leave your homes for that desert I'll never fathom. Now, you want to make a good living, you got to stay with what you understand, none of you-all know beans about that there dry-land farming. Cotton is what you all understand, in your blood like the nap of your hair. I can appreciate there's been hard times last few years, what with the price of cotton falling, boll weevil taking maybe more than his share, but things like that run in cycles, and what with the last national election things got to rebound. Now, I represent a planter not far from here, finer gentleman you'd never want to meet, and I'm not going to kid you, he's short of hands to bring in the crop. Therefore he's authorized me to make you an offer of a contract I think you will find in every detail to be the most profitable arrangement you have—"

A shot echoes back and forth across the river. An explosion of shouting, the crowd pushes toward the dock, another steamboat, this one putting ashore. The agent looks around, eyes bulging, glances at Spartacus again, pupils dilating fear, two more pistols discharge, somebody's got a civil war saber blade slashing at humid sunlight. People begin to leap from the dock onto the deck of the packet before the lines are secured, the captain runs across the bow, chased down by three men in coveralls, dragged writhing to the wheelhouse, the crew are jumping or being shoved overboard, rising shrieks collapse the silence bracketing gunfire. The packet rocks gunnel to gunnel, then lists near to capsize, smokes and chugs, a large African at the helm, pitches and yawls out onto the Mississippi River under the weight of the overload clambered on board, the whistle sounds. *We going to Kansas!*

The agent picked up his hat, which had somehow been knocked to the ground. "Great Christ Almighty, where those niggers get guns!" Saw Spartacus either could not or would not answer, set the hat on his head, and made for the trees.

But Spartacus did not want to go. Tried to imagine a tree-less landscape stretching flat and rainless in the wind. He couldn't do it. Until nightfall. A single kerosene lantern flickers in the corner of the room, a trembling black ribbon dispersed across the ripsawed boards of the loft, the children asleep, Brother-in-law and Sis trying to decide what was absolutely necessary to take, what to leave behind for Spartacus. Excited talk eddied with giddy laughter, the first family move in twenty generations made of their own free will. Until midnight. New moon, horses in the yard, curses and calls, the knock on the door. No need to answer, kicked in, five men wrapped in white robes, hoods. They've been out there all along, everybody knows it, since reconstruction, the bulldozers, night riders, you expect them when you register to vote, when you speak out, but the darkest expectation could never equal the light of the lantern on them now, breathing, stinking in the room: why another beating? For old times' sake, farewell and God be with you, that terrible pale Christ bless the seeds? Brother-in-law rises from the table, seems to shrug, resigned to play out the ritual one more time, Spartacus struggles through the inevitable, vis-cous terror, but not to be knocked to the floor as he thought: dragged outside, both of them, to the woodshed, Brother-in-law to the chopping block, *going to Kansas, huh, nigger, tired of cotton, plant a little wheat, that what you think?*

Stretch his wrists across the block, the ax, rented from old Master with the bale of cotton's worth of tools, Spartacus pulls at the arms holding him, kicked in the stomach double to his knees, can only watch the accelerating arc, one, two. The hands twitch and dance upon the ground. *Let's see how much farming you can do in Kansas now, nigger. Tell all your friends about the promise land.*

Spartacus and Sis stop the blood, get Brother-in-law asleep with corn liquor, stay with him until the sky turns white. Spartacus collects the hands in a gunnysack and buries them in the truck garden. But can't look at the blood-soaked soil, didn't want to leave but knows now he can't stay. They hadn't killed Brother-in-law, he knows the booming laugh will surely return, not choked off by bitterness, but he doesn't want to see it, couldn't, they've won, driven him from the land. The rooster crows his confident position in the rising dawn and Spartacus closes his eyes. No grassland yet, no thunderstorms gathering across the level plains. But the emptiness is there.

Spartacus left it all behind. Nothing in his pockets, it all comes round, on the lam again, but this time no one to meet at the four corners, running, not *to* something but away. The packets stopping again after organizers threatened to charter boats, but Spartacus didn't have the fare, left all his cash with Sis, flying helter-skelter, no more conscious direction than a fallen leaf caught in the wind, and the wind become a gale and it was blowing toward Kansas. Not even tears, the land too saturated with blood to absorb them, the Anchor Line going upriver, that's all he knew or cared, push on board the *City of Vicksburg*, hug the rail, not really seeing the shoreline recede, the brown water roll and wake, the landing, people still shouting and waving handkerchiefs, nothing to do with him, the trees the same trees of home, but strange trees now, the same Mississippi River, strange, the woodsmoke-choked air is the breath of exodus and exile now, the shuffle and flux of three hundred exodusters on deck, throbbing paddle-slap and steam, a soothing nothingness till the shrill whistle sends the shore-birds flapping.

"That'll be four dollars, Uncle."

"Huh?"

"The fare to St. Louis, Uncle."

His senses numb, but he's got his story straight. "I been told this ride is free for us going to Kansas, sir."

An indulgent but exhausted smile on the skinny kid's face. "I suppose you think free land waiting for you when you get there, too."

"That's what I been told, sir."

"You been told wrong, Uncle. Four dollars."

"I don't have any cash, sir."

The kid exhales, scratches his ear looking away. "Going to have to put you off at Skipwith's Landing."

Spartacus waited beneath a twisted oak, an old man and two children shared their hoecakes and cold boiled sweet potatoes, until the *Gold Dust* put ashore and they crowded on board.

"That'll be four dollars, Uncle."

Got to have your story straight in this life. "I heard no charge for transportation, sir."

A wizened man, pointed goatee. "You heard wrong, Uncle."

The crew hustled him down the ramp at Bullit's Bayou. Another wait for the *Grand Tower* to Waterproof, the *Colorado* to Delta, slowly steaming north. Sun pressing down on the deck thick with passengers, the steam engine throbs, bells clang, shouts and laughter. Spartacus curled up on a coiled rope, hungry for a while, then beyond, the weight of sun, the wind off water, trees along the shores often lost in shimmering humidity, a big meandering river, never out on it before, one steamer to the next, each landing off, each landing on, the position of the sun losing all meaning, a dull sadness, then vague discontinuousness, a falling away of sky and clouds.

Hot. At Good Hope he slowly pulls himself up from the trunk of a hickory to force his way on board, keep the story straight, gains the deck of the *Fanny Lewis*, his back a knot of compressed pain, shoulders and arms grown monstrous in his mind, the heat, but the sun is almost gone, the river golden red, blackbirds cluster and call back and forth to roost on the opposite shore, his legs tremble, he finds a bucket near the railing to sit, queasy heat showers around him, sweat beads sudden cold icy chills shivering over neck and spine. He sits, huddles, heart pounding rapid thrusts of concentric cold, the packet shudders, dips and bobs, water slapping the sides, teeth and jawbone cringe and tingle, abdomen convulses what little there is in the stomach splattering over the side.

The present is burning and freezing away, dissolving into pestering leadmen, piney woods, cotton fields, his woman and old Master's hounds, Spartacus cut off and floating, delirious, they told him later, eyes gone yellow with fever, shouting out threats to anyone from the crew who approached: *where's my forty acres and my mule, nobody going to get no four dollars off of me, going to Kansas, got family there already claimed the land the government owes us, John Brown set the bees a swarming can't nobody hive them now, this boat taking us to the promise land, stand back, I ain't lying, stand back.* And they stood back, they told him, the ones who wiped his brow and gave him water to drink, told him when he blinked open the eyes, clear for the first time in days, when the smoke rising up to heaven from the western bank clarified, the river stench, boats and sails, barges and ferries, when he asked *where am I now?* they told him St. Louis. Do you think you can make it ashore.

"I been doing rather poorly."

"Yes sir, that is right."

"I believe I'm better."

A woman on one side of him, her daughter on the other, helping him down the gangway. "You got to be careful with this fever, it'll fool you. Just when you think you got it licked it'll creep round and put a foot right up your backside."

Low sun in the sky over red brick warehouses to the west of the levee, they find room at a small smoky fire kindled from what scrap and driftwood could be scavenged, getting scarce, everybody arriving from Mississippi and Louisiana the last couple of weeks got the place picked clean. He's exhausted. The short distance from the boat, the chill of the air off the water, his own inner chill, she puts her shawl around his shoulders.

"You try to warm yourself, mighty poor fire to do it with, Lord knows, but we take it as we find it. I'm going to look around, see what I can learn."

Watches her walk, soft purple violet along the levee, the way she carries herself, shoulders square, the buttock. Seen it years ago, the daughter the age their youngest would be now, he reckons, the one with the array of purple birthmarks across her cheek like a constellation of difficult stars. How long has it been, damn, before the war, the look in her mother's eye, determined to make it away. Something wells up, can't tell if it's health or sickness returning, but the symptom unmistakable, after all these years: it was laughter, mirth, the sudden pall hung weblike from the casing of his brain, burnt loose perhaps by fever, settles, drifts from the mind, the warm smell of her in the shawl draped over his shoulders, the evening light. Rests his head on his arms folded upon his knees, glad the world does not swell and sink with the river, chuckles *lord lord lordy*, and sleeps.

The voice confused him. Very dark, low-burning campfires along the levee, she was back, a baby crying somewhere, he looked up and blinked, his stomach churned, nausea or hunger, a little of both, the pungent aroma of a piece of brown bread she was offering him. Rye. Never had that before, but better get used to a whole lot of things you never tasted, seen, or heard tell of before, you're not in Mississippi anymore, nigger. He blinked up at her again. It's not her, not his woman, it's the one from the steamer, their daughters the same age, but she won't stay put in the mind, some trick of the eye in this light, a touch of the fever, she stoops beside him and places a soothing cool hand on his brow.

"This German bread a little too sharp for you?"

Looks hard at her. "This is St. Louis."

"You need to eat something, get back your strength, we hardly halfway there, got to get the next thing smoking. Heard tell a locomotive waiting to haul us on to Kansas, but no sign of a train, no sign of anything, those with some cash got on all right, the *E. H. Durfee* took a deckful up the Missouri. People got no money spend a lot of time loafing around the docks, some of the men wander off into town looking for food, a place to get out of the weather, lot of them don't come back, don't know what happens to them. Town folks helping as best they can, St. Paul's African Methodist Episcopal Church got a committee up, bringing out what few loaves of bread circulating, trying to raise the money to get everybody on their way west."

It isn't her, night air off the river cleared the sleepy from his head, but she keeps forming, someone standing behind a plate-glass window in the reflection of the woman outside. "Where we going?"

"Right now the Eighth Street Baptist Church got room for us, but we better hurry. Tomorrow I think I got enough cash to get us on the *Joe Kinney* up the Missouri."

They sat in the corner of the basement of the church, bedding and bodies spread over the entire floor, the daughter asleep. The reverend, his wife, and several women of the congregation passed out bread and chicken soup, large gooey dumplings. Spartacus managed to keep down a half a cup, began to sweat, removed the shawl, had forgotten it was still around his shoulders, carefully folded it, glancing at her smile, handed it to her.

"Where you hail from, woman?"

She rolls the shawl and stuffs it between the small of her back and the wall. "Memphis."

"How come you leaving there?"

"I was a cook in a hotel."

Should have known, cook in the big house, she's lurking in everything, the way she moves her hips, floats her hands before your face when she talks. "A cook."

"Best there was in all of Memphis, but they fired my ass when my husband started registering people to vote."

"Where's he now?"

"They fired me. But killed him."

The way she looks askance. "Didn't think they were much inclined to do that sort of thing up north."

"When it's you they lynch, seems often enough."

Uneasy coughing and mumbling all around, very warm and dank. "Why you going to all this trouble helping me?"

Not looking at him the way she does. "I reckon you remind me of somebody I used to know."

His sudden laugh causes the daughter to jump in her sleep.

The sun burns it out. Everything. The direct rays heavy on the deck, the air thick with water vapor and smoke, tremor and glare. The Missouri, worn through limestone escarpment, wide valleys, rolling growth of hickory and oak. Two hundred seventy-five travelers swelter in the hold of a leaky wooden barge, towed behind the *Joe Kinney*, an oven, rancid, oily bilge, urine, sweat, vomit, quick with flies. Desperate, disoriented, some of them, delirious and dying, but most hang on to this constant necessity—all that remains of all that's been of Mississippi and Louisiana is confused detritus—hang on to this stark need to reinvent yourself, as the unknown ancestors had done before.

Spartacus gave in to it. The fever-distilled clarity of the present moment, the woman next to him his woman, that woman, all at the same time, long hours staring at her, dense insufferable heat, two days moored below a cutbank while the crew dismantled and reassembled the engine, eleven days out on the river, a stupor of droning afternoons and fitful fever dreams.

Midmorning of the thirteenth day out from St. Louis a mumbling anticipation spread, people stood, tried to peer out of the hold, we're in Kansas! Kansas City! The town of Wyandotte up ahead. Gathered their bundles, tried to rally the sick, the steam whistle sounded, the engine shuddered, Spartacus climbed up on deck, weak and stiff, squinting against the intense light, the levee lined with people shouting, waving rifles and pistols, several men running alongside the barge.

The *Joe Kinney* bumped against the wharf, ropes tossed and secured: *do not come ashore, make no attempt to come ashore!* A delegation climbed on board, met with the captain in the wheelhouse, a few people in the crowd started handing baskets of bread and cheese, a little sausage, some hard-boiled eggs and jerky up to the barge. Spartacus watched the captain and a man in the wheelhouse, angry gestures, the delegation hurried ashore, the captain shouted orders, the crew, confused, finally loosed the lines, and with a jerk the barge moved away from the landing, full steam upstream past jeering townfolk along the shore. This was Kansas, the promise land.

The next day they approached Leavenworth, docked, the crew preparing to lower a gangplank to unload everybody when another delegation came on board. The captain signaled a halt to the disembarkation. Spartacus watched again, the captain and a man in the wheelhouse, he's the mayor, counting, no two ways about it, greenbacks, the captain putting them away, the mayor hurrying ashore, the captain shouting orders, the gangplank withdrawn, the packet and tow steaming back out into the channel.

The captain didn't blow the whistle, didn't dock at the Atchison town landing, came ashore below Ketchem's mill, ran everybody off the barge, splashing through the shallows, mired in mud, slip-sliding up the embankment to the promise land. In fifteen minutes all two hundred seventy-five were sitting along the levee blinking in the sun, tending the sick or walking back and forth stretching stiff and cramped muscles, getting the land legs, checking the lay of the place, already pushing the river from the mind. The Atchison mayor arrived with little time to shake his fist and curse at the captain, steaming away.

Spartacus and the woman sat on a large piece of limestone, she wiped perspiration with a red bandanna, tied it around her head. He picked up a handful of small rocks, looked at them carefully—not like what you see in Mississippi, these rocks, this dirt—began pelting them out into the water.

"Well, we got this far, where we going next?"

"One step at a time."

Looking closely at a small sunflower and a thistle sprouting among the riprap. "This is some place we're at now."

She laughs.

The wind tossing the sycamore and cottonwood. "By the way, have you ever told me your name? I been out of my head so long can't seem to call it."

"Sojourner Truth Willsdotter."

What did you expect. "Sojourner. Ain't that something."

"You got something against it?"

"Lord no. Some of my favorite people been named that."

"For instance?"

"It's been a number of years now, but seems like my woman had a child went by that name."

"You have a daughter?"

"My woman had five kids that I know about, she always did say they were mine. Leastwise none of them's eyes were blue, near as I can recall."

"How long's it been since you last saw them?"

Pulls a grass shoot, turns it in his fingers, examining the head. "Lord, that was before the war."

"Where they at?"

"Could be they made it to Kansas. Where *we* going?"

A murmur overspread the levee, the first of a steady stream of people along ruts worn through the trees, news of the arrival already reached town, everybody coming to look. By late afternoon the African Methodist Episcopalians and the Ebenezer Baptists clattered wagons up to give out food and clothing, began taking women with small children and the sick to sleep in their churches. The sun burned the sky vermilion behind the mill, the wind died on the water, people hunted up wood and lit fires, twilight caught in the bluffs and faded, the moon rose, dew condensed, Spartacus, Sojourner, and her daughter sat, insects and frogs, fireflies, some women and men singing a song to the river, monstrous stars across an enormous sky.

"You think, Spartacus, so far this beats chopping cotton for old Master?"

He looks at her. Sees clearly for the first time. An emptiness seems to fill, all that's gone before is gone. "This whole trip sure been a lesson to me, I can tell you that. Every place we been, St. Louis, Wyandotte, now here, think we the first niggers to leave the delta for the wilderness, come to find whole communities of Africans already settled, two or three churches surrounded by houses, family buried in the ground, extra pork chop and a clean shirt, even a few dollars to help a poor wayfaring stranger on down the line."

"I swear to God, you country from the get-go."

"You can say that again. By the way, where *are* we going to?"

She leans away from him. "We? What about that woman you chasing after?"

This Kansas not the place it was in the Mississippi imagination, time to fish or cut bait. "Come this far together, maybe I found her already."

Throws back her head and laughs, leans in and touches his knee with her fingertips. "You got another surprise coming. An entire town settled by black folk: Nicodemus."

A Time to Leave

Autumn Tallgrass | She looked for New Mother when the wind dropped and the snowfall lessened. There had been no omen. *This* was the sign: the blizzard. And the pox brought in with the traders and the soldiers. The folk were weakened, hunting had been spare, too many unable to hold a bow, unquiver an arrow, too many dead, both man and buffalo, how much more devastating will be what is portended.

She found New Mother frozen beneath her collapsed tipi hide.

It had been mild, a sunny turning, children not sick on their mats stayed out past sundown, a warm forgetfulness, like the return of good health and abundant game, like the season had forgot to change. Autumn Tallgrass and Coyote Dropping were lying in their tipi naked on buffalo robes. It had been still, a quiet movement from the south, the stars revolving across the smoke hole. They sensed the wind come round. Uncertainty in the air, the sides of the tipi went slack, fluttered, then snapped and sucked at the lodgepoles, the rawhide tether hummed, the sky turned turbid, unstable, smoke from the cook fire swirled and fell to earth, their skin gone cold. A rumbling in the north, growing there awhile at the boundaries of consciousness, swelled suddenly and burst upon the camp, roared and screamed, hurled cold dust, leaves, and sticks from the river bluffs, uprooted trees, crashed tipis to the ground. They scrambled to collect pots, gourds, and utensils scattered before the wind, gathered wood to feed the fire, the floodplain quickly blown full of snow, the shallow backwater overstruck with thin crystal, by morning solid ice.

Folk too weak from fever, too indifferent from hunger to go for fuel, frozen in their blankets. Some had begun to flee even before the blizzard had blown itself out, many of them found within bowshot of the encampment when the thaw came, huddled in ravines where they'd stumbled, blinded and confused.

Autumn Tallgrass and Coyote Dropping, too exhausted and hungry to mourn, laid New Mother on a travois and drug her to the high ground above the river where the wind had blown most of the snow away. The sun was out for the first time in many days, pale and low in the sky, their breath clouded and lingered about their faces.

"I don't want to vex the spirit of the dead. But it sure would be better to die in summertime when the earth is easy to spade."

"You don't die when you want to, you die when you can." Coyote Dropping gazes off over the drifted plain, takes a few futile chops at the frozen grass, then looks out again. "Death's not just in the shadows that lengthen in the woods and washes. He's among us, at our council dances and in our dreams."

"You've been talking too much to rum dealers and buffalo soldiers, Fancy Dancer."

Still staring out across the flat river valley. "Too many dead. I can feel it in the marrow of my bones, the ghost sickness. We got to get away from here, Autumn Tallgrass."

"Where will we go? The other bands must be suffering as bad as we are, last thing they want to see is a bunch of half-starved cold-crazed cousins around their meager fires."

"Ha! Your Texas kin wouldn't be very glad to see us either. Anyway, Death likes company. I've seen it before in my travels: the folk try to flee and he hitches a ride on their travois to the next camp, they unpack doom with the beadwork and antelope spoons they bring as gifts. We have to do like the traders and fur trappers, go off alone, out where the foxes say good night, where a gregarious scoundrel like Death isn't likely to drop in."

"Get so lonely we can't even die, huh."

"That's what we'll have to do."

They paint New Mother black and red, clear the mound of ice and snow to dance and sing, with what little energy and spirit they have left, two more plaintive voices mixing with the wind, death songs rising like fever around the snow-struck camp.

They traveled toward the rising sun where the settlers are, the light dazzling over crusty snow, the yellow, red, and gray tufts of grass. They came upon the farthest claim. All they saw was the livestock shed at first, drifted full of fine powdery snow, a mule and a cow suffocated inside. Then the footprints wandered off through drifted ridges below the abandoned dugout, slowly obliterated by the wind.

"This lonely enough for you, Big Dancer?"

"But too far from water."

The dugout was blown full, a cramped ice cave hollowed around the small hay-burner stove. The bed, straw-tick mattress, chairs, and table had all been fed to the fire. Both stood and stared awhile at the paltry belongings left packed in the snow.

They butchered the animals, took the steel traps and whatever else they could carry, and continued their way east to the headwaters of the Ninnescah. Followed downstream until they found a small cabin built close to the shore where a creek ran in. Autumn Tallgrass dismounted: no smoke from the rusty stovepipe, the latchstring hanging out blowing in the strong north wind, a cowbell rattling from the eaves, no tracks in the snow settled around the door. She called out. No answer. Coyote Dropping rode up and down the river, looped out across the floodplain. No sign of other buildings, the sky turning dark, a menacing scent in the air, weak winter light dying on the translucent water roiled unfrozen at the channel.

"Well, woman. This looks like it."

"An empty cabin where two streams merge, at the end of the day, a blizzard hounding your heels, be foolish to pass it by."

"Death have a hard time finding us here."

A rusty stove, dry kindling, even a blanket on the bed, all covered hand-deep in fine powder snow. They scavenged wood along the river, a violet dusk congealed into sleet, the wind fell long enough for it to thicken, then rose again to drive it down the watershed. They brought the horses inside, the wind whistled, moaned, and sighed in the cracks between the warped board siding, the stove glowed red, the horses snorted and stamped.

When the sun returned, they set their traps along the river and the creek. When visitors dropped by, Coyote Dropping stayed inside the cabin while Autumn Tallgrass talked. In the spring she took the pelts into the nearest settlement, Blackstrups Mill, to sell. When she got back, he was gone.

Coyote Dropping | He had come back to the cabin early from his rounds checking the traps, before Autumn Tallgrass had started off for Blackstrups Mill. He was afraid.

There had been unearthly singing along the river at night. That early spring morning he had seen two creatures precipitate from the mist along the river, and his spirit broke. Nothing he could tell himself, no explanation or interpretation, settled him, not even a steaming bowl of coffee and chili juice, not her insistence it was a trick of light and moisture hanging in the air, could ease his distorted thought. He could see beyond the fragile surface mixture of Texas obduracy and folk ridicule in her eyes that Autumn Tallgrass was worried too by what she saw. What she saw was him.

He was a fancy dancer, storyteller, conjurer, a man who had traveled, seen the prairie north and south, had held long discussions with Autumn Tallgrass, a growing facility in her other tongue. He knew of things beyond the limits of the folk's encampment. But the encampment had always been there, a long tangled sleave of story and event, embattled maybe, hungry, sick, wounded, but there when he returned. Now he wasn't sure. The omens, despite all efforts to twist them to his liking, were ambiguous, confusing at best, disturbing to his usual calm sense of the world as a severe but harmonious unwinding, a sacred, inexorable process to be decorated by movement and words. This winter he had seen the abandoned burrows of the settlers in the clear harsh gray light of blowing snow, begun to recognize the forlorn terror they must have felt, utterly lost and desperate, thrust out, small and exposed, onto this indifferent expanse. Not home. Not anywhere. The land throwing up phantoms no one of their kin had yet dreamed of, no amount of deft decoration could subdue.

Autumn Tallgrass left with the pelts. He waited in the cabin, the air thick and dank, the smell of cold ashes billowing into the room on the downdraft from the unlit stove. Constricted and dark. The silver mill, sycamore bed, opaque sun at the narrow window, thoroughly small and troubled, the fixity of the walls, absolute and strange, confounding his sense of transitoriness and flux. The random clanging of the cowbell outside, the world wouldn't look right to him again until it was moving. He packed his bundle and started out.

Thunderstorms rumbled from the southwest every afternoon into the night, thunderclaps pulsed and rattled, lightning flashed across the broken plains, the grass came on lush and green, and Coyote Dropping's spirits rose. The chopping stride of the pony mile after mile, the cadences of stories and songs told and sung by generations of horsemen, the patterns of thought, the small rituals of the trail—it all came back, reunited him with them, even though they are scattered now like fallen cottonwood leaves before a bitter north wind. The land, rumpled hills sprawling away to the horizons on either side of a low divide beneath the turbulent sky, supported him everywhere.

He found Spotted Tail's camp. Everybody was excited, making preparations for a hunt, some big man coming to Fort McPherson from across the salty waters that separate the woods from the rising sun, lots of powerful people coming along for the sport. Coyote Dropping has nothing more important to do than to join in, there's going to be a lot of stomp-dancing done.

The fort lay sprawled below the Platte River. Log and frame structures painted fireproof brown around a dusty desolate parade quadrangle, the officers' quarters to the north, stables, corrals, and log barracks for the enlisted men to the south, a jointed cedar pole in the center, sun-bleached flag popping in the wind. Spotted Tail's people set up their lodges at the periphery. Coyote Dropping wandered among the laundry quarters behind the barracks, soapsuds row, sod roof, straw strewn over the floor, large numbers of mostly young women of all builds and hues after a hard day at the tubs. A good place to find out what's going on, he thought, until set upon by a pack of sentries and hustled back to the lodge. Knowledge would have to be gained at a distance.

He rode off to the town of North Platte just to walk around, take it all in. This alien people moving onto the plains, following the iron rails yellow men sweated to lay across the land for the monstrous steaming and hissing contraptions that rolled on them belching smoke and embers into the heavens. They were impressive. He watched one come into the railyard at the edge of town, take on water from the large wooden tank blackened by the stove that heated it in winter, watched the black iron engine whistle and chug, spin its driving wheels, rumble out onto a bridge in the middle of a bright red-brick structure, round like a tipi, set on a circle of limestone torn from the earth: the roundhouse where they housed forty engines. They swung it to an empty lodge and backed it in, a sharp pungent bite of burning wood, oil, and steel.

Coyote Dropping looked on. The wood-frame depot, log hotel, a long movable box on wheels where the yellow men slept who slaved in gangs to lay the iron trail. Mule skinners, fur traders, cowpunchers, speculators, Conestoga wagons, stacks of smooth-cut lumber, nail kegs, sacks of flour, side meat, beans, rifles, plows, shovels, pickaxes, all surged about him, lost in thought, a turbulent glee, alone, individual, lost from the considerations of the workers swarming like red ants in tall grass gone to seed, a better dance, it seemed, than if they'd contrived what every step should be.

The street a series of wagon ruts through prairie grass, lined with the one-room shacks the strangers build. The stench of horse manure, pigpens, beef ribs, eggshells, potato peelings, onion skins, and melon rinds thrown onto the ground, hogs, dogs, chickens, and children running loose, piles of hay rotting on the corners, enormous buzzing swarms of opalescent flies in open sun.

Coyote Dropping stopped in front of the Cedar Hotel. This is where they store the bottled spirits he'd heard much talk about. Stood and contemplated. The people on the street paid him no mind. He laughed, a low whoop, and walked on in.

Nobody raised an eye. Invisible. The shadowy inside seemed small and remote, a vague unfocused threat, smoke and dust, irresponsible amounts of tobacco being consumed, but the men and the few gaudy women distant from him, he loomed in their midst unnoticed, fought off the notion to slap the nearest loafer upside the head and dash for the door. Stood until his eyes adjusted, a flood of details jumbling up his perception, the tables, chairs, oil-burning lamps, the moist heat of the place, strong conflicting aromas caused the mouth to slaver and the nose to burn. A few dusty bottles of firewater lined below a gigantic streaked mirror, the entire place thrown back reversed.

He did a modified bull-buffalo gait to the bar. The man with a white cloth tied around his midriff ignored him, continued wiping a clean and dry expanse of wood, no bared teeth or bristling hair on the nape. Coyote Dropping stood his ground. Two men playing a game with cards and a perforated board nearby, shouting out what Coyote Dropping recognized as numbers, laughing or slapping their forehead and moving pegs. When everything had settled to what seemed normal proportions, the wild emotion controlled inside, and he'd observed how things went along the bar, Coyote Dropping attempted that fragment of language he'd garnered from Autumn Tallgrass.

"I have thirst." The man behind the bar, only a boy it turns out on closer inspection, florid, pockmarked, scrofulous sores, skinny as a lodgepole and not near as straight, moves a little like a turkey vulture, not many teeth left to bare, continues wiping the three glasses in front of him, stops to swat at his ear, maybe a mosquito humming around it. Coyote Dropping swallows a time or two, the place looking much bigger than it did, anybody with any sense would slink on out of here while everybody still acting like he's no more than an unpleasant odor floated in from the piss place out back. But damn, that firewater looking good, and this would be quite a coup for a dancer not given to martial exploits to tell about, squatting around the campfire on the floor of Hard Stick Canyon beneath the liar's moon. Speaks a little louder against the laughter and that cowboy in the corner started up playing some small wailing, shiny metal-encased collection of flutes, the inclination to fly. "I have thirst, please."

The bartender bats at his ear again, then turns to look, glances out at the room, the cowboy playing, the card and peggers, the women just standing there glowering, all satisfied to keep on what they're doing. He picks up the rag he'd put down to attend to his nails, moseys along the bar to where Coyote Dropping stands.

"You seem to have strayed into the wrong establishment, the Agency's over to Fort McPherson."

The kid moves slow but talks fast. In the face of incomprehension, Coyote Dropping smiles and repeats. A little sign language wouldn't hurt. "I have thirst."

The bartender's eyes turn up quickly in the sockets, flick about the tavern, still nobody giving much of a damn one way or the other. "You got money?"

"Money?"

A little sign language of his own. "Greenbacks. Dough. Wampum."

"I have thirst."

"That much is clear. How you going to pay?"

"I have thirst, I ask, you give me to drink."

"It doesn't work like that."

"It doesn't work?"

"You buy a drink."

"I don't know that."

"You don't have money?"

"I have thirst."

"But what can you give me in trade?"

"What do you want?"

For some idle reason taking an interest in this conversation, he looks Coyote Dropping over head to foot. "What's that hanging from your belt?"

Coyote Dropping at a loss for words, not sure he wants them anyway, perhaps a bit foolish to wear this trophy into town in the first place, to wander in here. But has come this far, too late to back off, pats himself on the head. "How do you say?"

"Well I'll be go to hell." Leaning over the bar real close to get a good look in difficult light. "That's what I thought it was. Whose was it?"

Better do some fast thinking, one mistake piling up on top of the other, instead of working himself into a drink of firewater, his first, it could turn out to be his last draft of the light and substance of this life. Fast thinking one thing, but also requires some fast talking, a precarious procedure in the other man's unwieldy tongue. The skinny bartender's interest seems sincere and not hostile, willing to listen to anybody's story, but how good are you at judging these people's intentions, their sense of humor, tolerance, and they yours, the intricate structures of intercourse where a man can get hopelessly hung up if he doesn't know where to step, whose eyes to avoid, and who he can yell at. It's suddenly, chillingly clear to Coyote Dropping he's in a very strange place surrounded by strangers. Maybe too late to explain, even if he was able, the trophy didn't belong to him originally, given as a gift in return for a step he cut during the games celebrating a successful hunt, he was only kidding, and a poor joke at that, about it being a scalp, really thought anybody could tell by looking it was a horse's tail. Feeling a little like the part of the horse it covers.

"Whose is it?"

One final, fatal look into the bartender's eyes, some sign how to proceed, what it was he wanted to hear. It sure appeared to be open-faced curiosity. Besides, he didn't have the language to tell the truth. "I one time in Texas was jumped from hiding by a pack of savage dogs."

Coyote Dropping is now aware the others in the enormous room are beginning to take notice: the board peggers have stopped counting, the cowboy has stopped playing his peculiar instrument, the idlers moved a little closer, more dangerous now to shut up than to keep on talking. "On a horse, making war along the river. I kill all seven of the flowing-hair sons of a distempered mother, unarmed." A pause to assess effect. They still want more. "*They* were unarmed. *I* had a plenty long knife and . . ." Can only finish off the story with vivid gestures.

The bartender grins, others in the room grin, he plunks a bottle and a tumbler onto the wooden plank between them. "I'll swap you even up, one drink for one scalp."

Has this man, has anybody in the place, ever seen a scalp before? The firewater a valuable commodity, from all you hear, but like tobacco, they squander it. Even so, not sure they'd be too happy trading it for a horse's tail. "I take it."

The bartender pours, Coyote Dropping lays the trophy down, grabs the glass, the bartender hasn't even touched the horse's tail, he and everybody else watching real close. Coyote Dropping looks to both sides, gulps the whiskey, wheezes, eyes water, a sudden welling up of feeling through his entire body, a big smile, then a laugh, everybody else laughs, the bartender pouring another tumblerful, he tosses it down, a surge of desire, jubilation, the cowboy gives out a yell, starts in playing a strange but thumping music, Coyote Dropping whirls around, a quick hop, stutter step, kind of a horse's-tail dance. And that's when he sees the woman. A long-legged big bear of a girl, frilly costume high on her hips, large as a north mountain grizzly and twice as mean, jump on a man like a camp dog on a buffalo bone, fixing him with an unnerving, disdainful, and lascivious eye. She grabs him. Doesn't know if she's going to eat him alive or throw him down to rut, a wrestling match of some sort, but he soon realizes her punches and shoves are in time to the wailing cowboy song: one step, three turns, two spins, and a bump. Cutting the pigeon wing, a money mask, a goat-house dance of some kind, so simple it eluded him.

The bottle spirit took full possession, fractured him, he saw it all as it occurred, participant and observer in and of the dance contained within the dark middle of a structure of planed boards, walls, and puncheon floor, prairie wind blowing at the swinging doors, light extending out across the sand hills to the forest rivers, the mountains, to the fabled world of salty oceans, forever till the start of time. It ruptured the petty limits of a hard existence, was what drew him to Autumn Tallgrass, this knot of strange dancers stomping and singing out blindly this rhythm, this simultaneous love and alienation, the unspeakable, unknowable all.

The observer of all this was keen-eyed enough to see the bartender, who'd been cutting his turkey-vulture step, flapping his long skinny arms and cawing behind the bar, see him stop to catch his breath, reach down and pick up the horse's tail. Was able to read the change of mood in the expression that flowed from the eyes across the sharp, bald, red-faced features, understood what they all held in common, what bound them together, was mighty delicate stuff, could be very quickly exhausted, saw it was time to break off this ceremony, collect his coup, whop the nearest cowboy atop his hat, and make for the door.

The shots discharged as he hightailed it down the dusty main drag of North Platte among scattering, honking, and hissing geese, between the boardwalks filled with men, women, boys, and girls watching, the shooting more in jest than earnest, lofted with lusty yells and curses into the windy sky. As close to a chase as anybody cared to mount.

The hunting party was forming when he got back to Fort McPherson. Important men arrived at the North Platte railhead, washer-women worked extra hours to get the parade best ready for close-order drill and military review, handlers exercised greyhound dogs, recruits loaded large tents, oriental rugs, pillows, buffalo robes, potatoes, onions, peas, mushrooms, carrots, tapioca, tables, chairs, linen, china, glassware, silver cutlery, candles, evening dress, brass and woodwind instruments, ale, whiskey, claret, brandy, champagne, and several long tons of ice onto sixteen four-horse wagons. As the sun disappeared in dust suspended at the horizon, the military band struck up music for the dance. The quartermaster handed out a thousand pounds of Virginia tobacco to Spotted Tail's people, and they picked up drums, gourd and turtleshell rattles, and joined on in: a giddy festival, no two ways about it.

The next day before sunup the bugle sounded, a clatter rose with the morning birds that scavenged the dump. Spotted Tail and Coyote Dropping watched the buffalo soldiers saddle horses, yoke mules, line the wagons up on the parade ground, three ambulances to carry firearms and ammunitions. A cheer burst from officer's row, they maneuvered their ponies to see, General Sheridan, then a tall man, silky mustache and goatee, hair flowing almost golden, buckskin pants and vest, long rippling trim when he moved, the angle of the early light catching in the porcupine quillwork, the weave of the crimson shirt.

"That's Buffalo Bill."

A shorter man, grizzled beard covering his face from the ears and nose down, stiff-collared jacket, golden ropes hanging from the shoulders, and knee-high black polished boots, joined the two others on the porch.

"The Russian Grand Duke Alexis."

Then came the rich tycoons, railroad builders, and newspaper men, all dressed for the hunt, lined up to see the troops parade, the wagons roll and clatter past, and finally Spotted Tail, Coyote Dropping at his side, followed by his band of a thousand men, women, and children trailed out of the fort, the rising sun at their backs, a low tissue of dust slowly sliding south across the plains.

Autumn Tallgrass	She waited at the cabin. Coyote Dropping didn't return. Listened to the coyotes howl, the creatures joining in, she fought

off the terror struck down her spine, echoed from her feet and hands to nestle in the brain. She forced herself out to find the source of this singing, convinced herself the dogs are always loose, it's the silent ones you need to fear, not those who make their presence so earsplitting obvious. After she found them, she went every night along the creek to observe. Grew fond of her loneliness, had never lived away from people before, but her nurturing of the language she'd brought with her to the folk had always set her apart, the time in Texas when she'd lurked back deep inside herself had prepared her for it. She grew used to the cabin, close to Old Red, Long Tooth, Tore Ear, Gimp, and the creatures who shared the watershed.

One day a god-speaker came. He talked with her under the tarp in the drizzling rain, used tobacco, drank hully gully. Wanted her to help him capture them, rescue them from the beasts, he said. She understood the creatures taking on the ways of God's dog and making them their own. She knew what that was like. Didn't know why she did it, disrupted their lives, uprooted them, destroyed their coyote mother. Loneliness, maybe, an unsuppressed susceptibility to the common work of the group, maybe the memory of her Texas grandmother, whose honest desire and longing for lost family on the desolate prairie led to the near destruction of Autumn Tallgrass's life. That same lost longing she recognized in the god-speaker's haunted eyes. She brooded, as perhaps her Texas grandmother had, when it was too late, the pack dispersed, when he had gone with the one he called his brother. She wondered at the fate of Black Woolly, cast out, the enormous silence of the night, beyond the singing of frogs and crickets, where the coyotes had been.

The moon waxed. She remembered what Coyote Dropping would do. She stripped naked, smeared her face and arms, breasts and belly, buttock and thighs with fine silt from a still backwater of the river to protect her from mosquitoes, followed the creek bed to the den. Huddled in deep blue shadows till the full moon was in the very middle of the sky, moved out onto the level floodplain across the tepid flow of water from the bluffs into the pure lucid light and began to croon a song. Howled and yodeled nonsense, then words and phrases, eyes closed to capture some canine vision, camp dogs, Texas hunting hounds, foxes, wolves, transform them from the mind to motion, imagination to dance. All around the coyotes joined in, but from distant watersheds, and not the voice she wanted to find.

When the sun rose she crept exhausted into the ruptured den, the deepest chamber where the creatures had cowered, curled into a tight ball, and slept.

The next evening she hunted field mice for her food, went hungry, lapped water at the creek, smeared on a new layer of mud and waited for the moon to rise. She did this every night, and on the seventh the voice rose close behind her in the sumac, locust, and grapevine along the ridge. The hair bristled on her neck. She continued her singing, the dance, to make sure of what she heard, that it was Black Woolly out there and not her mind starved and half crazed with loneliness. Does nothing different, the same melody, words, and movement, nothing sudden to spook her prey. One more trilling yip-yowling call from the bluffs, it is there, then dissolves in the incessant evening drone.

The next night the same. Autumn Tallgrass growing weak, eating nothing but sorrel, peppergrass, and cottonwood sap, but the fast had not gone over to delirium, she was sure of that, the ritual was strict, the world palpable, and Black

Woolly out there again, could even believe she smelled her on the warm breeze funneling down the channel of the creek. At sunrise when she'd returned to the inner chamber to sleep, could hear rustling outside, something prowling, sniffing at the mouth of the den.

The next night she appears. Autumn Tallgrass is out on the floodplain, the sickle moon not yet risen, the wind high overhead, a hot, dry flowing, the air crackles in the treetops, heat lightning flickers along the horizon, she doesn't see her until she is almost upon her, a darkness in the tall grass suddenly formed into woolly mane, black body nestled low to the ground, an abrupt *woo-oo-woo*. Autumn Tallgrass drops down on her knees, face in the dirt, arms stretched out flat, flops her head back and forth. Black Woolly creeps forward on her belly. She holds a young rabbit in her teeth.

Autumn Tallgrass grovels, but it seems to confuse Black Woolly, like she might bolt at the slightest sound or twitch of the hand. Autumn Tallgrass rises up slowly on her haunches. Be dominant, replace Old Red, like New Mother once, she chortles and coos: *I will save your life.* Black Woolly sits, tense and suspicious. Food. She's brought her kill to share. Autumn Tallgrass must go to her, one hand forward, woofing and wooing, not sure whether to look her in the eye, glances side to side, at the ground, halfway there when Black Woolly drops down, seems to have decided it's safe, she will not run. Autumn Tallgrass fighting for control, hunger and fear, electricity, she inclines her body, leans in close, sniffs, Black Woolly doesn't flinch. Autumn Tallgrass licks her nose, her cheeks and lips, Black Woolly rolls over on her back, stretches and squirms. Autumn Tallgrass laughs, Black Woolly springs up on her hands and feet, retreats backwards into the tall grass, panting, eyes wild and wide. Autumn Tallgrass doesn't move, looks into the sky, Black Woolly relaxes, drops down again, circles to one side, rolls over, circles to the other, sniffing, then shaking her head, finally approaches and sits, head tilted back, nostrils flared, sensing the air, her eyes squeeze shut and open. Autumn Tallgrass nuzzles her again, she rolls over, grabs the rabbit in her teeth, and lays it in Autumn Tallgrass's lap.

They devoured it, then lay in the grass beneath the wind until the sky turned white. They moved to the den, slept balled together until midday heat woke them. Autumn Tallgrass began to groom her, removed lice, fleas, and ticks, they slept again till dark, went out to hunt along the creek.

After several days Autumn Tallgrass led her down the channel toward the cabin. Black Woolly became agitated as they approached, held back, Autumn Tallgrass had to stop and go fetch her, cajole, coax her on. She refused to continue where the bluffs opened out onto the flat river. Crouched on all fours, the cabin in sight, she whimpered and whined, sensed something that seemed both to fascinate and to frighten her. Autumn Tallgrass realized it was the scent of her abducted brother. Left her there and went on alone. Curiosity and loneliness would overcome fear, by dawn she would be pawing at the cabin door.

It was a long difficult task to train her, to work from snorts, howls, yips, and yowls, snarls, frowns, and bared teeth to words, to raise her to her hind feet, straighten her spine and square her shoulders, many days alone in the cabin or the fields along the Ninnescah before she'd consider giving up her coyote ways, at least modifying them to the ways of the folk, before she'd tolerate clothing, at first just the vest made from Old Red's hide, then finally dungarees and a red flannel shirt Autumn Tallgrass had found, before she'd move from the floor to sleep in the bed and eat her meat cooked instead of raw.

Whenever travelers stopped by she would run off to hide in the saplings and tangled grapevine along the riverbank or creep into the dark corner of the cabin. The strangers would see her, sometimes naked, smell the wild musk, then quickly ask directions, or for a drink of water, a bite to eat, not linger to pass the time of day, hasten on their way, furtive glances across the hindquarters of their mule as they trotted out of sight along the river trail. Before long the neighbors stopped calling, a new path beat an arc over the high ground above the cabin, a resting spot beneath the old lightning-struck elm to view the peculiar goings-on below.

They passed the winter walking trap lines, Black Woolly in charge of the coffee mill and chili juice. An expressive sign language, a series of sounds taking on syntax and grammar, their lives fallen into a sequence of rituals and rites, all of which conspired to keep Autumn Tallgrass's mind channeled, moving, to keep her from thinking too much on Coyote Dropping, New Mother, the folk, even her Texas grandmother. The images settled so vividly sometimes in her dreams she'd start awake, disoriented and confused, bewildered until the warm scent of Black Woolly cuddled beside her calmed her back to sleep.

In the spring the grasshoppers came. A sunny, wild windy day, then suddenly the northern sky turned black, large great flakes of snow it looked like, but it was hot. Black Woolly the first to hear it, stopped stockstill, her ears raised. Autumn Tallgrass saw her, bluestem tossing about, an intent look in her eyes, a concentrated listening beyond the wind, turned to look, and saw them descend. They slammed down like hail against the worn siding of the cabin, began to eat, the world gone dark, the close throbbing screams, rising and falling, contained within a larger dome of a constant, impacted droning, the entire prairie resonating hundreds of miles around. Black Woolly leapt high into the air, snapping at them as they flew, a feeding frenzy quickly gone over to pure frenzy, the grasshoppers crawling into her shirt and trousers, wriggling and eating the fabric away from her body. Autumn Tallgrass, slapping, spitting grasshoppers from her face and eyes, the air viscous with them, fought her way to Black Woolly, had to subdue her, scratching and biting out wildly, dragged her to the Ninnescah, splashing and stumbling in the shallow water to the middle of the river where the air was clearer, sat down in the warm current on the sandy bottom, and watched.

Everything a locust will eat was gone by the time a strong wind came up and blew them away. Devoured it: the fields of corn and wheat, oats, hay, sugarcane, the truck gardens stripped to the ground, carrots and onions even eaten out of the soil. Many of the hard-luck settlers packed what was left, hitched the hungry oxen and mules to the wagon, abandoned the homestead and headed east. Those who stayed had to sell the livestock or butcher it before it starved to death, had to stand in long humiliating lines for handouts, a few sprouty relief potatoes and some weevilly flour, youngsters got the spuds, oldsters the peel, nothing to eat sometimes but bean water. Hard-working, self-reliant people on the dole again, one damn thing after another, beg for loans from the grasshopper bonds voted in, grafters, swindlers, vagabonds, and drifters, idle time to kill.

The presiding elder at Blackstrups Mill called prayer meetings, preached sermons about God's will. Farmers who'd never had to deal with a world like this flat, unearthly desolation started coming from hundreds of miles around, shouted amen, sang and supplicated, bemoaned their helplessness caught up in the enormity of creation's wrath. Mumbled and whispered of devils, how else explain it, nothing in their experience or that of the parents or the grandparents was up to it. Two miscreants stalked the Ninnescah just last summer—knew nothing good would come of it—the dark woolly one still hereabouts, seen her often, holed up in the cabin with that strange-acting trapper woman, seen them both cavorting naked in the moonlight, a heathen service to Beelzebub. They're the ones called down God's own angry retribution, caused all this deprivation, suffering, and pain. I don't know what the Good Book says, but in my book only one way to handle a witch and her demon, one place for devil dancers, and that's dancing at the end of a rope!

Black Woolly, sitting in the corner staring at the reflections mirrored on the surface tension in a bucket of water, rocking slowly back and forth, was, as usual, the first to hear the noise outside the cabin. A distant cough, footsteps along the trail. A new moon and overcast, total darkness pressed upon the eyes, whispering borne by the slow-moving river water and wind, she growled low in the throat. Autumn Tallgrass started awake, flickering torchlight on the oilpaper window, a sudden blood-chilling scream the other side of the door. An ax blade split through, another, Autumn Tallgrass grabbed what she could, whatever was near, a steel trap, the coffee mill, the old butcher knife, stuffed them in a gunnysack, the door broke open, and Black Woolly sprang, confused torchlight and dark, ax blades and clubs, howls, barks, and snarling. Autumn Tallgrass swung the loaded sack wildly, the circle of men beyond the doorway seemed to give in panic, and she broke clear to the trees on the higher ground. Couldn't see Black Woolly, not in the dark safety of the woods or in the globe of firelight growing larger around the cabin as they put it to the torch.

She watched the sparks fly upwards, eddy, and die in pitch-black night. At dawn the men left. She hauled the gunnysack up the creek to the den, then returned to search for Black Woolly. A mist, water vapor and smoke, hung over the river, the embers smoldered. A trail of blood led to the underbrush, then out onto the prairie. She followed as far as she could, lost it in a ravine. When she got back to the ashes of the cabin, two men on horseback were waiting, came up behind her before she was aware of them. She ran for the river, was roped and tied, tossed up on the rump of a horse.

How many times, she thought, as she was carried off to Blackstrups Mill.

The Coyote Trials

Brother | He sits at the table staring at his hands, clasped but fidgeting in his lap, a droning prayer, the half-hearted singing of the 512th and the 234th hymns, looks up finally when the Committee of Trial is called, takes a deep breath, fights back the supercilious smile beginning to twist his lips, can hear the mumbling shuffle of the crowd outside in the street, all Brother can do to keep from laughing out loud.

Bishop Wiley takes his Brown's Tar Troches to clear and strengthen his enfeebled voice for the strenuous task, strides past the anxious congregation, his jaunty posture, the cut of the Bible resting in the crook of an elbow, belying the spiritual exhaustion, the dread. Eighty-seven circuit riders, supernumerary preachers, and the effective elders have convened to discuss the ninth, the third, and the tenth questions, to hear reports from the Auditory Committee and the committees on Missions, Popular Amusements, Freedman's Aid, and Tobacco, to expedite transfers, to grant permission to trustees of booming town churches to sell their property and reinvest—have done all the tedious business of the annual conference preoccupied, in rapt anticipation of this final consideration: the judiciary investigation of dram drinking, dalliance, and consortation with the Devil.

Bishop Wiley places the Book on the lectern, lips puckered, chin pulled down to the Adam's apple, eyes peering over the wire spectacles, leafs through the thin pages held carefully between gnarled finger and thumb, a slight palsy in the hand. He finds the proper mark, looks up at the restless house, hot, dry autumn air trapped in the narrow dusty building, clears his throat, and reads. The text seems to be chosen to plant seeds of doubt, an implied condemnation: the fourth chapter of Second Corinthians. Floating fragments dissolved in the diaphanous voice, in the expectations of those come to judge: *we have this ministry . . . have renounced the hidden things of dishonesty, not walking in craftiness, nor handling the word of God deceitfully . . . but we have this treasure in earthen vessels . . . we are troubled on every side . . . perplexed, but not in despair, persecuted, but not forsaken, cast down, but not destroyed . . . we look not at the things which are seen, but at the things which are not seen: for the things which are seen are temporal, but the things which are not seen are eternal. Amen.*

The annual conference had never attracted attention before, had run its course in hay-tent churches or balloon-frame meetinghouses, cottonwood siding springing in and out with the wind like an old horse with the heaves, indifference the best to be expected from the clodhoppers, molasses lappers, and professional squatters haunting the makeshift land offices and the taverns of the dusty prairie towns, sniffing out rumors of warrants to be purchased and sold or claims to be contested, trouble to be avoided or engaged, some way to collect the revenue to cover the whiskey consumed, anything to avoid aggravating the dirt too much on the places they were supposed to farm. But this year was different. What little fat there was stripped from the soil, first the economic panic, then the infestation of grasshoppers come down with the wind blowing in from the Dakotas, like all bad news, like an avenging angel darkening out the sun, the sudden realization the powers in this world descend upon to destroy you so vastly large, you can only sit in resigned religious awe and await your fate. And when word spread of the circuit rider holding truck with the Devil, claiming even to be his kin, it all came clear. Now they understood.

Brother hears them whisper and gawk outside, the people he had wanted to guide and enlighten, now caught up in concentric circles of fear and ignorance. Will sits stiffly beside him on the bench, rocking gently forward and back, staring at the sun shrouded in early morning haze above the heads of the idlers and the curious crowding the open windows.

The presiding elder rises to read the charges and specifications: drinking spirituous liquors in cases other than necessity, a habit, it is unfortunate to note, of a worthless father visited upon the son. More serious still, while under the ruinous influence of demon rum, engaging in licentious conversation, fraught with lewd suggestion, passing perhaps from suggestion to consummation, with the comely daughter of a class leader, whose hospitality he thereby sorely abused. And finally, the most heinous crime against God imaginable, seeking the Devil's company with the ruse of ridding the country of his evil, making common cause with the Prince of Darkness, having the audacity, some would say plain orneriness, to bring the miscreant among us at this convocation, Beelzebub himself, even claiming, unrepentant to this very hour, as the proceeding will show to everyone's satisfaction, to be his brother.

A gasp spreads across the room, due not to the shocking burden of the indictment, perhaps, but to the sulfurous fart Will cut to punctuate the gravity of the charges. Bishop Wiley rises and clears his voice. He will be the first questioner.

"Before we get down to the specifics, which some of the younger brothers are eager to pursue, I'd like you to relate to us something of your Christian experience and your call to the ministry."

"I'm not so sure I've had a Christian experience."

"Come now, son, you mustn't let your present darkness of soul obscure your vision. What led you to seek out the Church?"

"I grew up on the prairie. The Ole Woman always told us there's no Sunday west of Grand Junction. West of Salina, there's no God. The Ole Man never told us anything much, doubt if I would recognize him if he were alive and sitting in the front row today among the righteous brothers."

"But he figures in the charges. And he did, I believe, in his fashion, lead you to the ministry."

"His absence did, more than anything. When the drought hit and the Ole Woman decided it was time to move on, the Ole Man nowhere to be found, it fell to me as the oldest son to take charge. I wouldn't have been responsible if the Ole Man'd been there, or at least wouldn't have been distracted by so many other things, the dry axle bearing, the nigh wheelhorse's galled neck, on the lookout for rabbits, deer, and prairie chickens for food, buffalo chips for fuel. If he'd have been there, just maybe my brother Will and little Sojourner wouldn't have been lost. I wouldn't have had to bear the weight of my own grief along with that of the Ole Woman and of the African, and the guilt on top of that, the nagging notion I should have prevented it pounding down like a rail-splitting wedge to drive me from the family.

"As soon as I'd helped prove up the new claims out west, I left. At the time I reckon I didn't know what I was doing, drifting, but now I look back on it I realize I wasn't running away. I was looking for the Ole Man.

"I figured out real soon the prairie yields up her treasures very grudgingly. It's easier to get wealth from men than from the land. Got pretty good with a deck of cards, one thing led to another. Come into some sod road ranch, sometimes no more than a forked stick holding a pole running to the wall of a godforsaken trading post, wagon sheet draped over it sheltering a couple whiskey barrels. Usually not enough stock of goods to make a wheelbarrow load on a bumpy road: a few decanters, some cans of pickled oysters, and two or three boxes of sardines. You had to hunch over to walk from one side to the other, which didn't take very long anyhow, no more than six or eight feet any direction you'd want to go. I'd sit down at a whiskey barrel and get out my well-worn deck of cards and start playing a game of solitaire. Man offer me a drink, I'd take it. Knock the chill off, or thin the blood to cool down, depending on the weather, definitely cut the alkali dust, and pretty soon somebody would come along and suggest a game of chance to break the eternal monotonousness up.

"Soon had enough confidence in my deal to move up to the taverns and saloons in the bigger towns, near the army forts and railheads. Really hit the big time, a whole shelf full of dusty bottles, a box of cigars, whiskey barrels had a plank or two across them for the gaming table. Some of the fancy hotels even had furniture made in the East hauled all the way out by rail, steamboat, and freight wagon, kerosene chandeliers, a fiddler hanging around to play an occasional tune, and whirligo girls. But these people take their gambling a little more serious, had to lay on a side arm to demonstrate my earnestness and, as usual, lots of nux vomica and tanglefoot to be sold, bought, and otherwise consumed, and for the more abstemious there was always Hostetter's Bitters or Diamond Dick's Mountain Man Sagwa and Wizard Oil."

Bishop Wiley, who's been standing during the testimony, arms clasped across the chest, right hand holding the chin, staring down at the floor in a rapt attention drifting into reverie, now looks up, brings a chair over to Brother and Will, sits, his back turned two-thirds toward the conference. "How did you get to the Church?"

"It was troublous times. As you know. Easy to collect enemies, bands of border ruffians, bushwhackers from Missouri, Jayhawkers from Kansas, vicious, thieving pillagers is all most of them were, both sides, and I guess I might have ridden a mile or two with them. Lots of moral chest-thumping and highfalutin talk about freedom, but the truth of the matter is most were out to get what they could in the turmoil, just as always, grabbing horses and land hand over fist. Fighting not so much to keep slavery out of Kansas, but to keep out the blacks."

"You say you rode with the Jayhawkers?"

"I was with Jim Lane when he sacked Osceola. We both served under Lane."

"How's that?"

"Lane was with the steadfast third in the Mexican War, same as the Ole Man."

Bishop Wiley removes a kerchief from a pocket, dabs forehead and cheeks. "I see. Following his footsteps, it looks like. Did you ever find him?"

Brother looks about the room. The air is hot but promises winter. Harsh sun washes the colors of the listeners outside the windows, Will rocks to and fro. "I heard from a woman at the Roaring Gimlet Hotel he was bedridden, staying with a family ten miles southwest of town. One night after a very successful evening at the poker table I went out to see him. Frail, unshorn and unshaven, sallow, a devitalizing sweat dankening the bedclothes, they kept feeding him Osgood's Callagogue and sarsaparilla to fight off delirium. He didn't even know he had sons, much less that I was one of them. As usual, he wasn't much help when I needed it. I gave the family my winnings and left. He passed on that same night." Looks wistfully at his boot propped up on the left knee, somehow, even in a time of no rain, the crease between worn sole and cracked upper filled with mud. "I think you know the rest."

A faint smile. "Yes, I do. But tell the congregation."

Comes forward in the chair, both feet on the floor, forearms resting on thighs, hands clasped between the knees. "The next day, after I'd heard the Ole Man had died, after a night of drinking and dice, I was sitting in the hotel eating side meat and grease, pickled cabbage, cucumbers, corn bread, and dried-apple sauce, heard a terrible commotion in the washroom, loud talking, some singing, even a little scripture quotation. I was in no mood to be reconciled, couldn't abide my supper interrupted just as I was about to light up the cigar came with it, head a little oversensitive after all the bad news and the bad whiskey I'd had to deal with, got up to investigate. The place was full of molasses lappers in b'iled shirts, wearing their entire wardrobe on their backs with their feet sticking out, standing around the water bucket and tin basins, the roller towel, getting happy, on their way to the camp meeting along the river out south of town. You know how the revivals were in those days."

Bishop Wiley's smile constrained, but less faint.

"The way the farmers carry on enough to disgust a sizable crowd of intelligent sinners. What the hell do they know about sin and guilt and loss. Decided then and there I was going to put a stop to this nonsense. Picked up my pistols, good for twelve of them, I figured, and a bottle or two of snakebite medicine, never know what you might run into out there in the woods, and headed down by the riverside.

"Beat anything I'd ever seen, could hear it a mile off, see a plume of dust rising. Snake-oil salesmen, petty thieves, drink peddlers, a few whores, even members of the respectable religions gathered at the periphery talking about God and the soul, milling through the tents and wagons in the camp trying to get a good view of the proceedings, best show to hit town since Old Dan Castello's Great French and American Circus.

The trumpet had just sounded calling people back from supper to public worship in the oval clearing when I arrived, so I worked my way through the crowd, women to the split-rail benches on the right of a fence run down the center aisle, men to the left, my mind made up to wreck a little havoc among the converted. Don't know why I was feeling so mean and evil that day, or any of the long string of days since I'd left the Ole Woman—when you get right down to it, since Will and little Sojourner fell from the wagon crossing the Ninnescah. A dark evilness descending upon me like a winter fog on the evening of the longest night, slowly the light goes until, without realizing it, you're cold and lost. Angry at the world that doesn't give a damn and at yourself for trying to fight it. Nothing to do but strike out blindly until the morning comes.

"But when I got inside the fold, saw all those dirt-poor, half-starved, downtrodden people crazed by distance, failure, privation, fear, and loneliness, heard the hymns they bellowed out, the service the same order as when I was a kid and the Ole Woman would drag us all out, travel several days across windblown flatlands and sand hills just to see other human beings, to sense a spirit larger than the congregation yet at the same time a creation of it, a manifestation, an emanation of common suffering, ambition, and desire, power was there to heal and to justify. I wasn't alone. Overcome with tears, love welling up, an unheard-of joy from the toes of my boots snapping the ends of the hairs on my head like the fur coat of a cat stroked in winter darkness, like the tips of a range cow's horns on a windy dry spring night, like Saint Elmo's fire, blue-violet sparks burning the soul clean of the dusty residue settled over years of aimless wandering across this desolate empty plain. Everybody shouting and singing, taking up a call and response, the hymns washing over the clearing, *come ye sinners, poor and needy,* one preacher after the other, each one outdoing his predecessor in unpremeditated rapture, and then an exhorter. You remember."

"Yes."

"You were that exhorter."

"Yes I was, son. But tell the elders."

"You got up. Walked to the platform beneath the canopy of native elm stirred by the evening remnant of a dog-day wind, stood there soaking it in, gathering strength, it looked like to me, a meek man at first, gaining stature and power from the assembly pleading, praying, shouting out before you. When you raised your arms to speak you appeared ten feet tall, a terrible angel spreading his wings to collect his brood: *It is a feast of fat things, brothers and sisters, our souls sweetly drawn out this morning, before the trumpet first sounded, in private meditation. And tonight we yokefellows are pulling the Gospel cart, praise God who suffered for us sinners on the cross, feel the presence of the Lord Almighty conjured up among us!*

"You paused to let the amens and hallelujahs settle: *and yet I am troubled as I stand before you, buoyed up though I am by your joyous thanksgiving, your harvest collected, dry and dusty as it is, the Lord has provided, and it would be of little consequence in a land of milk and honey to praise God for the bounty all around us, what meaning do devotion and pledges of infinite dedication have at the bell of the cornucopia. No, it is hard times that test our faith, prove our worthiness to serve the Lord, it is faith that survives the dust storms, whirlwinds, prairie fires, the grasshopper plagues and depredations of God's savages, this faith that shows us worthy of God's love and grace and eternal salvation, this faith that has brought us*

*through the long summer to this love feast now, and this faith
that steels us against what is to come. Even as we celebrate, the
winter storm clouds are gathering in the north. It is this joy
that will bring us through! But I am troubled as I stand before
you by what I see. It may be a very painful duty, but a very
solemn one, to reprove vice, misconduct, and sin whenever
and wherever you see it. But especially my duty at camp meeting. That is the duty to which I am about to attend. That man
over there who, between amens, takes out his barlow to clean
and trim his fingernails, leaving the hard labor of salvation to
his wife, he would do better to complete his grooming on Saturday night. But I don't mean him. This young girl, the one
there in the third row, with the red ribbon tied so prettily in
her flaxen hair, glancing sidelong at the young swain the other
side of the aisle, giving the skirt such delicate tugs to expose,
quite unintentionally, I'm sure, petticoat ruffles, the top of her
shoe, the ankle, she thinks I'm talking about her. But I'm not.
And you in the back, in the shadows of the sinners' corner, yes,
ma'am, the flowered calico bonnet, spend more time praying
and less gossiping about your neighbors, get you a lot closer to
heaven, but I don't mean you either. Now I reckon you all
want to know who I do mean. I mean that dirty, nasty, lower-
than-a-snake's belly, whoring and gambling scoundrel who'd
dare come into the presence of the Lord with his pistols still
strapped on, foul whiskey breath and that demon weed, that
devil's tool, tobacco, rolled into a fat cigar stinking out the
place! He's the one I do mean!*

"Our eyes met. You were talking to me. Everybody turned
to look. I broke into a sweat, I'd forgotten all about my intentions, but before I could react one way or the other the clearing

exploded in song, *praise God from whom all blessings flow*, and you were inviting all those who were convicted of sin to come forward to the mourner's bench, you were inviting *me* to prayer.

"My mind went quiet, like the eerie blue-green vacuum before a storm, then the violent wind of remorse and regret, the Ole Woman and the Ole Man, Will and little Sojourner, the profligate and vagrant life I'd been leading—or, rather, had been leading me—twisted memories of my dissipated existence swirling up like tumbleweeds and dead leaves before the front of God's wrath, a thunderclap and a cloudburst of tears. I take the cigar out of my mouth, a foot of dog-leg chewing tobacco from my pocket, unstrap my pistols, sling them all into the underbrush—vibrant song trembling the dust rising up to the enormous cold stars like a votive offering to the heavens—and join the sinners groping their way forward to testify. Falling to their knees shouting for purity of heart and strength, some of them, prostrate on the ground, rolling and moaning, pounding the earth, some passed clear out still as death. Everybody around in earnest prayer, pleading, wringing the hands, rolling the eyes, woman next to me lets out a shriek scare the Devil away on a moonless dark night, begins to laugh, jumps to her feet and dances circles back down the aisle, the man beside her watches her go, turns back to the altar, face contorted in desperate supplication, an agony of effort, wan and covered with sweat. His eyes finally turn in his head and he swoons away, a dead heap at my feet. I don't know what to do, the first thrust of emotion brought me up deteriorating into a mixture of ridiculousness and fear, something dangerous going on here. A woman on the other side bends down to take his hand, mumbling some incoherent incantation, I take the other, more from the desire to crouch and hide than any concern for the immortal soul of the fallen brother. The pale lips quiver, the eyelids flutter, then pop open, a blank stare of amazement, his cold fingers suddenly clamp mine hard as a smithy's vise, he jerks up on his elbows, pinning my hand to the ground, whispers *sing*. The woman, her arm, like mine, held flat, hesitates, confused, he shouts *sing!* She sighs, settles on her back, head resting on the man's stomach, and bursts forth with *o happy day that fixed my choice*. Looks like I've got no choice but to join in. By the third verse he's relaxed his grip, I look up at the rejoicing around us, a vibrating in my head, the overtones of the singing, I think at first, amazing, but only singing, but now become a voice, running powerfully from northeast to southwest through the bones of my skull and teeth: *you must declare my counsel faithfully!* I thought I was going mad, confused and exalted at the same time, frightened at the power taken hold, shaking me like a hound dog with a prairie rattler in her mouth. I struggle to my feet, clothes clammy with sweat, cold, trembling, try to follow, to start off to the southwest.

"The next thing I remember, I wake in your tent. Voices chiming around us like a country church at Eastertime, laughing, weeping, shouts of *praise the Lord* and three or four different hymns sung in four or five different keys, flickering torchlight dancing across the canvas walls. Everybody saying goodbye, Godspeed, wanting to get beyond the next rise before it all collapses, spent and solitary, around them. This congregation will never come together, this specific spirit never manifest itself, again. I sit up on the edge of the cot, the compulsion, like a compass needle toward the pole, an abiding thirst to water, a nigh-on-overwhelming urge to the southwest. I could not deny it any longer: it was a call to preach."

Bishop Wiley, his back turned completely to the ministers now, looks at Brother. "And I gave you your exhorter's license."

"Yes, you did."

After a brief silence, Bishop Wiley rises and faces the conference. "Who is the first accuser?"

Will starts at the sudden sound beyond the bar, his lips draw back from his teeth. A young man, fine-tailored jacket, sharply pressed trousers, ruffled cuffs, and polished half-shoes, maneuvers toward Brother in a wide arc to avoid passing too close to Will, a hostile grumbling out in the street. Will lets out a low, throaty growl, staring, stiff-legged, hair bristling, hard at his eyes. Brother utters what seems to be a low woof, leans over to say something, nudges him with his nose and cheek. Will turns several times on the bench and sits. The accuser glances over to Bishop Wiley, who gestures him to continue. Still uncertain how close he should get, wiggles his nose side to side, makes an unusual sign of the cross in Will's direction, finally approaches from downwind.

"Are we to understand you traveled to the southwest to preach?"

"I rode hard and preached hard, the Big and Little Arkansas, up and down the Ninnescah. My first sermon was in the Golden Rule Saloon, where Wichita is now. Kind of a nice place, even had a piano, but the clientele weren't all that disposed to prayer."

"Did they not offer you a drink when you entered?"

"They did."

"And did you not accept it?"

"These rough-and-tumble plainsmen aren't going to listen to what you say if you begin by insulting their hospitality. They were all thinking they're going to get the preacher drunk, run him out of town on a rail, maybe, like the brother first tried to bring the word of God to Atchison. You, sir, are probably too young to remember this, the rabble caught him up, tied him to a beer-barrel raft, and sent him down the Missouri River toward Kansas City. Folks were not all that inclined to contemplate the errors of their ways. So I toss down the hooch with the best of them, starting to make an impression by the third or fourth shot, walk past the gaming tables, step in behind the bar, set a small butt of sack up for my pulpit, lay out the Bible Bishop Wiley gave me along with my exhorter's license, my two pistols, one on each side of the text, and announce: by the grace of God and these two revolvers, I am going to preach."

"I understood you to say you cast your weapons away the night you found the Lord."

"At the time it seemed the right thing to do. Reading the Good Book makes it clear the Almighty appreciates the dramatic gesture, but upon reflection it seemed to me prudent to collect them from the underbrush when the meeting was over, especially since my southwestern route providentially led me right past the spot they lay. If God had not wanted us to carry side arms, he would not have given Mr. Colt the inspiration to contrive such a machine. In any case, it sure got the attention of the riffraff hanging out at the Golden Rule that day, and they, for the most part, were an attentive and respectful audience. An occasional irreverent aside, a volatile explosion of swearing when someone drew two to an inside straight to beat three queens. A dogfight during the scripture reading—it seems a bluetick hound been sleeping by the spittoon thought the bread really did turn to the flesh of Christ—but all in all I'll have to say my first public sermon was a success. To talk to sinners you've got to know something other than theory about sin, it seems to me. Few people more knowledgeable than your committed heathen—a word, by the way, whose origin is tied up with the notion of wide-open land, the prairie, space for the soul to wander, people not wont to submit to a humorless, cantankerous, and bullying deity. Anyway, I felt qualified to discourse on the subject because of the special path the Lord had led me down, and the denizens of the saloon recognized and appreciated that I knew whereof I spoke, and a couple of them, well schooled in the order of service, got up at the appropriate moment to pass the hat for collection—the generosity of the congregation stimulated, perhaps, not only by the power of my rhetoric but by the unsheathed six-shooters the ushers were toting, as well."

"And did they offer you a drink as you left the saloon?"

"They did."

"Did you accept it?"

"An unpardonable incivility not to."

The accuser turns to the conference. "He does not deny it: dram drinking." He brushes the cuff of his coat with his fingertips, returns to Brother, pulls a neatly folded sheet of foolscap from a jacket pocket to consult before continuing. "You have testified, Brother, that your circuit took you along the Ninnescah River. Did you ever stop over at a molasses mill on the South Fork near Neola?"

"Yes, I did. Many times. Home and business of Brother Blackstrup, class leader in those parts."

"Could you relate the circumstances?"

"First stopped by there one very dark morning, been raining three days and nights, all the creeks out of their banks. I hadn't been exactly lost but I sure was bewildered. Taken the wrong shoot around midnight south of Grasshopper and brought up in water lapping at the horse's side. My wagon would take to floating now and again, finally drifted up against an abutment of some kind, I got out to investigate, was able to ascertain it was a bridge someone was building. All there was were the abutments and stringers laid across for foot traffic, the river, about thirty foot above flood, caressing the bottom side. Well, I couldn't stay there, the way the water was rising, and it looked like if anybody was going to use this bridge it would have to be me, cause not much chance it would ever last till dawn. I found lumber under a wagon sheet, started laying planks athwart the stringers. Ever now and then the skeleton arm of an uprooted tree would rise up and grab at me, catch the bridge, and scoop a rush of water over. I'd fight it off and keep on laying planks. The rolling mass of the river, the droning growl, vibration, the inexorable indifference of current and slope, and me compelled to push on into the abyss of absolute liquid darkness and sound. A joy in this blind compulsion the other side of fear. I suppose the damn horse was the only one with any sense, when I was done, she refused to cross. I unhitch her and pull the wagon by hand, bridge getting mighty buoyant by the time I get back, tie a lariat to her bridle bits. My idea is to walk on the bridge alongside her swimming. I drive her in downstream, slack in the rope taken up like it was lashed to an anvil thrown out a hayloft door, I'm yanked in behind her and towed on across. Had to walk a quarter mile back upstream to find the wagon. The bridge was gone.

"It took till sunup before I found someplace to light. Smelled hickory smoke from an evaporator, came upon a field of Chinese and imphee sugarcane, a one-horse mill with wooden rollers, found Blackstrup's dugout by the river."

"And he didn't live alone."

"No, he didn't. I was half asleep at the reins when I heard him hail me. Still soaking wet, only outfit I had the one on my back. He was busy getting the fire stoked, told me his wife died of fever and ague a few springs back, but go on in the dugout, his daughter, Prissy, would serve me up what fare there was for breakfast."

"Yes, Prissy Blackstrup. Was she comely?"

Looks up at the accuser. "That, sir, is a question a town fellow, surrounded daily by the pulchritude of civilization, would ask. To a man been wandering three days alone, beclouded and without compass, it never occurs."

"But she was—is, in fact—beautiful. And young."

"Looked mighty good to me, especially with that mud trickling down her cheek dripped from the tarpaulin strung up over the cookstove to catch the rainwater still seeping through the sod roof, the gumbo oozing between her toes from the floor. Above all else, the plate of grits and fatback, and yes, that molasses melt over your tongue make you dream still awake of the hills of Cathay, of a far savanna bathed in African sunshine.

"Anyway. I had to shed my clothes to dry by the stove, found a corner not dripping and, huddled under a buffalo robe, slept until early afternoon. I joined them at the mill, helped feed the stalks between the rollers, tended the fire under the evaporator pan. A pleasure in this: the dull repetition, revolution, the mare at the horsepower swishing her tail, plodding round and round. Routine. Prissy collecting the juice from the rollers in hundred-gallon barrels, dumping in bushel baskets of alkali from the hickory-bark fire to fine out the green debris squeezed from the cane sheath, draining the juice down the wooden trough into the iron-bottom evaporator pan, clear as water when the alkali settled. Hickory smoke, the constant sweet boiling of cane sugar, meadowlarks, sparrows, dragonflies, and sweat bees. I tell you, sir, I was a long way from the world of evil and sin."

"You returned often to Blackstrup's homestead."

"I brought him into the Church. That night, after cooking molasses all day long, we had to build a dike around the door facing the river to the south to keep the high water out, another thunderstorm moving across the floodplain. We all three sat in the one room, twelve by eight, burrowed four foot deep into the bank, the mosquitoes land on you and bark. Prissy cooked up the meal on the smoky old stove in the corner, hard to keep the cow chips dry after so much rain. Salt pork and water gravy, mashed potatoes, bread, pig fat instead of butter, and dried peaches, rain pounding on the roof so hard could hardly hold a decent conversation, water percolating through the sod almost as fast as it was falling outside. We all huddled on Prissy's bed, the only dry niche in the place.

"Blackstrup and I talked. Told him about my life on the circuit, Prissy sitting silent, very intent on the food in her plate, it seemed to me very self-conscious, fidgeted with the damp hair

kept falling into her face, we were very close together. The only
light the cow-dung fire flickering through the grate, discharge
as powerful as the lightning outside, when all of a sudden she
reached over to brush a mosquito from the back of my hand."

"Have you no shame, man?"

"Shame?"

"You admit your lust!"

"You misunderstand the Lord's will if you consider desire a
sin."

"That is for the conference to decide."

Stares at the accuser, a quick glance to Bishop Wiley, then
settles in his seat. "Somehow I doubt it."

"Continue, please."

"Blackstrup said he was more philosophical than religious,
but on a night like this, with the water rising, it sure couldn't
hurt a thing if I wanted to lead us all in prayer. Well, I was
embarrassed. The fire wasn't there, God's mysterious workings
his wonders to perform the farthest thing from my mind. This
flood more a matter of the size of the watershed, the amount of
moisture suspended in the air, the capacity and slant of the
draw outside our door. The vagaries brought me together with
these people were the consequence of a lost compass, the
choices my horse made in the pitch dark, and the fact somebody wanted a bridge to help them get to the molasses mill,
more than anything the Lord had done. But I did my best. You
can always mention brother Noah in circumstances like these,
and I eventually warmed to the task, a resolving peace finally
settling over us, a calmness of spirit, owing more, I would
guess, to the strenuous labor of the day and the passing of the
storm outside than to any emanation of the Holy Ghost.

Whatever the case, Blackstrup and Prissy well pleased when I finished, and our roles switched, him gone religious and me the philosophical one. As wet as when I came when I went off to sleep in the molasses shed."

"Nothing passed between you and Prissy?"

"Not a word."

"No furtive glances, additional touches?"

Leans out closer to the accuser, a slow, bitter smile. "Sir, I sense your interest in this matter goes beyond the judicial."

Throws up his hands, almost a pirouette toward Bishop Wiley. "We cannot proceed if the witness does not take these matters more seriously."

"Answer the question, Brother."

"Well, I was—am—a healthy man, it was springtime, she was young and nubile, huddled close on the dry end of the bed, our thighs pressed together, both of us without human contact for an extended period."

"You saw her no more that evening?"

Growing more agitated. "Is she here today to bear witness against me?"

"No. How would that make a—"

"Her father?"

"No. They could not attend."

"If they are not here to read what happened into the record, I would consider it a violation of the code of honor of a gentleman and a preacher for me to do so."

"This is contemptuous! What do you, or any of your catfish aristocracy, know of honor!"

Springs to his feet, going for the accuser's lapels. "I'll show you contempt, you good-smelling dandy!"

Scuffle among the chairs, Will snarling and barking, lips curled back from the teeth, much commotion in the house and outside the windows. Bishop Wiley has to separate them. "Gentlemen. Decorum, please."

They stand there, each shoving against an opposite shoulder of the bishop, whose glasses have been knocked awry. Brother finally laughs, more a snort through the nose, returns to the bench, nuzzles Will to calm him, adjusts the collar of his shirt, brushes at the dried mud on his boots, then looks up at the accuser. "I see no relevance in the answer to your question."

"The charge, sir, is dalliance. I find it highly relevant to establish that she, after her father had fallen asleep, slipped out to you in the molasses shed."

"If it were so it would hardly be evidence that I led her astray. And you are not going to hear from me that it was so."

A long pause. The accuser still flushed and flustered from the assault. "We will return to this."

"You may. I doubt that I will."

Another pause while he smooths his ruffled clothing. "You made many subsequent visits to Blackstrups Mill."

"As I said, he took a religious turn. Soon became a class leader. I am a circuit rider, it is my task to visit many such stations on a regular basis."

"And what of your dealings with Prissy?"

"I was her minister."

"Nothing else? You spoke to her, and never in private, only of matters concerning her salvation and the glory of the Lord?"

"Now and then about the weather." Rubs the side of the nose with extended first finger, a tight, sly grin developing across his lips. "May I ask a question or two of you, sir, before we continue?"

"I believe the rules allow it."

"Have you ever ridden a circuit?"

"No, I have not."

"Preached every day at a different station, three times on Sunday in order to make the two- or three-hundred-mile loop every couple of weeks?"

"I said, sir, I have not."

"Slept in the saddle, or a settler's haystack in a prickly pocket of prairie feathers?"

"No, sir."

"Taken your pay in spuds, a sitting of eggs, a jug of home-made whiskey, whatever the class could hardly afford to do without?"

"I said no, sir."

"Just what *have* you done to reform the nation and spread scriptural holiness over the land?"

"I have been the pastor of several thriving congregations, in Leavenworth, Lawrence, Topeka, and Wichita."

"So your flock are town folk. They don't have to leave the raw and difficult farms on Saturday to seek relief from monotonous drudgery in gossip, horseshoes, footraces, raffles, wrestling matches, to get drunk and maul each other with their fists. I daresay you preach against such people, you're what the town speculators are after when they say they seek a star preacher to supply their pulpit."

"I fail to see what bearing this has on the case being adjudicated."

"I daresay, sir, that you were given town lots to come in and preach, that these could be resold at a handsome profit. Serving the Lord is not always loneliness, suffering, and pain, is it, sir. Some speculators willing to give up quite a bit to get a church and a preacher to quote in the booster newspapers they send back east to beguile unwary folk to abandon their farms in the old states and to head on out to the prairie. That's no doubt what led you, sir, to give up your stable but modest pulpit and come here, the Lord helps those who help themselves, is it not so? You live in ever-improving parsonages with your lovely wife, collect town lots and shares, even have a small interest in a sawmill, I understand, no conflict between leading the flock and speculating on land values, the Bible is silent on the point. You know nothing of spirit, a God created from the common longing of worn-down, isolated sodbusters clinging to the empty soil with broken fingernails to keep from being blown away. Why bother with the inclement weather, the saddle sores, and the hunger to carry the word out to the unschooled masses scattered across ominous spaces, you preach long-winded sermons explaining God and his demands, his laws, to the pious city folk, in town where the women, wives and daughters of lawyers, merchants, and bankers, in their fine dresses, appreciate the learned pastor's well-crafted discourses, where the firewood is neatly stacked and the money good. Is it not so?"

"The Church is not on trial here, sir."

Brother laughs and settles back into his chair, a chorus of hoots and catcalls from the windows. "Quite so."

"I do not believe rousing up the ignorant rabble with fiery ravings to be the aim of the Church, rather to fight against such emotion, to control it, to bring order and predictability to the affairs of men. Such fits of enthusiasm are, I am certain, the machinations of Satan himself."

"Then I stand condemned already."

"That is a reasonable assumption. To think otherwise would be to challenge the notion of lordly authority. To believe, as you would have us do, that this creature there beside you is your brother, suckled by the most cowardly of dogs, is to cast out our religious underpinnings altogether. No longer could we maintain man is made in God's image, holds dominion over the beasts of the field and the air and the sea, it would be to admit that we are just another of the dumb animals roaming the earth in brutish search for food and fornication. This we will never admit. What is this monster then, human in outward appearance yet lacking in every trait that marks us as sacred, that reflects the divine spark within, the holy fire of God's love and salvation, this hollow mockery of the Lord's creation? It can only be one thing on the face of it: the work of the Devil. And you, his—it would appear—willing tool."

"It is you, sir, using the Devil as *your* tool. This entire trial is a travesty, you no more believe in the Devil than you do in a spiritual God. You are incapable of understanding how the Lord could be subtle and complex in his design and execution—or should I say quite capable of understanding that most other people cannot grasp it—and quite willing to take advantage of that, use any weapon at hand, including your bogeyman devil, to dumbfound the congregation to gain power in the Church. Order is what you believe in, preaching is not a calling for you but a career, and you use the specter of Satan to help you rid the organization of your enemies, anyone with any passion, because passion is the enemy of order and predictability, and for you and your kind to prosper, and I mean that word in its meanest sense, there must be that. After circuit riders like me have sown the seeds, done the dirty fieldwork of the Lord, you and your kind move in, moral claim jumpers and speculators, to reap the harvest—and not of souls, and not for the Lord, but of dollars and of power for yourselves. Bishop Wiley knows what I'm talking about. And he knows, after I'm gone, he is next."

The accuser looks over to Bishop Wiley as if asking for remedy, a ruckus, garbled shouts, a fistfight maybe, out in the street. Bishop Wiley, pale, feeble even, pounds on a table to restore quiet, stands, his eyes clenched shut, as if fighting off some pain. A shout from outside the window: *let the brother talk!*

He opens the eyes, one corner of his cracked, bloodless lips resisting a smile. "I must admonish you both, gentlemen, please drop it. Continue with your questioning."

The accuser adjusts the coat on his shoulders, turns to Brother. "We were discussing your conversations with Prissy Blackstrup."

Brother leans back in his seat, legs fallen open before him, scratches his head. "It was shortly after my first visit to the Blackstrup homestead that I found Will, my lost brother, after many years thinking him dead, miraculously saved—by the grace of God, it would appear—by a pack of coyotes." A murmuring, both inside and out. Brother leans over to Will, a low crooning deep in the throat, lifts his wrist to show the jayhawk tattoo, then exposes his own. Gasps and whispers spread from one to another across the assembly, some standing to get a better look. "This is the mark the Ole Woman made when we were kids."

"The bestial sign of the Devil! And who helped you find him?"

"The heathen woman! He saved her neck!"

"Let him speak!"

"I was at a loss. A brother I thought long dead, untutored in the ways of civilization, uninterested in learning, had to be held by force. The only things that commanded his attention were food and his absolute desire for freedom. It was clear the unknown life in the wild held more appeal than any regulated, domesticated existence ever could. He had been quite a talker before he was lost, only three years old but jabbering away, everything went through his mind came out his mouth, but now all he could do was howl and whimper, growl and snap. It gave me pause to contemplate what I believed.

"I had nowhere to go. The congregations fled in panic when they saw us coming. It made no sense to continue on the circuit, the world, which had seemed to cohere in God's omni-science and omnipotence, had come undone. The only people would take us in were the Blackstrups. Prissy. Old man Black-strup was against it.

"She tried to invent ways to teach Will to be human again. She was the only one, in the beginning, who had much faith it could be done. At night when the moon rose and the light pen-etrated the room to the pallet where he slept, he'd wake, prowl restlessly, sniff the corners, the door, then finally, after giving up his attempts to scratch his way out, he'd stand, the spas-modic movements and swaying would give way to tranquility, his vacant face take on a sad and melancholy gaze, stand motionless, head high, eyes fixed on the moonlit land. Any sudden change in the atmosphere would excite him: the sun coming from behind a cloud, a thunderstorm, snow flurries. During the day, at first, while Prissy and I labored at the mill, we'd have to tie him to a tree down by the river, a deep pool of slow-moving water beneath a cutbank, he'd stare at it for hours at a time. Not at his own image reflected back but at the sky and trees, water bugs, tadpoles, phantom forms of languid minnows moving beneath the surface. Time to time he'd throw in a stick, a handful of dried leaves, to contemplate the slow, random drift.

"He appeared to have no human passions, his desires didn't exceed his physical needs: food, rest, and freedom. When he wasn't sleeping, curled up in the sun, knees and balled fists pressed against the eyes, he was searching for food. Prissy gave him potatoes, walnuts, and acorns to eat at first, but he would still chase field mice into their dens and wait for them to come out, and she would have to pull him away before he could catch and eat one. The first sign she was making headway was when she taught him to cook his own potatoes, to throw them into the campfire and quickly pull them out. Prissy got him to eat bread, to drink a little soup, and finally she let him have meat, cooked or raw, it didn't seem to matter to him. He took quite a liking to sausage, when we had it. Prissy would offer him a piece, he'd come up lickity-split, reach out with the left hand to get it from her, distract her attention with his panting and slavering, and snatch the rest of it clean off her plate with his right. We couldn't help but break out laughing, watching him over in the corner wolfing it down, looking at us between gulps like an egg-sucking hound. What he didn't eat on the spot, he'd carry out and bury in the truck garden. Prissy taught him to stand up straight by hanging his food from the ceiling on a jute cord. Another step toward civilization, small to be sure, but a step: she got him to shell beans. He'd get his pot, set

141

it to his right, the beans on the left, open the pods very nimbly, put the good beans in the pot, reject the moldy ones, pile the empty pods beside him. When he got the pot filled, he'd pour water in, lift it onto the stove, and throw the pods into the fire. If the fire was out he'd grab the shovel, put it in Prissy's hands, start looking for kindling. He even learned how to fry his spuds, he'd go over to the larder, start sorting through them, pick out the biggest ones there, pluck the eye sprouts off, sniff around until he found the knife to give to Prissy, make a sign like slicing, go get the frying pan, and point to the cupboard where the lard was stored. If he'd had a tail it would've been wagging."

"You were staying at Blackstrup's homestead all this time?"

"Yes."

"Even though Blackstrup was against it?"

"Prissy . . ."

Turns to the assembly, as if that point were made yet another lay hidden. "Of course. Prissy." Casts his eyes askance at Brother. "What was the nature of your disagreement with her father?"

A shout from the street. *"Did you lay down with her?"*

"He freed the heathen woman!"

The corner of Brother's mouth twitches, one elbow propped on the arm of the bench, the other on his knee, finger-tips pressed together, staring at the toes of his boots.

"He eventually ran you from the place. Something to do with Prissy?"

Brother looks up at the accuser. A long pause. "Yes. She was afraid of him."

"Because she was afraid of her father she invited the Devil in!"

"She invited me and my brother in because I had comforted her and was now in need of comfort."

"Comforted her."

"The first night I stumbled onto the mill in the middle of the flood—"

"Then she did come out to you in the molasses shed!"

The answer hardly audible in the uproar from inside and outside the meeting hall. "Yes. She came to me."

"And what sort of comfort did you tender her?"

"Damn little. I was a preacher, I gave her preacherly advice. What comfort *could* I give, when you get right down to it. My worldly experience extremely limited, a misspent youth, then constant wandering over the prairie preaching wild exhortations but learning nothing, except that my role was to understand sin, to be tempted, to be lost, and to find salvation again. She came to me because she was afraid, she sat there in the shed, a damp shawl wrapped around her shoulders, shivering more from confusion and indecision, didn't know if she could trust me, sat in the hay by the horse's stall. It was the rain that did it. The long lonely days at the mill after her mother had died. Alone two or three days at a time when Blackstrup was off to the nearest town laying on supplies, she would cry, lie down with the sheep for companionship, sleep with the horse in the stall. And then the rains came, soaking the sod roof, dripping through on Blackstrup's side of the dugout in the middle of the night. He had to move. Move to keep dry. To— to Prissy's bed. She lay there with him on that narrow cot, she . . ."

"Go on, man."

"At first she was grateful for his warmth, she said, the nearness of him in the damp dark, the thunder and pounding rain, water rising outside the door. His breathing increased, from sleep she thought at first. But then . . . I guess it was grief, bereavement, loneliness, his little girl become a woman, the way she moved, voice, the shape and smell of her, all this unhinged his judgment."

A hush in the room, the street, except for the distant barking of a dog. Brother looks up from the floor, takes out a handkerchief to wipe his forehead. "She told me all this."

"What?"

"I think you can imagine it."

"No, we cannot imagine it. Go on, what happened? What led—who led this young woman to league with the Devil?"

"Who's talking about the Devil?"

"Who indeed. What counsel did you give, you said comfort, what deal for her soul, this vulnerable tool of the Prince of Darkness, temptress of God's clergy, her own father even, grateful, you said, for warmth and closeness in the wet night, was it not damp and dank in the molasses shed when she came to you? Speak up, man!"

"I must object." Bishop Wiley steps between them, arms raised to calm the sudden clamor in the house. "Brother need not speak of that told him in confidence by one of his flock."

"It is for his confidence that he is on trial. And that child of Satan beside him."

"Let the man finish his story. The judiciary committee is not or should not be interested in what went on between Prissy and her father."

"But among Brother, her, and her father. And this miscreant! Why were they driven from the place?"

"Let him go on."

The accuser steps back. Brother settles Will on his haunches on the bench, his mouth twitches from side to side, finally faces the presiding elders again. "Prissy seemed to be able to understand my brother. She said because her only companions for so many years had been farm animals. He was used to getting his point across by gesture, by physical posture, so Prissy worked out a complex set of signs. When those seemed to come easily to him, she took a plank and hung tokens on it, each representing an object, say a potato, for which they already had a sign, and ever time this sign was used she would go to the board and show the token until he finally would do the same, and then she would say the word for the sign, the token, the object. When he began to repeat the words, she replaced the tokens by letters of the alphabet to spell out the thing he wanted."

"You mean to say he can speak?"

"Yes, he can, better and better as time goes on."

"Devil's work!"

"Quiet. Continue, Brother."

"After a while we didn't have to lock him up or tether him. She petted and massaged him, he would roll over and squirm with pleasure like a little puppy, she gave him hot baths—"

"With him while he was naked?"

Long pause. Brother looks from the accuser to Will, his nostrils flare. "That is the normal way to bathe, I believe. I can understand your concern, I shared it. Especially when it became clear the massages and baths were, were—well, arousing him."

Even the distant dog is silent. "Arousing him?"

"Yes."

"What was . . . did you pray for God's guidance?"

"I . . . I was confused, didn't know what to do. He'd been doing so well, I didn't want to break off, after what Prissy had told me, didn't feel, but it was clear: it isn't God's guidance makes us human, makes us divine, even. It is our fellows, our rituals, our personal bonds, the community is our identity, why Will had been a coyote, not God's will, the company he kept, and if there was any hope of getting him back, neither God nor I should intervene."

"You didn't stop this lasciviousness?"

"I would have been stopping his progress. It was a natural consequence, the central human ceremony."

"To spread her legs for the Devil!"

A sudden outburst, hoots, hisses, howls, and scraping furniture, shattering glass, a large limestone block hurled through a window clumps and rolls over the wooden planks to Brother's boots, Will hunched on all fours, the door at the back of the hall kicked open. Bishop Wiley tries to hold the crowd swarming across the line of the bar, down-on-their luck speculators, drifters, town ladies, even elders and exhorters joining in, scuffling toward the front. The accuser has disappeared. Brother and Will wait, Bishop Wiley, overwhelmed, gives way, a last desperate looking. They see each other, from somewhere smoke in the room, a choppy stasis, some enameled icon of martyrdom. Brother holds his gaze, and they both smile. Like in the good old days.

The Last Hunt

Coyote Dropping | He smelled the stench for miles before they came upon the bones. They'd watched the sky looking for a sign, a gauze of dust at the northern horizon, the squabble of crows feeding on the insects that live off the buffaloes' hide, but saw nothing. Not even turkey vultures in slow, fatal vortex above the plains. It was too late even for that.

Young men were growing restless, anticipation turning to edgy resentment. They'd spent the bitter winter, the long summer, cooped on Cache Creek bickering with the Agency about issue, scrawny beeves, weevil-infested flour, sitting around smoky cow-dung fires passing what tobacco there was, listening to the tiresome stories the old farts kept telling them about a prairie vast and open. About the war dance, the long full-moon rides, a hundred miles without sleep or food or water across the Llano Estacado, stolen horses, war whoops, and scalp dancing. About buffalo herds make the earth tremor when they move, the wild chase, hanging from a pinto pony, sweat showering in the wind, every stride an arm's length from the heaving flank of a charging bull, drive the mulberry shaft just behind the short rib deep into the heart. Women and children with flint knives scramble behind to fall on the steaming carcasses, suck up warm blood, devour the liver, gallbladder, draw the entrails through the teeth, blood and milk from cows' udders, curdled from the bellies of unborn calves, hack off large steaks to broil, strips to dry in the sun. When the medicine was strong, the world fraught with potent signs, every detail of an urgent existence confirming it: this is the way to live.

Their lives hung heavy now. They cracked jokes about the old geezers' medicine bags laced too tight around the dick, the medicine of the buffalo soldiers, black as Death, water of earth, firewater to fire vision from the fetid present clinging to their skeletons, fenced in, the empty sky growing pale with coming snow, the waxing of the hunger moon.

Coyote Dropping never had liked to hunt, never had the enthusiasm others showed for war games and raids, counting coups, and taking scalps, the only reason he liked the scalp dance was that it was dance. The man could move and had a voice clear and distinct as any on the plains, his performances excused many peculiarities not tolerated in folk of smaller talent, and he could tell a story. Not the man you'd expect one day to take on medicine to lead the people to try to run ever goddam stranger there was off the plains.

Coyote Dropping had had a vision. When he was coming back after the wild celebration with Buffalo Bill and the Russian duke, caught up in the reverie of it, both exhilarated and downright puzzled. Duke Alexis, the business tycoons, and the newspaper writers from the East gone hog-wild, charging out over the prairie at the first sight of buffalo, like possessed children turned loose from confinement, infectious, especially oiled by the spirits they carried with them, champagne, whiskey, brandy, and ale. They wanted to commune after every single kill, buffalo, antelope, jackrabbit, it didn't matter, even a grasshopper brought down by a finger flick was reason for ceremony, spirits, which at first they kept to themselves but by the time the chase was on full gallop they shared with all. The duke had an eye for Spotted Tail and his clan and not just the bow hunters, especially interested in how they lived, how they mated, couldn't keep him away from the young women. Coyote Dropping marveled at these people, laughed and cast his eyes to the heavens, the unbridled lust they expended, not only when bringing down animals but in camp in the evening. Amazingly wrought silver dinner utensils, plates and bowls lined with gold, faceted glasses, candlelight, cooks from France across the salt ocean serving buffalo-tail soup, broiled cisco, fried dace, prairie-dog salmi, stewed rabbit, filet of buffalo with mushrooms, yams, mashed potatoes, green peas, and tapioca pudding. Then they would sing and dance. Coyote Dropping was set loose, no constraints of folk and custom, cutting figures he'd never imagined before, the Drunk Buffalo Gait, the Soldier Death Stalk, the Loco Scout Dance, and finally the Buffalo Bill Hunting Circle Gallop, in honor of the man clearly in charge of this ravenous horde, no longer of this earth, unconnected to the daily struggle for sustenance, marauding with the powerful spirits over a grassy plain extending out forever.

Buffalo Bill sat beside him at the fire after the dance, his blue eyes aflame with reflected light and frenzied by the essence of the large bottle he now proffered for Coyote Dropping to imbibe.

"God damn, you should be in show business."

Coyote Dropping nodded, the medicine from the bottle bubbling within like the liquid in the long-stemmed cup, looking for meaning in the confused mirth, a sign in Buffalo Bill's finger pointed toward the sky. These people can make business out of anything. Reached out and gave the finger a pull.

Cody farted. He was his brother.

After the expedition was over, farewells to Duke Alexis and Buffalo Bill properly marked, Coyote Dropping was in no hurry to find the folk, the people he had abandoned, sickened and hungry, in the winter storm. A mild sunny mass of air lay on the rolling green-grassy hills. He heard gunfire nearby, could tell from the report, a .50-caliber Sharps rifle, a crew of buffalo hunters. He slipped from his pony, crept to the top of the rise overlooking a shallow four-mile-wide watershed, several small stands of buffalo grazing both sides of the draw. Twelve wagons waited at the bottom of the valley. The shooter, buffalo skull cap, robe hanging down the back, walked out among the sixty or seventy animals calmly eating, stopped in their midst, raised the rifle, and fired. The nearest bull jumped straight up, all four hooves off the ground, collapsed limp in a cloud of pollen and dust. The others continued to graze. The shooter stood there, firing, reloading, then slowly moved on. The hide skinners pulled up behind him, stripped the carcasses, cut out the tongues, tossed them on the wagons, left the rest to rot, too much even for the hundreds of vultures already soaring in downwind. By the time they were done, the shooter had finished off the next stand, gone on up the draw. When the sun fell beyond the opposite hills, the long light washed the green grass orange, every buffalo the entire length of the valley was dead.

Coyote Dropping watched the skinners finish the bloody work, the wagons roll and bounce into the gathering darkness: this has been going on a long time. He'd seen bleached bones littering the prairie but had never seen the relentless execution up close. This is business. Buffalo Bill and Duke Alexis, sitting around linen-covered tables, wind ruffling the surface of the claret in their crystal glasses, had talked and joked of such a thing, Autumn Tallgrass, who knew about Texans—she herself was one—had often spoken of it. Coyote Dropping hadn't really comprehended what they meant. Buffalo hides to make shoes for multitudes of people living east beyond the grasslands, tongues for the powerful to eat, trade them for greenbacks, silver, and gold.

He had stayed all night on the rise above the valley, could hear coyotes and wolves tearing at the carcasses, the dense buzz of flies. Stayed through the early morning, lightning and thunder flashed and boomed across the watershed, and he could finally see it: these people, these silly, incompetent, bungling people, wandered out on the plains with no idea how to live, rigid. Once you figure them out and you know what one of them does under certain circumstances, you know what they all will do, good for a laugh to watch them try to scratch up the grass with cows and mules pulling sticks, cower in dank warrens dug into the banks of creeks, covered with dirt, half starved, crazed with distance, sun, wind, and loneliness. Good for a laugh—but they just kept on coming, red-faced, relentless as a ferret going after a prairie dog, like red ants, stomp on them, burn them out, they pick themselves up, dig themselves free, just keep on coming. And the folk laugh. Likely, in the end, to laugh themselves to death.

The folk are like the buffalo, eternal past numbering, you think, one with this undulating world like fleas on a dog. But they are killing all the buffalo, and when the buffalo are gone the folk will die, like the buffalo, too dim-witted to look up from the luscious grass to see the slaughter all around. They are killing us, not for the honor of catching a coup, the prestige of providing kith and kin with meat, but for what Buffalo Bill and the powerful men from the East, surrounded by buffalo-soldier servants, toasting each kill with flutes of champagne, say is business. We must make medicine to drive the buffalo killers out.

"I sat on the hilltop, the storm parted and passed on either side of me, the sun rose green and yellow, caught the backside of the clouds dark blue and dazzling white. A red-tailed hawk hovered in the enormous air, a prairie rattlesnake writhing from her claws, floated above me and called. I am the one must lead the folk away from the black brink of death."

When Coyote Dropping got back he began to ride out to the elders of other bands to talk. The red-tailed hawk gave him medicine, he said, makes him immune to the Texan's bullets, we must strike out now. The ancestors came from nowhere, grubbed for food among the heartbreak foothills of the western mountains, froze and starved long winter moons, but the magic sustained them. Came from nowhere out onto the plains, found brothers and sisters wrangling horses for the Spaniards, learned from them, traded, trained, bred the ponies that made themselves the lords of the prairie, the most magnificent horse people ever to ride this windswept earth. Drove the Spanish, the Mexicans, the Texans, Those-Against-Us from the land. But now the buffalo hunters keep coming, the buffalo soldiers drive us back, folk on folk, corral and fence us like ignorant beasts, the days to come dark and bleak, a horror stalking us like wolves a feeble elk. Our children and grandchildren, what will we teach them? How will *they* win glory and honor, whom will the people praise?

A streak of fire appeared in the sky at the end of winter, a long snake come to devour the world. It will linger five days, Coyote Dropping said, and then no rain for the entire summer. When the fire snake was gone in five days and the rain didn't come, when the creeks ran dry, catfish squirming and slithering in evaporating puddles, the mud banks shrunken, curled, and cracked, when the grass turned white and brown, people began to take that medicine of his seriously and to watch him dance. Might as well, too dry to hunt, they say he belched up a whole wagonload of cartridges along the Salt Fork.

All through the snowless warm winter he spread the word: build sweat lodges, burn seven ritual woods, haul creek water from the east, heat it with pink sacred stones, and purify yourselves. The time of deliverance is near.

Spring again, the folk restless, remnant, wandering the parched earth looking for buffalo, looms of multicolored dust blown swirling across the prairie. Coyote Dropping called them together north of the Red River to perform a ceremony they had never done before, one he had seen and learned on the northern high plains: the sun dance.

Autumn Tallgrass didn't know what to make of it. But she too was caught up in it now, no choice but to ride it out, it was she who cut the cedar tree for the sacred center pole, played her part though filled with dread. The omens she was seeing did not augur well, but she did it, they all did, the three false starts, the final raising of the pole, just as Coyote Dropping told them. They dragged a fresh-killed buffalo across the circle and hung it in the very center.

The first omen: it was hard to find a bull to kill, and even harder to kill him, the first arrow struck a short rib and shattered the mulberry shaft.

Old men and young boys prowled around the grounds, up and down the river, elaborate hunting games, turkey dance and prairie hen, fought sham battles, women and girls sweeping along with them shrieking chants and tongue trills.

The evening of the fourth day, sun scattering through floating dust, a rider went around to the encampments and called the people out: stand in front of the tipis, chant the songs of your band, and dance. When the dance is done we will fall upon the strangers, and the buffalo will return.

Another ill omen: dawn the next day, the leaders considered most wise packed their travois and moved their people across the river south, didn't want anything to do with it, headed for the fastness of the Llano Estacado.

A hot, dry, south wind. The people circled the sacred pole, turning the universe, Coyote Dropping said, three days long, sang, beat deerskin drums, elegant-strider-shell rattles, eagle-bone whistles, red-cedar flutes, danced in unison till the earth shook and dust obscured the sun. Till Lone Wolf, Woman's Heart, Stone Calf, White Shield, and Coyote Dropping, naked, bodies painted yellow, faces the color of Death, led them into the Texas panhandle to reclaim ancestral lands.

The third bad omen: a bear charged toward them from the windward as they forded a stream through a narrow wash, saw them, reared up on its hind legs, raised a paw, and waved, a warning the wind blows down, waved again, a beckoning, then circled round them and disappeared down the gorge. Everybody drew rein and sat in silence, watching Coyote Dropping. He stared where the bear had disappeared. Finally wheeled his horse to face them.

"If you're afraid, you can turn around. I will go on alone. No doubt many people will entertain you when you get back to camp, help you dance around the fresh-taken scalp of a cottontail."

They all pushed on.

The fourth evil omen: that night a violent storm, wind tearing out trees and knocking over tipis along the creek, thunder and lightning-struck fire whipped through the dry grasses, tumbleweeds turned balls of flame tossed high into the air. But no rain. Large blood-red globules splattered over the buffalo-hide tipis when morning came.

They move on Adobe Walls, an old fort where the buffalo hunters go for shelter. Coyote Dropping sees it in vague morning twilight, pulls back his horse, a sudden dread settling over him. Something wrong, it should be dark and asleep. The wind in the night has ripped off part of the roof, they are awake and working and can see us coming. The others yell and goad their ponies on. The hunters scramble down the scaffolding to grab their Sharps rifles, open fire, bag three riders at three hundred yards, easily fend off the eight or ten men who push the first crazed charge.

Spirit and strength seem to drain from the attackers, to crumble in screams and dust, spent gunpowder, nostrils, mouths, and lungs congested with it, dying moans of fallen men floating on the air. Lone Wolf, bleeding at the foot of the wall, calls out: *don't let the bastards take my hair!*

Coyote Dropping holds back, numb in the confusion of the unexpected volleys from the fort: what are you doing, tricked out here, naked, painted yellow and black, a dancer. Woman's Heart and Stone Calf ride up to him, wild-eyed stares of realization: the magic is flawed!

"What are you looking for back here, the fight is before us." Woman's Heart reins in close, the others milling about in south-wind dust, sun just clearing the horizon. "If your medicine is strong, turn the bullets of the buffalo hunters' long rifles, go fetch our brother's corpse before his soul is ripped from his head with his hair to hang as trophy in some draft mule's shed."

Silence. The wind stops, a flash and puff of smoke from the top of the distant wall, the report then echoing along the trees of the far creek, all heads turn, a high-pitched whine, Stone Calf knocked from his horse. Cohesion and will dissolve, Woman's Heart contemplates the dead man, looks back at Coyote Dropping, raises his quirt, and strikes him across the face. Horses rear and jump, a flurry of manes and tails. Then Coyote Dropping is alone in the empty field, blood quickly seeped into desiccated soil.

He made his way back to the creek where they'd spent the night, Autumn Tallgrass and the disheveled band the only ones left. They broke camp and headed out on the desultory trail. The summer was long, brutal sun, dust storms, each morning fewer tipis, families deserted in the night, or starved, or simply wandered away, never to be seen again. They were hounded by the cavalry through the fall until the final massacre in Hard Stick Canyon, the sacred place cut deep across the rim of the high plains, where the folk had always wintered, confident and secure. The buffalo soldiers, before daybreak, swarmed screaming and cursing down the walls, a murderous fusillade cutting through the panicked people trying to flee over smoldering embers of last night's fires. They killed the horses, piled them rotting in the weak winter sun, jerky, pemmican, sugar, flour, rifles and ammunition, buffalo robes, blankets, tipi poles—everything was burned. There was no place left.

The children died. Huddled, horseless, in stick shelters dug into the draws, no tools or weapons, just what they could fashion from flint, sticks, and rushes, Coyote Dropping silent, churlish, and withdrawn, his medicine dry and ephemeral as winter dust. Reduced to the skulking ways of the ancestors before they ventured out on the plains to get the Spaniard's horses, on hands and knees digging for grubs, worms, and ants, eating the bark off trees. What magic is this, sets us up in glory to better demonstrate our final frailty and doom.

Toward spring he begins to chuckle, give himself over to it, useless to fight against these forces of the spirit, the universe of the stinkbug and the dung beetle as amazing as the golden eagle's and the buffalo's. This world on foot the ancestors thought blessed, saw it as confirmation of their power, what's led us then to think it now as utter desolation. The buffalo gone? Everything has its time, the cottonwood leaves yellow, sumacs turn violent red and drop when it's time and are swept away by the north wind, left drifted beneath cutbanks of creeks, rotting in backwaters, food for fishes and water bugs, turning black mud and muck where the tule cattails grow. Coyote Dropping begins to laugh out loud. The starving folk back away. They know it is the end.

Autumn Tallgrass She had thought at first the hunt would be good. Word had spread along Cache Creek, through the Agency compound where they were penned: the Quaker agent might grant permission to haul down the tipis, load the travois, run down the ponies, and head out onto the plains, a specious hope, giddy excitement, the old buffalo butts' stories took on interest, young men and women began to sense how it was and is to be. She had hoped it would rescue Coyote Dropping from the dark spirits deposing the easygoing storyteller he had been when she was young, from the evil taken hold of him, of her, of all the folk, ever since the pox and the blizzard, since the medicine went bad, the magic evaporated, fighting the buffalo hunters at Adobe Walls, ever since the folk were chased down by buffalo soldiers and scattered in the early dawn attack along the twisty creek on the floor of Hard Stick Canyon where they had camped secure for every winter that ever was.

The fabric had unraveled. A stultifying summer, harsh winter, disaster beyond imagining, a stink with the spring thaw transcending physical decay and crowded latrines, the stench of decomposing souls. What made it terrifying, the folk grow used to it. A routine, an everyday life, talk and laugh, desperate couplings conceive children among a senselessness deteriorating into sense.

Autumn Tallgrass had gone to the Quaker agent to convince him to let the people hunt. Not just for buffalo but for that life, that meaning, justification, fallen away in just a few short seasons into the irretrievable past.

It was a mistake.

They had tried to conjure up the old buffalo medicine, put on buffalo skull bonnets, if they still had them after years of turmoil and flight, made substitutes as best they could from cow horns, beat rhythm for the buffalo dances with spoons and broken hoe handles on cooking oil cans and crates, even the young beginning to sigh for marrow bones.

Early September, fifteen hundred folk packed tipis and headed west to the buffalo plains, accompanied by a platoon of Agency soldiers, set up camp along the south fork of Little Water Creek. Scouts rode out with great excitement, even Coyote Dropping caught up, telling all who would listen how it would be.

They sit around the fire sharpening arrows, replacing rawhide strings on bois d'arc bows. Wait, watch the sky. Hours at a time. Day after day. The storytellers fall into silence. No smoke signals. Finally dust rises in the distance, the scouts return.

"What do you have to report?"

"We're hungry."

"What have you seen?"

"Empty prairie."

"We must go out again."

Coyote Dropping rode with them. They saw no buffalo, the wind switched to the north.

"They will come when the leaves begin to fall."

Searched every creek and draw. They found bones: skulls, vertebrae, ribs, white and bare, broken and gnawed, powdery and dry, stretching sometimes as far as they could see across the plains.

"They always come when cold north wind drives the leaves."

Rode until the hardtack and bacon gave out, people in camp restless when they returned, frost covered the brittle grass and cooking pots in the morning, all along the horizon they saw nothing but orange-brown grass. Children began to cry. The hunters made more medicine, Coyote Dropping went out at night above the camp, the stars large and cold, fasted and prayed to the buffalo spirit, to the wind, to coyote and red-tailed hawk to stand by him. The wind howled, rattled the bluestem and foxtail, coyotes laughed all around, the smell of snow. He returned at dawn, shivering cold, crawled under the Agency blanket beside Autumn Tallgrass.

"I saw nothing, nothing came. The magic is gone."

"You've known for a while."

"Yes. Since Hard Stick Canyon I've been dancing. Imitating myself, like I once did pronghorn or prairie chicken in the hunting dance to summon them."

"Families are packing up, going back to Cache Creek."

"We will not."

"The buffalo will not return."

"Nor shall we."

Autumn Tallgrass, Coyote Dropping, Woman's Heart, and a few other old hunters slipped off before the Agency soldiers were awake. Rode the hills and the streambeds, saw nothing but bones. They sat around the fire. There was nothing to eat. It began to drizzle and freeze, sleet, then hard dry snowflakes. Woman's Heart stuffs the last of his tobacco into a catlinite pipe, lights it with an ember from the fire, inhales, holds and rolls the smoke in the mouth, blows east, south, west, and north. Passes the pipe.

"You know, Coyote Dropping, I'm sorry I struck you at Adobe Walls."

Rubs his hand across his face. "Not as sorry as I was, I'll wager."

"I was striking out at what I could not hit, you were the closest to hand."

Looks out into the swirling sphere of campfire light. "The buffalo have forsaken us, but this still beats chasing down those docile, worm-infested cows the Agency gives."

"Sure doesn't stick to the ribs, though."

Autumn Tallgrass takes the pipe, rekindles it, lets smoke slip through the nostrils. "What will we do now?"

"Buffalo Bill makes what you call business of the buffalo, he now collects greenbacks from people settled in the eastern woods doing a kind of war dance powwow. He will give money to those who help him. I talked with a man up north who's done it. Says it's more interesting than gambling away Agency rations or trying to prod a sick cow into a frenzied chase, cooped up behind wire fences. And lots of whiskey, loosen those visions right on up."

"They give you greenbacks to dance?"

"These people can make business from anything."

They laugh, stare into the fire, snow beginning to eddy and settle downwind of the tufts of grass.

"My father always said it's a bad sign to be this hungry before the snow has even drifted."

"He should know. Starved to death two winters ago out on the Llano Estacado, didn't he?"

Autumn Tallgrass brings out her butcher knife from beneath her blanket. "When we were doing the hunting dance before we left Cache Creek Agency, kind of a vision came to me. I knew I was going to grease my chin with the fat of a fresh-killed animal. Never figured on it being my horse."

The wind howled for three days and three nights, drove heavy snow.

They killed their ponies for meat.

Paradise

I looked with all the eyes I had. I couldn't see it.

Slate gray and brown, sky and brittle grass. I was ill, three miserable days from Ellis in a Conestoga drawn rattling and banging across emptiness so vast and forsaken the world seemed to fall away, the here-and-now dissolve, nothing, not my Maker, not the Devil, nothing but hollow eternity remained. The menfolk scurried around the oxen, the dogs began to barking, and my husband raised my head from the folded wagon sheet I was using for a pillow and pointed.

Hortense S.

"There it is!"

Low rolling pasture. "I cannot see it."

"There!" As if insisting would make it appear.

I blinked: some dark spots on the earth, curdled smoke twisting to the colder heavens. "They're living underground?"

"Dugouts and soddies."

Others clustered around the lead wagon, silent at first. W. R. Hill, who'd brought us out here, sat on his horse pulling the corners of his mustache. I began to weep.

We pitched our tents, but the north wind blew so bitterly it tore them down, whipped the little dab of flame we had from sunflower stalks and willow switches scavenged on the way, churned showers of sparks across the darkness. Some didn't bother to unpack much, already made up their minds to turn around at first light and head back east, Kentucky full of peckerwoods looking better all the time. A circle of men sat about the campfire and passed the snakebite medicine.

"We been snakebit all right. And I reckon I know the snake that did it."

"Where I come from only one thing to do with a snake."

"Ever since he tempt sister Eve, only one thing."

"I got a good length of hemp rope right here by me."

"What we waiting for, then."

They moved through the night, I saw them disappear from the bowl of firelight, heard them, the mournful keen of the constant wind. Shouts and curses from where Hill had been sleeping, I couldn't miss this, sick as I was. I wrap an old star-pattern quilt around my shoulders and stumble through waist-high grass out after them. Hill bout knocked me down running like hellhounds on his tail, sock feet and one boot in each hand, a passel of brothers and sisters like hungry prairie wolves on a hare. I forgot the desolate plains, the double crud, all my worldly woes, and joined in the chase, that little squeak of a man the focus of all God's troubles. Never stopped to think if we caught him not a tree within a hundred miles to string him up on.

We came to a mound of grass and milkweed, turned out to be a dugout, murky light through the one oilpaper window. We kicked the door open and as many of us as could entered in. The place smoky, a tightly braided flannel lantern wick smoldering in a tomato can full of grease, sitting on the shipping-crate table in the middle of the dirt floor, a large woman standing with her arms crossed, a meat ax held firm in a hand looked like it knew what to do with it.

"If you-all come for tea, you'd best wait till I can rustle up enough cups."

"We want Hill. Where he at?"

A shawl draped over a woven willow chair in the corner by the stove seems to tremble and breathe, something small and lumpy and maybe scared underneath, but the woman doesn't take her eyes off us.

"He ain't here, makes it a habit to do his socializing in the daytime."

We stand, the edge of rage worn smooth by the bits of roots and dust drifting down from the roof through hazy deep orange light, the futility of striking out blindly at whatever might be hovering beneath that shawl, and, to boot, the big woman's cleaver.

Nobody says a word as we walk back to our blown-down tents. The moon has come out from behind a cloud, not a Kentucky moon, a cold, lucid blue light tossing the prairie grass, the meager buffalo-dung fires trailing embers, an incessant moaning all around, distance, and garbled coyote calls.

This is Nicodemus.

Spartacus He looked. From the cave in the bluff running along Dibble Creek just outside Stockton the world was yellow and flat, treeless, sand mounds held together by crane grass along the shores. He was disoriented and lonely, couldn't even recognize many of the people he'd been traveling with, knew the path out there led to Nicodemus, knew the fever had struck down the woman and her daughter but not sure which woman now, Mississippi dissolved away, a confusion of memories, but graves were dug, and it was his loss specifically, he remembers that, the pitiful soil they planted them in, his tears as much for it: how could anything ever grow in this, magnesia somewhere between clay and a rock quarry. And wind to blow your soul away.

They'd traveled, all of them, hand-to-mouth, plenty of people to help them on their way, but that was it: on their way. Nobody wanted them to stay, wanted them out of here, somewhere else on down the line, send them all to Niggerdemus. The woman bought the train tickets to Ellis, joined up with this ragtag bunch in wagons moving up to the Solomon valley toward Nicodemus, sat around the bonfires at night firing guns ever so often to keep the wild animals off, the fever passing one to the other. First the daughter gone—or had she left in Lawrence, found something better to do than travel into the void? Spartacus couldn't remember now, the woman dead for sure. Knew the way she moved, and the form of her in the shroud, infertile sand and clods rattling from his fist into the narrow grave. The lone prairie. Alone again, broken, in a cave in a bluff, he's got to decide: does he want to live or to die.

People seemed to come and go, gave Spartacus food, his companions in the wagons gone on, they said. Some lived in the caves all the time. Some had claims in Nicodemus, out looking for work, they said, to tide them over till they could get a crop in, not enough cash, not enough farm equipment, some paid men passing through with a team and a plow to break the plains, two dollars a day but worth it, mighty hard to turn the sod with a spade and a grubbing hoe. But things looking up, can get twelve–fifteen dollars a month doing farm-work in Stockton, they said, even get railroad work in Ells-worth and Bunker Hill. Last year, grasshoppers got most of the corn and wheat. This year looking like a good year long as the rain comes, Nicodemus climbing out of her burrows, rising up from under the ground.

It was summer, warm again, a brilliant sky outside the mouth of the cave. Spartacus woke, felt his knees, thighs, balls, and cock, the mind cleared of inchoate images, snarled voices. A body was there, at least that was certain, but his self, his spirit, buckled and bent, did not adhere, but tethered now at least here and there to this chilled flesh. He stepped out of the cave, first time in God knows how long, an agony he recognized as hunger, his legs trembling under the weight, surprised what seemed so insubstantial had such actual heft. He walked along the path but was soon exhausted, stood with eyes closed facing the sun. Going to have to get ahold of yourself, pull it back together, not even enough left to die right now, what a man needs to let him know that he is, is some Mississippi side meat and grits.

Spartacus chuckled to himself, hands in the stiff pockets of oversized coveralls, whose they once were he didn't know, eyes still shut, red-orange glow around him, wiggled the toes, the fingers, ran the tongue over the teeth, sniffed air, felt it taking form through the nostrils and throat, in the lungs. Sure wasn't Mississippi out there, that's for damn certain. But knowing what it's not a good step in finding what it is, first time in a long time much interest one way or the other.

A startling darkness fell across the face, he opened the eyes, a jolt through his limbs. A man standing right in front of him on the path.

"Good morning."

Large high-yellow man, big head, two rows of very white teeth, well-stitched jacket, golden rings on the fingers of plump hands. Spartacus not used to seeing such drapery on a man of color, came to him suddenly how loose and crusty his own clothing hung on his feeble frame.

"Morning, sir."

"Are you on your way to Nicodemus?"

His eyes fill with unexpected tears, he blinks them away, overcome with loss, found and lost again, he *was* going but not now, not enough left. "Sir, I have been doing poorly."

"So I can see."

Hortense S. The first thing we had to do, all of us together, was build a house for Mrs. Henry. The woman was big with child I mean to tell you. The next morning, after wishing those fifty or sixty families heading back east farewell, we all of us who chose to remain were feeling better. My fever had broken in the night, slept mighty well, in fact. The wind lulled me, seemed to nestle me even more securely than the Kentucky mountains but at the same time promised wild, unhindered freedom, and the sun rising over the monstrous flatness gave such volume of light you couldn't help but feel blessed. When I woke I'd made up my mind: this is going to be my home. Also glad we didn't kill Mr. Hill the night before. Generally satisfied, when we watched the last wagon fall away east beyond the low sand hills, that we could have cut and run with them. Nobody was making us stay. We had chosen not to go and, more important, chosen to make our stand.

Most of us had no idea where to start, never seen, much less built a house out of sod before, and there sure weren't nary a tree to be had anywhere. Those already living here helped us out and we got it done in time for little William to be born in what soon would pass for comfort for all of us.

I'm telling you we had some learning to do. Nothing we knew or thought we knew applied. But some things we didn't leave behind either. Lots of folks in Graham County didn't much care for the notion of Africans settling on the prairie. Many of them helpful, friendly even—my God, live out here long enough you damn happy to see anything alive that can talk—but there were enough hard-asses to cause trouble. We couldn't get anybody to survey our claims for love nor money. We didn't have no money and plenty of the old settlers had no love. Finally got a man come all the way down from Norton to do it. On his way home, some pack of cowardly cur killed him from ambush.

It was hard. But what doesn't kill you makes you strong. The prairie people coming back home along the Solomon from their hunt in the western mountains gave us some of their meat, some of the U.S.-issue flour and lard they get from Fort Ogallala. The founders of the town company went east to get help, brought what they'd collected back in wagons, we built a stone-front dugout commissary to give it out to whoever needed it. Emigrants heading farther west made Nicodemus a stopping-off place, helped us plow our fields, plant our crops. My husband and lots of the other menfolk and some of the women walked hundreds of miles to work in eastern Kansas or Colorado. We picked up buffalo bones to sell for six dollars a ton. We became plains people. By God we did.

Spartacus He was in the Burley's Union House, near Washington Street, Nicodemus. The man who'd brought him there from the caves, J. W. Niles, sat with him in the kitchen. Spartacus still ill at ease, lost, the fever cleared again but a confusion accumulated over the last several months, or was it years, an entire lifetime, or just a matter of weeks, and then there was the building itself. Made out of dirt, a sod hotel, smell it all around you, permeating the coffee, greens, and fatback, corn bread, the dank smell of earth. The walls pargeted with magnesia, three rooms where the guests stayed, a large structure as things went in Nicodemus. Niles had pointed everything out as they came into town: the general store, generally out of everything, at Third and Washington, things booming so much even got the white folks moving in. Right here at the northwest corner of the public square, Third and Main, which is what we call Washington, Wilson's putting up a stone structure two stories high, William Green building on the northeast corner: like the rats, mice, snakes, and centipedes get into the sod houses, we try to kill them, and if we can't we sleep with them. Got two livery stables, I'm certain you can hire on, cause I run one myself over on First Street, you dealt with mules, you say, back in Mississippi? Need a harness maker in a boom town like this one, good hand make two dollars, two-seventy-five a day, maybe even get a job skinning mules for the freight company hauling in cargo from Stockton, Hill City, and Webster, no time at all have what you need to pay your filing fee, stake you a claim. Man not expecting a handout like some of those folk making their way upriver from the old states, we don't need that sort, man willing to sweat and hustle a little got opportunity out here on this prairie, this Solomon valley going to grow big let me tell you, a railroad coming, no question about it, and we're here from the get-go. Real estate office, two hotels, and I'm going to be starting up another one myself early next year right over there at Second and Adams. You don't know anything about carpentry or stone masonry, do you, look at these limestone houses and stores going up, Jonas Moore can sure use the help, pocket two–three dollars a day, easy. Two churches, if you're in need of spiritual sustenance, Reverend Silas Lee tends his flock at the First Baptist, little sod church over at Fourth and Main, and the African Methodist Episcopalians going to settle west of town at Mount Olive, and we got six schools in various soddies around town. Spartacus, it was your lucky day you ran into me.

Hortense S. | If it's not one damn thing it's another. Just when you think God smiling on you, got the locust plagues licked, enough rain to keep down the prairie fires and bring up a little crop, industrious neighbor like Spartacus proved up on a claim next to yours, hardworking man, skinning mules for the freight line between Stockton and here to get him a grubstake, good friends with Mr. Niles, helps out with the plowing and the sowing since my husband off in eastern Colorado doing what he can gathering a little cash money. Just when we got a good-looking stand of wheat, the Lord forgive me for evoking his name to curse, the god damned drovers from Texas run ever longhorned cow they got right smack-dab over our fields, turn untold days of toil into a muddy quagmire, and, if that isn't enough, steal ever last one of our farm animals.

We'd been having trouble off and on with the cattlemen from the first, they're a mean and lawless lot, no doubt about it. Think the river water and ever blade of grass in God's green creation belong to them by right, been known to cripple folks' draft animals, tromple down their dugouts while they sleep, but this year the first time they took it in their heads to run ever god damn one of us off the land.

I was out tilling in the truck garden when I heard them coming up from the south. I knew a herd had been watering down on the Solomon, and I knew there'd been a frascas about it but didn't know how serious it'd gotten till I looked up and saw this wasn't just a herd of cows moving past, they were on a dead run toward me and my fields. I set out for the shed, stumble, and fall, and before I can get to my feet the stampede is upon me. I think about praying, already on my knees, but realize yelling and screaming, flailing away with my double shovel at the beasts as they pass, do me more immediate good. Crouched down to stay below those nasty horns clicking and clattering overhead, slaver, chunks of dirt, and hooves flying, tails slapping across my face, I manage to split them, like Moses parting the Dead Sea waters, and keep them split around me, don't ask how. Lucky, I guess, I was at the edge of the herd. The last steer leaps past me and a horse skids to a stop, prancing and snorting, eyes wild with excitement. I look up and see a gold tooth flashing in a face black as the Devil on a moonless night.

"Howdy, ma'am. What are you doing out on these dangerous plains?"

"Trying to grub a living, and they weren't all that dangerous till your boss sent you lackeys out to tramp us down."

"Please, ma'am. You're talking to the newly appointed Segundo of this operation, the best damn cowhand ever ride up the trail from Texas."

"Just confirms my low opinion of you all."

"You'd better pack up and get on back to the safe farms and plantations in the east and south. This country out here meant for coyote and prairie dog and the longhorn cow."

He swept down and grabbed me around the waist, the horse whirled as he slung me up on the rump, and we went bounding over the ruined wheat field to the shed. He dropped me, pulled open the stalls, untethered the mule, ran our two cows, the goats, and three pigs off, then sidesteps up to me, big smile showing his gold tooth like he's mighty proud of what he's doing. I stand there hissing and faunching like a mother goose, a powerless rage.

"You can't fool me with all that Texas cowboy talk, nigger, you from Tennessee, your mama probably still down there doing her best to outsmart Jim Crow. You ought to be ashamed."

He laughs, tips his hat, and gallops off.

I walked into town to look for help rounding up my stock, found a big bunch of folks congregated at the public square.

Miles was there, Mose, and Spartacus just pulled in from Stockton with a wagonload of lumber, everybody milling around madder than a whole coop full of wet hens, their fields trompled and the animals run off, but not knowing what in the world to do about it. Just like chickens, we run in circles, scream, and shout. Finally, somebody came in from the south told us the cowboys had regrouped their herd and had them bedded down on the Solomon, probably contemplating the same romp again tomorrow on the off chance a few stalks of corn, row or two of wheat, maybe a pig or banty rooster they missed the first pass still needed to be ground into the mud.

Lots of mayhem threatened, but the fact of the matter was, ever last one of us on foot, only livestock in sight the team of six sumpter mules hitched to Spartacus's freight wagon. After a lot of cussing and not much else, lot of imaginary backsides kicked, a group of us crowded into the kitchen of Burley's Union House, brewed a pot of the real Colombian coffee Spartacus had managed to scare up in Stockton, even had refined white sugar to go in it, and after a while the aroma of that coffee filled the place, drove out the smell of damp sod, sweetness and warmth began to restore the ravaged spirit, and we got down to plot us some serious revenge.

Spartacus sat at the head of the table, such as it was, three warped cottonwood planks laid across two sawhorses, with woven willow chairs. He's a peculiar man, quiet, hard worker, but a cloud of loneliness seems to hover over him like river mosquitoes in the spring, like he's never really left Mississippi in his mind, or at least never made it all the way to Kansas, his eyes that faraway desire of a man constantly longing for a tree. Looks at a stand of winter wheat in the fields, a wistful smile, handful of tilled earth running through his fingers, you can see it in the way he lingers there rapt, something at the very center of his being knows it will never be so magical, never so satisfying, as tobacco or a cotton crop, as the Mississippi dirt. His Mississippi soul just can't quite hold together in all this Kansas wind.

"What the hell we gonna do?"

"Only got six mules among us, never be able to corral all the stock scattered across the valley, looks to me the thing to do is to get those damn Texans to round them up for us."

"Yeah. Just mosey into their camp and ask them please, if they don't mind interrupting their stories how they mashed us into the ground today, and their plans to do the same again come sunup, could they take time off to collect our cows, mules, horses, pigs, goats, and chickens for us. Give them something to run off tomorrow. Sounds like a good idea to me."

"We'll take our guns."

"What guns, nigger? That rebel contraption you picked out of old Master's trash heap? That ain't going to scare nobody. We ain't got three good bird guns or squirrel rifles among us, nor the shot to load them with."

"What do you think, Mose? You were cook once on a drive from Texas, weren't you?"

"Sure was. And I can tell you, six of us bareback on team mules against ten or twelve of them on cow ponies not going to be a pretty sight to behold. But I know what we *could* do. While all the hands sitting around the campfire yarning, there is one of them usually all by hisself, usually the youngest among them: the horse wrangler, at the back of the herd with the remuda, sometimes a half mile off from the rest. If we was to sneak up and grab him, we'd have us something they might be willing to trade our animals for."

Well, everybody got real excited, happy even. Like this was a welcome breakdown of the daily drudgery of trying to scratch a home out of this indifferent country. Decided Mose would go, he knew about herding cows, Spartacus would have to be in charge of the mules, Niles as president of the self-governing organization, two others with shotguns. I was getting riled up myself.

"I better take that last mule."

"You?"

"Not only am I head of the Nicodemus Chapter Number Seven of the First Grand Independent Benevolent Society of Kansas and Missouri, but a lot of the stock out there is mine. I better help get it back."

"But you're—"

"I been breaking sod and cultivating crops by myself most of the time what with my husband gone off to Colorado, that don't seem to bother none of you-all, and I'm as good a mule skinner as some of you and better than most. Now, Spartacus, the freight company going to be mighty put off if something happens to one of their sumpters, you want the best we got on them. Isn't that right."

Finishes off his coffee, sets the mug on the table in front of him, even he's appearing friskier than I've ever seen him, looks up at me. "That's right. Let's go unhitch that team."

And it's a good thing I was along. Cause we sure had a surprise coming.

When You Go to Herding Cows

Cannonball | It wasn't your ordinary drive. He knew that when he learned they were taking an unruly herd of twenty-five hundred short yearlings, tail-ends, and scabs for the Big Bellies, all the way to Montana. Knew it from the time he found out back in Texas crossing the Brazos that *el coyote* was really *la coyocita* and decided to keep his mouth shut about it and to bring her along, best damn horse wrangler he or anybody else straps on a saddle ever saw, disguised as a greenhorn boy.

The first day out they discover the trail is full of Africans on foot, carrying the sum of their worldly goods on their heads and backs, children and a few dogs strung out behind, barefoot, dust-covered, thirsty, and near starvation some of them, but by God on the way north out of Texas, following the longhorns to Kansas, the land of milk and honey. Well, of corn whiskey and molasses anyway.

He knew for sure things won't be going the way a man'd want them to, and more than likely never going to go that way again. Why he ever thought he could get away with a stunt like this one, on a drive like this one, was beyond even his fertile imagination's ability to grasp. Been around machinery long enough to realize things start to vibrate when they're falling apart, and that's what this drive was doing, the entire trail starting to rattle from one extreme to another. Just like his innards: things shaking on down.

Bad enough him sneaking back to the rear ever chance he gets, see how Coyote doing, his first drive, better make sure he's got it under control, feel kind of responsible for him, kind of my protégé. Sure thing, Cannonball, you go check him out, we know how it is, Cannonball, you been out in that coastal brush country too long, hornier than a three-peckered goat. Should have spent a little time in town before you started on a two-month push, blown off a load or two, not a good thing to leave them rusting inside, man's nature come down on him get him in a lot of trouble. Better hope that stone cathouse still there in Mulberry Pass, cross-lipped, mouse-haired Matty with the lazy left eye. Way you been carrying on not even Jojo the whorehouse monkey safe.

They all laugh. Cannonball tells them they get theirs in hell and moseys on back to find her among the horses, to point things out to her and give their name, to teach her to talk, to snuggle and rut in the coulees, Big Mouth Henry singing his soul out in the distance beneath the endless spindle of the stars.

But even in the draws you have to be on the lookout. Wayward bands huddled against the wind, some sneaking up on the remuda convinced a cow pony much better way to the promise land than shank's mare, even some with the idea burning in their heads and bellies horseflesh taste pretty damn good. The damn lone prairie not as lonely as it used to be.

Not as dry either. It's drier. Man owned both Texas and hell, he'd rent out Texas and live in hell. They throw the cows off the bedding ground early, first light across the horizon, get them going before what pitiful dew there was evaporated in that hot, static air going to be lolling across the trail. Let them lie down and rest for an hour or more two or three times during the middle of the day, dull, aching heat heavy enough to drive the strongest, mean-temperedest steer to his knees. Didn't take long to ride your horse to a shadow, had to change mounts four times a day. What moisture you had in your body caught in the bandanna across your face, trail dust turned to mud against the nose and mouth, evaporating to exquisite coolness whenever the stagnant air would stir. By late afternoon the herd beginning to get a powerful thirst on them, growing surly, impatient, and restless, they're sniffing, smell them some kind of water somewhere, if not here, up ahead, and the faster we get to where it's at, the better we gonna feel. The point men had to ride in the lead to hold them to a walk. They wouldn't graze, too damn hot, till twilight, brutal condensed sun diluted through haze, a kind of suspended calm, an ecstatic relief you'd made it through the Devil's anvil, cows and men both glad to let the mind empty in the long golden red light before the stifling darkness fell. And dawn the same as before, three times the distance traveled yet to come.

The longhorns wouldn't abide anything near them, took three times the space, three times the time to bed them down, milling about aimlessly, scarcely half the cows settled by midnight. No sleep for anybody, double guard circling the herd, trying to hold it in one place, a hopeless task, Coyote and Cook up all night to keep the hands on horses and full of coffee, Big Mouth Henry and Cannonball fallen silent, no singing, no funning, just tedious, endless drifting, the cows over a mile from camp by the time the morning comes.

The next day is worse. And the third is hot and clear. The herd never stops, can't get them to graze or lie down in the torrid middle of the day, the cook unable to prepare the meals, each man given a can of tomatoes and sent on his way. The cows' tongues hang hopelessly from their mouths. A sullen yearling in the rear lets out a desperate appeal, those around her take up the complaint. It surges through the herd to the lead and then back again: a piteous, ominous admonition, repeated, as if marking time, throughout the day. As they approach the river they begin to trot, the Segundo calls up two more cowboys to the lead to try to hold them in check, the herd spread out now over two miles down the trail. You can see over the series of flat hills and the floodplain the line of trees winding through, dusty, brown, and withered. The river is dry.

"What do you think, Cannonball?"

"She's dry."

The Segundo squatted in the sand of the riverbed, idly sifting it through his fingers, then funneling it from the palm, the long reins from his horse held in the other hand against his thigh. "Drier than a popcorn fart. You might say we're in a tight spot."

Cannonball, still mounted, leaning on the pommel, looks down at him. "I've seen worse."

The Segundo getting on in years, a man meaty in personal experience, the enthusiasm of youth replaced in the green eyes squinting against the glare on the sand by defiant resignation, a fatal acceptance. "When?"

Like trying to read omens of what's ahead instead of recollecting the past, his future somehow bound up with this man's fate, and it all indicates water some kind of way. Instead of tea leaves or the roots Mama used to work, it's the puckered folds and wrinkles of skin around the Segundo's eyes. Everything under this insolent sun, no question about it, starting to vibrate apart. "Gimme some time to think on it."

Slowly fights his way up from his haunches, hangs on the saddle horn taking in quick gulps of sere air, head cocked toward the painful chaotic lowing of cows spread all around. "You do that, Cannonball, and while you're at it, get a shovel from the chuck wagon and dig us a well. Least have some water for the horses and for us. Hotter than a fresh fucked fox in a forest fire. No way in hell we're gonna ever get these dogies to lie down."

When he'd finished digging, Cannonball leaned at the edge of the five-foot hole on the shovel handle watching damp sand seep water, sharp reflections glare from the surface. A clutch of Africans seemed to congeal from rippling heat around him, approached the well, and stood silent, heads slightly inclined in polite supplication. He looked at them with idle curiosity, dust-covered apparitions, indistinct portents, hants that seemed to mean no harm other than the harm the world does. He thrust the shovel into the sand, turned and waded across the dry riverbed to his mount, tethered to a sycamore, took his tin cup and a couple of cans of tomatoes, a few sticks of pemmican from the saddlebag, and returned to the well. The one closest to him, who he just now recognized was an old woman, took the cans and pemmican, passed them to the others to be packed away in canvas tote sacks they carried over their shoulders, took the tin cup. Cannonball pulled up the shovel, leaned on it again to watch. She filled two goatskin bags, waiting after each cupful for the water to replenish itself, then passed the cup to the others to drink, then drank herself. She wiped her mouth on her sleeve and handed the cup back, stared awhile at him, hard to tell if taking or giving strength or just confirming some fragile cement bonding the chaos together. He watched them retreat up the sloping bank, shimmer and shake and disintegrate, then incorporate again, giants on the low far hills.

The herd stretched five miles over the prairie on either side of the streambed by the time the horses and riders had drunk, feverish and out of control, lead cows turning back, wandering through the confusion behind them, rear overtaking them in a tight bunch, bawling and clacking horns together, then spreading out again, a random search for some scent of water. The Segundo, Cannonball, and Big Mouth Henry rode out to the flank to try to break up the mill, spurred their horses and charged, a V-shaped wedge, Segundo in the lead, whooping and hollering, swinging lariats, breakneck gallop through the cows, who broke at first, opened passage for them, then shuffled, finally hemmed them in, momentum turned to mill and swearing by note and rhyme, energetic as the heat would allow. They regrouped and tried again, but the cows were turning, heading back south toward last water.

The Segundo rallied the whole outfit to try to stop them, strung out slapping ropes across their noses, firing pistols so close it singed the hair on their faces. The cows plodded on, morose and determined in their willessness, bumped and shoved until the line gave, pushed the horsemen aside. The cowboys regrouped farther south, were forced apart again. The Segundo flailing and sputtering, eyes that have seen ever damn thing betraying desperation, a realization beyond the normal acceptance of what befalls. Like the sudden breeze across a sweat-soaked flannel shirt, it chilled to the bone.

"Cannonball! We got no more chance than a one-legged man in an ass-kicking contest, these damn razor-backed barn-yard savages are going blind. We've lost control. You take three men, have Coyote cut you out two extra mounts apiece, stay behind to throw in the stragglers, the rest of us gonna have to ride the son of a bitch out. Meet you back south at the water."

Sure enough. Things shaking on down.

He knew it. When they got the herd back together at the lake, waded out, water up to their sides, moaning and bawling for a half hour before they took a few laps at it with swollen tongues, water, just to feel it all around them. Came out after an hour and lay down to rest, regain the strength lost, then in again to drink. Finally enough faith restored to graze, their eyesight slowly coming back.

Knew it when it started in raining pitchforks, things oscillating, one damn extreme to the other. As wet now as it had been dry, hell and high water. They pushed the cows back north and ever dry gully was now a raging torrent, ever low spot a muddy bog, and by the time they got to Doan's Crossing on the Red River, cows thick as three in a bed in front of them, waterbound for over a week, waiting for the flood to crest.

Nothing to do but skulk. Not the kind of inactivity would restore vigor to the logy cattle, horses, or men. Cringe under your water-soaked slicker, fingers and toes pale and wrinkled like a drowned man's, the saddle made ten pounds heavier by the moisture taken on, the waxy mud balled on boots and fetlock, bedding ground off the trail, the trail itself churned into gumbo thick as hod and tenacious as horse-hoof glue. Can't strike enough fire to keep your damn cigarette lit in the constant damp, much less warm a cup of coffee.

The drovers getting edgy, especially the Segundo. Doan's Crossing the meanest there is, swallowed more Texas steers, horses, men, and mules than all the other rivers put together. It just looks ornery. Steep red-bluff banks, in times of no rain dried silt up above a man's head on the trunks of the timber marking its course, driftwood and sedge hanging, bird feathers and animal hair on the branches, just to show you how churlish it can get. And the water red as fresh-spilled blood.

It finally cleared up long enough for the flood to fall and the outfits in front to ford, but started raining again like a cow pissing on a flat rock by late afternoon, no time at all, the river back up past dangerous to the apocalyptic. The Big Auger called the Segundo and Cannonball over to the chuck wagon to discuss the situation, not only serious but getting tense. He wanted to go on across but the Segundo didn't think so, huddled close to the cooking fire, put up quite a mouth about it. But the Big Auger is the boss and had made up his mind: those longhorns going to be on the other side by sundown tomorrow. When the Big Auger rode off, Cannonball thought he heard the Segundo murmur through the vapor rising from his tin coffee cup: *damn right about that. But the other side of what.*

The rain had let up again, looked like the sun could even break through before it went down, the Segundo and Cannonball left alone at the fire. Cannonball getting ready to leave himself, but something about the Segundo's demeanor, crouched, arms resting on his knees, his cup of coffee in both hands held close to the chin, seeking relief in the aroma from a vague disorder, his eyes staring beyond the fire to the rippling tree line at the river, fixed there since the Big Auger rode off, something Cannonball had never noticed about the Segundo. Not much time to notice anything, but these waterbound days get a man to thinking and seeing things he don't ordinarily dwell on, something about him, transparent light saturating the space contained beneath the clouds, air smelling uncommonly clean after so much rainfall, the succulent grasses and distant rush of water, something made Cannonball stretch his shoulders back, roll his head around, shrug a couple of times, shake each leg out, and sit down again.

The Segundo didn't move for a long time. Finally gave a start, you'd have missed it if you weren't looking as close as Cannonball was, ever since he got to know Coyote, been observing things a lot closer, a quick dilation of the eyes is all it was, a sudden return, then the entire body settled, a tension released, and he drained the coffee gone cold in the cup, looked into it, frowned, shook out the dregs.

"You know, Cannonball, I been herding cows a long time."

"Anybody on this drive been at it a long time, even if it's their first go-round."

A pause, as if assessing the truth of it. "I reckon if we stop what we're doing too long, sit on the woodpile or the sunny side of the corral staring at our boots, scratching lines in the dirt with a stick or digging holes with our barlows, sit down and think about it all very much, we'd all go crazy." Gets up and pours another cup of coffee. "I always did what was expected of me, never shirked. A man don't get to be second in command any other way. But I just got a bad feeling about this river crossing."

Watches him sit again. "Could be a pisser all right."

Silent for a while. "You know I had two brothers in the cattle-driving business."

"I have heard that."

Looks distracted now, or is it the smoke from the fire, reaches inside his cowskin vest and pulls out a worn, folded piece of paper. "This is a letter from my mother. She's asking me not to cross no swollen rivers. My brothers both drowned. The youngest trying to get a bogged longhorn out of the quick-sand on the Cimarron, rolled over on him and pinned him under, been two years ago now. The other went down last year with his mount. Stepped in a hole crossing the North Platte above Forty Islands, be a year tomorrow. Never found him or the horse."

Cannonball is looking at the toes of his boots, nothing to do now but wait for him to go on.

The Segundo reaches in the other side of his vest and takes out a worn edition of the New Testament. "My mother give me this when I left on my first drive." Holds it in the fingertips of both hands, finally offers it across the fire to Cannonball. "I want you to take it for me in case. In case anything goes wrong. I'd like you to see to it my mother back in Texas gets it."

Cannonball hesitates, uncertain. "That old Red River not going to get you. You too ugly, spit you right on back out."

A weak smile, but still holding out the Testament. Cannon-ball finally takes it. "Thanks. Now get on over to the herd, be sure we hold those steers off water, want them nice and thirsty by morning."

Looks like Cannonball not the only one thinking things starting to quake.

The lightning flickering and flashing all night long in the north and west didn't bode no one no good.

Cold mist and fog hung along the river early dawn, the cows apprehensive and disorderly. Been that way from the start, ever since the dry run, they never did take instruction well, get into a routine, ever morning like starting all over again. Coyote cuts out the horses with the biggest barrel chests, the swimmers and floaters, cowboys strip down naked, hop on bareback, grabbing the mane and slapping the neck to guide them. Cannonball and the Segundo scout out a low spot in the high cutbank on the other side for the exit point, hardly see it through the saturated air. Estimate the current, damn if the rip isn't two feet higher than last night, but we ain't gonna let her whip us, the boss says to go, he's the one with the money to lose, so let's go.

They get the herd in a narrow line, enter about two hundred rods upstream, float down to the exit, half dozen riders on the low side of the drifting cows. River running faster than they figured, they overshoot the exit, come ashore thirty rods too long, yelling and splashing to try to get them back upstream and onto the high ground above the bluffs, starting to bunch and flounder in the shallow water and mud. The Segundo all this time back on the other side watching, high and dry. The river rising as the morning passes.

He has to cross. The chuck wagon ready to go on the ferry, he could ride with it. All the hands watching him, wisecracking, they'd all overheard the heated conversation yesterday with the Big Auger, easy to confuse caution with cowardice. He could try to stare them down, explain why it was necessary for the good of the herd and the drive that he ride the ferry, tell them about his mother and two brothers. But what would a desperate bunch of cowpunchers know about anything, hardly one of them older than twenty-two, not old enough to see more than a river out of its banks, a day's sport to break the monotony of a long difficult summer, what do they know of the fragile, unstable, temporary interplay of all this, of omen and of fate.

Cannonball saw it all from atop the red bluff on the northern shore, the broad churning red river frothing and swirling eddies of foam, sticks, leaves, and uprooted tree trunks, rising from mist to his right, spilling out over the floodplain below and to the left, and finally disappearing in an indistinct line of cottonwood, blackjack, sycamore, and haze beyond the far bend. The last of the herd splashed and milled in the muddy red water, angry and recalcitrant at some bovine slight the ignorant cowboys, hollering and slapping at them with ropes, couldn't comprehend. Saw the Segundo, removed and small yet immediate, compelling, almost a doll you could reach out and manipulate, saw him unsaddle the coyote mare, strip the bridle, his boots, chaps, blue denims, and smallclothes, fold everything neatly, arrange them on the bench of the chuck wagon, stand pale and naked. The ferry was readied to cast off. Cannonball shouted out suddenly against the rumble of water and distance, surprising his horse and himself: *don't do it, man, ride the damn boat across!*

The Segundo doesn't hear him but looks up at that moment and raises his hand in some kind of salute, farewell, die-dog-or-eat-the-hatchet, maybe just swatting mosquitoes swarming after his vulnerable flesh. Grabs the coyote mare by the neck, swings up on her, and plunges into the river. They look like good swimmers, both of them, barrel chest and belly, good floaters, bobbing and rushing with the current, two heads, thrashing feet and a tail in the wake, angling across the river, gaining and failing, but right on course toward the knot of irate longhorns in the shallows. The last steer lumbers out of the water, finds a soft damp spot in the bank, snorts and shakes his head, paws, and butts into the rise, digging side to side in the waxy red gumbo, down on his knees cutting vicious licks with his horns, the champeen horns of the herd, looks like, ten–twelve foot across. How the hell did he get in with the yearlings anyway? He spins around, clumps of earth on the horn tips, forehead matted with mud, on the damn prod, and the first thing he sees is the Segundo and the coyote mare just finding solid bottom. He charges.

The coyote mare sees that steer splashing out after them and jumps straight up in the air, clean out of the water, all four hooves, seems to hang awhile, the Segundo clinging to her mane, feet pawing to give some extra lift, wanting to drift a lit-tle downstream of those horns but can't quite make it, both of them losing their balance, left front foreleg doesn't quite clear the horn tip, a violent snap of the head topples them upside down into the river. The steer thrashes about, sputtering and sneezing, head and horns the only thing showing above the red roiled current, then horse hooves emerge, the mare floats up and flips, shakes spirals of water flying and bounds off to the shallows.

It would have been damn comical if the Segundo had bobbed up like a cork, spitting river-bottom mud, maybe a small carp or two, waded buck naked to shore cussing that longhorn's Mexican ancestors, and that's the way these things more often than not turn out, omens and dark forebodings rarely augur much. But sometimes, as sure as snake eyes, they mean exactly what they portend.

Cannonball and Big Mouth Henry left the others to gather the herd and started off downstream to find the body. It began to rain. They waded the wetlands, cutbanks, the snags, cattails, and bulrushes, fired shotguns across the water to try to bring him to the surface. The evening of the second day, crouched under oiled-canvas slickers, they decided they'd give it one more morning and then push on north.

The sun came out. They found him three miles downstream, caught in the crotch of a fallen cottonwood tree, bloated, catfish and river eels churning the water around him. Had to puncture his belly with his pocketknife to get his clothes on. A dry wind rose from the south, had to tie down your hat, nobody knew what it meant. The outfit stood scattered, pawing mud off their boots, pitching sticks into the river from the bluff, Cannonball and Big Mouth Henry dug the grave in the red dirt. An African family in a wagon stopped at the periphery to watch. The man finally approached.

"Pardon me, sir. I am an AME preacher on my way to Kansas. If you'd like, I'd say a few words to accompany this man on his way to his glory."

Cannonball looked up at him, at the scarf flapping, the brim of the hat vibrating in the wind, the sun over the left shoulder directly in Cannonball's eyes causing him to blink rapidly. "We would appreciate that, Reverend. We all could use an encouraging word."

"My wife and daughters will sing a hymn."

Cannonball leaned over, pried the stiff, swollen fingers apart, and put the New Testament between them. Who knows when he'd ever see Texas again. They lowered him down. The women started out timid in the sound of the wind, but picked up force as they went, voices leaving off the challenge and joining in chorus with the moaning sigh through the sumac, plums, and grasses along the river bluffs, and the bass voice of the preacher fought out against the elements, water and wind and the clods of mud they all pitched down onto the wagon sheet: *he has crossed that final river beyond all struggle and travail. Leave him, Lord! You've vexed his soul enough. We part from here. Continue our journey over this long troublous road, and even you, in your infinite wisdom, know not where it leads. Each of us on a highway no one has traveled along before, will ever follow down again. Who are we to wonder, when you, who could know everything, have chosen not to know.*

The sure-enough shake-em-on-down.

The herd was restless, the men moped, everybody hangdog, cowboys and cows, fallen into a ritual disintegration. Stampede at the slightest provocation, a cloud shadow quickly crossing the rump of the steer in front, coyote scat on the trail, the smell of the blood of a rabbit or turkey brought in for chuck, the uncertain light of a misty morning, or sometimes it looked like just for the hell of it, just to keep in practice, getting damn good at it, they'd take off running. The men brooded, the sharp memory of the Segundo going under, the steer that did it somehow insinuating his way in among the leaders of the herd. Nobody'd ever seen him before he capsized the coyote mare, some stray picked up in one of the runaways in north Texas, and an idle mind turned loose on such an animal can conjure up frightful fantasy, plus the fact they were now passing through the Oklahoma District made ever last one of them jumpy.

The Big Auger had come to Cannonball the first night out from the Red River, took him aside, offered him a cigar.

"I hear tell you a damn good hand."

"I am, sir."

"Good as those California vaqueros I understand carry a sixty-five-foot lasso?"

Scratches his ear and grins as best he can. "Ain't a man been born can toss a sixty-five-foot rope its full length. Without he throws it down a well."

Leans in toward him. "Cannonball, who is the best cowboy we got in this outfit?"

Takes a few quick draws off the proffered match, lets the smoke tumble from his mouth while he studies the stogie held carefully in the fingertips, then, to be on the safe side, a puff in each of the cardinal directions. "I don't think there's any question about it, sir. Me."

"Glad to see I can trust your judgment. I'm counting on you to get this bunch of no-account mavericks to Montana. You're the new Segundo."

"My judgment looks to be second only to yours."

His bravado belied the shaking going on inside, as hard as that all around him. And Cannonball knew it.

When they made it into Kansas they were feeling better. Had gotten rid of the devil longhorn, gave him to a band of horse nomads wanting a toll to allow the cows to pass over their hunting grounds, glad to pay it, but it took the two best ropers near half an hour to cut him out and chase him down. Cannonball a little nervous too to be in the same state again as Fort Dodge, had to take a lot of ribbing about his prowess with heavy artillery, the mood of the outfit much improved but things not settled by a long shot. Hardly been past the border a day when they ran into a stretch of fence hadn't been there before.

"What the hell is this?"

"Looks like barbed wire to me."

"You don't say."

"Man back in Illinois invented it, putting it out by the mile. Take a good look, cause you going to be seeing a right smart of it from now on."

"Did you ever see such a thing in your life."

"Vicious-looking stuff, ain't it. Get me the hatchet from the chuck wagon."

This is too damn much horseplay and cow shit. First have to travel over a desert, then navigate a damn flood, now ever nester can afford a few posts and a dozen yards of this newfangled cross between pig iron, rope, and a locust thicket, blocking off God's own pasture like it belonged to them, special order from the Big Auger in the sky, ever blade of grass got my own personal brand on it. Get down on your knees and inspect it if you want, and while you're down there with your hindquarters elevated, I'll demonstrate my post-holing technique. Get Cannonball to help, he seems to be getting mighty good at that kind of thing, teaching that young lithe horse wrangler of his more than how to ride a mean-tempered mustang, ain't that right, Cannonball.

Cannonball flailed away at the wire until it finally yielded, rode back to the chuck wagon, and slung the hatchet banging into the tool chest, causing the cook to jump.

"What the hell eating you, nigger?"

"Too damn much cow play and horseshit. Whoever thought herding Texas cows was a good way for a man to pass his time through this vale of tears ought to be tied to the nearest tree and bull-whipped."

"That won't be till we get to the Solomon."

And damn if the next day they didn't come upon Andy's Big Boggy, a deep narrow creek out of its banks. Two outfits in front of them waterbound going on three days. They all gather around the fire sputtering in the drizzling rain, not a dry sock in the bunch of them, decide what they needed to do was to build a bridge.

They round up all the axes they got and the three crews commence to chopping down cottonwoods, found a slow-moving spot and packed it full of brush, then laid the logs crosswise over the top of the pile. With the three spades they had they dug sod to cover it with, stuck saplings along each side, and tied rope stringers between them for guard rails. Queer-looking rig, but long as the cows don't spook and the water don't rise she ought to hold.

Got the oxen from the first outfit's chuck wagon to lead everybody across, it was a might touchy there for a while, cows not too damn sure they wanted to use such a contraption, starting to procrastinate, trying to turn and bawl, ones coming up from the rear not knowing what the hell is going on, begin to bunch up at the head of the bridge, push the lead cattle forward, approaching what could be panic, hooves skidding in the mud trying to backpedal, one or two shoved in, troubling the water, a couple of hands go after them on their ponies, damn, if you're not careful going to have the whole damn herd off in the creek bogged to their asses. All the long-horns paying mighty close attention, a real nervous moment. But the Segundo manages to convince the rest of the leaders there's nothing to fret about, look at those dumb oxen already on the other side munching that green grass, the commonest thing in the world, she don't look like much but she'll hold till—well, no way in hell to know how long she'll hold, best for everyone involved to get on across. And they went. And the rest of the herd followed. And the second herd. Bridge holding up damn well, rain a little heavier, sod across the logs turning to mud, trompled pretty thin, footing getting downright treacherous, but the longhorns stepping right along like every-body knows it was the bovine race invented bridges in the first place.

Until Cannonball's herd. Lead cow bothered by the light shimmering on the split bark of the first log from the low-hanging clouds where the evening sun should be setting, didn't like it, and didn't take long till the whole damn menagerie knew she didn't like it and had come to the conclusion they didn't take too kindly to it either. They balked.

That was it for the day. Just as soon move the creek as to get those stubborn animals over to the other bank. Things not all bad, though, the glowing that stopped the herd a sign the rain was about to quit.

Put on new sod before dawn, threw the herd off the bed-ding ground at first light, creek as high as it was last evening, but at least no higher, ground so soaked be a week before it goes down even if it doesn't rain no more. The first sight of water and the cows balked, started to mill, the cowboys could only sit in their saddles, shake their heads, and cuss.

"What we gonna do now, Cannonball?"

Picking his teeth with a locust thorn. "Circle the herd, get those in the rear haven't seen this damn creek before to go across first."

It didn't work. They just sulked when they saw the bridge, I know this ain't pasture, cause if it was pasture it would be wider than that. Big Mouth Henry hands Cannonball a tin cup of coffee, the horse cuts a quick step and sloshes half of it out, trickling beneath his chaps down his leg.

"What next, boss?"

Ain't this some shit. Keep a man down, all his work for the benefit of the Big Augers of this world, taking everything worth taking, run the outfit into the ground, and finally, when the whole damn shooting match on the verge of shaking completely apart, come up to you and ask if you'd like to try your hand at running the show. "Get a lone ox from the team, tie him on a long lariat, long enough to stretch over the bridge, you cross with one end of it, we'll get the cows up behind the ox, and you pull him to you. The rest will follow."

They didn't.

"Coyote, get your remuda together ready to run."

Looks at Cannonball, only the eyes show she understands, and then only he knows they do. She'll mutter a phrase now and then: *I do, Bah*—what she calls him—*stick thing in*. Knows all the vocabulary of coffee making and chili juice, in fact gets downright loquacious when it comes to foodstuffs: *pecan mighty tasty, want spud, have a cup, Bah, I grind it good*, also said when sticking thing in. Mostly practical matters, hungers, thirsts, heat and cold, but not verbalized, an attitude of the head, shoulders, downcast or steady eyes, rubbing and licking noses, woofs and woos, rolling over on the back and wriggling the arms and legs tucked in the air. Often unclear to Cannonball whether he's teaching her to talk or she him to shut his mouth. But sometimes she surprises you, sitting off at night at the rim of the firelight, quiet, the movement of air through grasses and draws, the restless cows a half a mile beyond the rise, rocking back and forth, more to herself than anyone: *moon looks good far away, make me want to sing.* And as if to verify the simple truth of it, the coyotes lurking all along the watershed rise up and howl.

She looks now at Cannonball on his horse, exasperation showing clearly in the fixed jaw and flared nostrils, bordering on hostility, she knows, at the cows. "I do it. What happens, Bah?"

"I want you to stampede all the horseflesh we got as fast as you can get them to run right on across that bridge, me and the boys going to throw the leaders of the herd in hard behind you, and if our luck turns a little better than it has been this entire God-abandoned drive, the rest will follow."

They didn't. Cannonball snaps over, it looks like. "God damned pitch of bitches!" Cuts out fifteen longhorns and runs them so damn hard over the hill to the creek they don't have time to stop till they're halfway out on the bridge, and he holds them there, yelling loud and hoarse enough to bring on rain. "Come on, you good-for-nothing shit-kickers, get some more cows up here!"

Big Mouth Henry brings about two hundred head, short yearlings not been bogged before, Cannonball lets the cows trapped on the bridge off the other side, the yearlings sniff and low, approach slowly, cautious and tentative, never seen nothing like this before, Cannonball, Big Mouth Henry, everybody holding their breath, keeping close check on their ponies, praying a sudden wind don't stir up the tops of the trees, a hawk strike a rabbit, a twig crack beneath some stupid steer's tread. The cows start across. The whole damn prairie still and tense, the only sound, the only motion the cattle one step at a time onto the bridge. And the cows leaving the other side. And the brush and the logs and the dirt and the saplings and the rope stringers starting to vibrate as they do, sudden alarm bawled out, the panic-struck longhorns feel the world quake beneath their feet, clatter and heave as they wheel and charge back to the body of the herd.

Cannonball ashen with rage. Whispers through clenched teeth. "Don't that beat hell."

Coyote saunters up beside him, bareback, barefoot, silent for a while watching the mayhem on the slope up from the creek, clicks her tongue, her mustang moves a few steps forward into Cannonball's line of sight. His dark eyes are turned inward it looks like, an uninterpretable opaqueness she's never seen before, sets the hairs on the back of her neck to bristling. She swings the pony around full circle as if to escape, at least dispel the gaze, he blinks, squeezes a tight grin over the teeth. She sidles up to him again.

"Little dogie go."

"What?"

Throws back her head and brays the most plaintive motherless-calf moan you've ever heard in all your born days, and the nearby cows in the mill stop and turn their heads.

"God dammit, Coyote, now you're doing some good thinking, you've got to be smarter than the stock you're trying to drive. Next to the smell of blood, nothing roils a bunch of range cattle more than the sound of a calf bellowing."

He spurs his horse up into the herd, finds a cow with calf, ropes the calf and pulls it down to the bridge, the mother following, calf bleating rage and confusion, stumbles and falls, Cannonball drags it onto the bridge, the mother right behind. Steers getting interested, calf back on its feet on the other side, still hollering. Steers very excited, the notion spreads through the herd, they all turn to the creek, begin to crowd and push toward the entrance of the bridge, everybody up front trying to slow them down now, hold them, get them in line: finally, stand back and watch them all cross.

A few days later, after a stampede set off because Big Mouth Henry broke rhythm in his singing when his horse stumbled in a prairie-dog hole in the middle of the moonless night, after a day and a half riding over twenty miles in all directions collecting them back together, they came upon the Kansas Pacific Railroad line. The herd had never seen anything like it before. The lead cows balked. Couldn't get them to cross the rails. After two days, Cannonball's eyes had the hair on Coyote's neck standing straight up again.

He had to drive them ten miles along the line till they found a culvert big enough to put them under. "You want to cultivate patience when you're handling dumb brutes."

Cannonball knew by the time they reached the South Fork of the Solomon and the nesters, Nicodemians, started carrying on about water rights. The place hadn't even existed last time he was up this way. He knew not only that this was not an ordinary drive, and that he was growing damn weary of herding cows—sell his horse, sell his saddle—but that this could be it, the last roundup. Barbed wire, railroad lines, trail cutters, destitute and desperate prairie nomads, freedmen, cattle thieves, and homesteaders, he knew that this could be the end of it all. In a fit of pique he sent the entire outfit, cows and all, marauding, knocked down every fence, trampled every field, run off every god damn horse, cow, mule, goat, pig, dog, and banty hen within ten miles of Nicodemus.

After they'd gotten the herd settled again on the north shore of the river, the stories told of the havoc they'd visited upon the clodhoppers, a warm evening coming on, a peace, the pent-up passions of the drive temporarily spent, after beans and bacon around the fire, Cannonball, feeling the best he had in weeks, not good but better, because maybe something had been decided, took a plate of grub with him back to the horse wrangler. *Go still that hunger, man. That hunger of another kind.*

Coyote took the plate and went to eat with the horses. A very hot night, she'd removed her flannel shirt, perspiration beaded on her forehead, upper lip, the breasts buoyant in the blue phosphorescent light of the prairie, too large to conceal much longer, the hips and buttock tight in the dungarees. Another sign. A few of the boys bound to suspect already, only thing keeping them in suspense the idea a woman could handle horses the way she does, but the secret won't last the drive to Montana. Cannonball lets out a low chortle, Coyote's ears perk, she breaks off her contemplation of light lingering along the low horizon reflected in the near horse's eyes and scampers on all fours over to him. They rub noses, nuzzle muzzles, he's up on all fours snapping his teeth, sniffing and snorting, she falls back on her haunches, he licks the chin and neck, each nipple with the tip of the tongue, she laughs and scurries backward.

"Hold the horses, Bah."

"You hold this big black snake."

"Time for coffee grind first, and chili juice."

"I don't know, Coyote. Time is getting short."

Moonlight glistening on the hard wet nipples. "What do you mean? Time is always tall."

"Things are changing fast. Look at you, look at everything around us. We'll never make it like this."

Head cocked sideways. "What we making, Bah?"

What you get for opening your big mouth.

Cannonball lay reclining on the saddle, back of the head cradled in laced fingers, still covered with sweat and breathing hard, naked but for his boots crossed, watched her move and counted them, the signs. Desire building again, for more, much more, but of what he had no better notion than a piebald calico mule has of the trans-prairie freight business. The woman whose fields he had trompled and whose animals he'd run off this afternoon was not right, standing by her dugout shaking her balled fist at him, yelling he ought to be ashamed of himself. Much to be proud of, and his mama back in Tennessee be proud too, but pride seems to mean nothing in the realm of the churning stars, the moving wind, the peoples wandering the land restlessly seeking out somewhere to have a home. If for no other reason, to have some place to leave the next time the lust to hit the open road mysteriously overcomes them, a fancied place to croon nostalgic songs about to sustain them in the actual void. Beat anything he'd ever seen or imagined, how could he·have conceived it all those years ago in the tobacco patch, Mama gathering nuts, hardly his mother anymore, not even a story to tell. A cowboy can't spin yarns about slavery and truck gardens. He has no mother now. Will he be able to conceive of longhorn cows, summer drives over vast open ranges in the years to come when circumstance has mothered another man to contemplate in the lulls what he was, the Segundo, his own feral woman loyal as a rambunctious pup. Who'd be able to think it.

Coyote got the pot and the coffee mill from the saddlebag, gathered dried grass and sticks to strike fire. Flames flickered around her, jumped over the silver planes and edges of the mill, the dark damp skin glowed, a dense aroma of Colombian coffee hovered and drifted close to the ground in the calm cupped beneath the wind. The mind trembled, decomposed, re-formed, and merged. The sure-nough shake-em-on-down.

He rose to go to her.

And that's when all hell broke loose.

I Can Tell by Your Outfit

Hortense S. Seems like I was the only soul ever took the time to explore the banks of the Solomon. Come down here often to fish, bring along a wicker basket full of hoecakes and fried prairie chicken if I had it, while away the lonely hours of a Sunday afternoon when my husband was off looking for work. Figured if I was truly going to be a plainswoman, had to get out and get to know something about this featureless country. It took considerable time and effort to appreciate that what you at first call featurelessness is itself a feature of respectable magnitude. Spent many hours with my pole and line watching the river flow, a sleepy reverie in the hot summer afternoon, or, like whatever kind of birds those are laying low beneath the north bluff out of the wind in weak winter sun, huddle there and toss in sticks and see them drift off out of sight, follow in my mind's eye all the way down the watershed, the Kaw, the Missouri, the Mississippi, deep into the woods of the old states, two thousand miles, at least two lifetimes gone. The menfolk all too busy standing around the public square of Nicodemus or loitering at the land office, speculating, loafing and lying, too occupied trying to concoct some scheme to get rich quick to ever take much interest—other than water rights—in the river. I knew all the best fishing spots and all the paths to get to them, so it ended up when Mose, Spartacus, Niles, me, and the others started out after sunset on the freight company mules, I was the one leading the raiding party.

The idea was to ride almost halfway to Stockton, cross over to the southern bank of the river, and circle back behind the herd. Mose said the horse wrangler would be bedded down with the remuda, probably didn't even have a sidearm, no trouble at all to cross the shallow ford there, stalk up, and pounce on him, have us a real good argument the cowboys ought to help round up our stock. And just to make sure nobody would interfere about the time we were ready to jump, Mose was going to stampede the cows.

He moved upstream shortly after we'd waded the river. The rest of us found our way along a dry creek bed to the high ground. Could see the two fires burning north and south below us, the wind so still we were able to hear the restless herd and the cowboys laughing a mile off, more than likely about us. The moon was in the middle of the sky. We put the mules on pickets and crept down a draw up close to the horses.

At first I could only make out the wrangler squatted in front of the fire, his bare back, glistening perspiration, turned toward me. Then I caught sight of something I thought was a pile of saddles starting to move, a man. Got off the ground, pulled off his boots, the onliest stitch he had on, I swallowed hard cause that's not the only thing hard out here tonight. I thought he was getting up to carry a big stick over to the fire, wondered why he had to get naked to do it. It was a big stick all right, and for the first time I began to feel a strong sympathy for Lot's wife, turned to a pillar of salt right here on the Kansas prairie. My husband been gone a long time, and these cowboys a sorrier bunch than I'd ever been told.

He came up behind the wrangler, who was pouring something from a glass vial into the tin cups of coffee he'd just brewed, came up behind and grabbed him around the shoulders, rubbing up against him. They rolled over wriggling and licking each other, he was pulling at the wrangler's dungarees. I forgot all about why I was out here lurking in the tall grass. Took awhile to realize the ground was beginning to shake and the thunder and shouting spilling all over was the stampede Mose had just provoked.

The cowboy jumps up cussing and grabbing for something, but all he can find is Niles, already standing over his saddle with his own pistol pointed at him, and Spartacus behind him, explaining he's sorry about interrupting in the middle of the down stroke. His partners'll have to handle the herd without him.

I run for the wrangler, not sure what I'll do when I get him. He's wanting to clear out for parts dark and unknown, would have made it too if it weren't for his trousers tangled up around his feet. I must have been out of my head, take hold of him under one arm and over the other shoulder, most peculiar-feeling man

I'd ever hung on to, snarls and spins, bites me on the wrist near to bringing blood, stumbles backwards into the grass, ears cocked back, lips curled away from yellow teeth, I swear the eyes glowing like a wolf in the dooryard. Sends a shock of fright exploding through all my limbs. It's a woman! And a wild one at that.

Somebody's screaming. It's me, sure I've latched on to the Devil himself—herself—some shape-shifting fiend, Spartacus beside me looking down on her, shaking as much as I am myself. She kicks her trousers loose, breaks free, and bounds naked on all fours out into the faint edge of the firelight, high-tailing it away from here and nobody much interested in stopping her. But she turns suddenly, drops close to the ground. Spartacus rigid as a corner post beside me, can't take his eyes off her.

She begins to slink toward the fire where the cowboy is pulling his clothes back on. I recognize now he's the one run off my animals this morning, the newly appointed Segundo of this outfit, we'd grabbed hold to more than we'd bargained for in more ways than one. I say something to Spartacus, he doesn't even hear me, staring at the naked girl like he's found something he's been looking for but don't know what it is, only that it's here, his eyes concentrated, the wayward searching been there since I first met up with him now bearing down on her, her face, the purple splotches across her cheek. His gaze seems to be what's pressing her to the ground so hard she can barely move. Stops right in front of Spartacus, sniffing at him, it looks like, fear and curiosity such a powerful mix her whole put-together threatening to tremble loose. He goes down cautiously on his heels, holds out the backside of his hand to her. She hesitates, then nuzzles it. He whispers something, sounds to me like he says: *So join her.*

I'm trembling myself. The earth is trembling, rumbling all around me, the herd of longhorns running wild over the prairie, drovers firing pistols and yelling, the night beginning to choke with dust. Everybody watching Spartacus and the girl, the cowboy trying to button his shirt, Niles, the cowboy's revolver hanging loosely at his side. I finally tell Spartacus to get some clothes on that girl for God's sake and let's get out of here. Reach down, for lack of something better to do, and pick up one of their coffee mugs and gulp it down. Strong, a spicy kick, sweat beads up all over my body, then my head blows off. I cut an involuntary series of foot figures, the girl gives a little yelp, rolls over, and squirms like a hound in her favorite wallow.

By the time we get back to Burley's Union House, Niles, Mose, and the cowboy are carrying on like they been main buddies all their lives, taking chaws from the same plug of tobacco and wanting to loan each other money. You could almost think he was relieved about something, the way he leaned back in the willow chair in the kitchen, boots kicked up on the shipping-crate tabletop, spinning out yarns like somebody who'd just completed a long and troublesome journey bubbling over with tales they so happy to be home, a little like a cluster of the Old South had all of a sudden fallen out of the Kansas wind. Niles even come up with a brown crockery jug of Kentucky whiskey. The problem was, if this boss of the trail crew was in no haste to get back to the herd, how would we ever get them to round up our livestock?

"Now looky here, cowboy. You know why we snatched you, don't you?"

"I suppose it had something to do with all the animals we run off. I also suppose you weren't planning on kidnapping the Segundo when you crept up on the horse wrangler."

"Didn't figure on him being a nigger, either."

"And I further suppose you didn't reckon on the wrangler being a woman."

"I can tell you're a perceptive man."

"And what's bothering you now is that Niles and I been carrying on here nigh onto two hours as close as two sides of a thin box and haven't once mentioned getting back to my herd."

"You sharper than a store-bought needle."

Slips his feet off, falls forward in the chair, slapping the tabletop with a bang. "And twice as hollow-headed. But I do suppose one more thing." Looks over at Spartacus, who all this time has sat subdued, paying more attention to the wrangler, removed and slightly lower at Cowboy's side like a faithful pup, than to the raucous talk. "Brother Spartacus got something on his mind concerning Coyote."

When he said this I realized Spartacus *had* been acting mighty peculiar since he first seen her, not enough that you'd notice till attention was called to it, a peculiar man hard to spot acting peculiar, but he almost jumped in his chair when Cowboy spoke, like he'd just been found out. Cleared his throat with a swallow of whiskey, eyes cast to the floor, kind of a guttural chuckle, a world-weary snort, then he looked up.

"You say you met up with her in the Texas brush country, don't have any idea where she come from."

"That's right."

"I think I know. Ever since I left Mississippi against my will, forced, it looked like, out on this desolate journey, seems like I been looking for, chasing after, my long-lost woman. Her ghost been haunting me, keeps rising up before my eyes, mis-shapen by fever and hunger and loneliness, to be plucked away again. All the while I thought I was wandering farther and farther away from her, deeper into a wilderness of the soul, thought I was lost, a churning cloud of black Mississippi dust blown across the plains, all the while I was being drawn to her. I'm sure this girl is Sojourner. But as strange to me as the flat Kansas horizon, wild, new, and vagrant, her ignorance of her birth, of her mother, as burdensome as my own, swallowed up in the vastness of this harsh, foreign country, the hurly-burly of a desperate here-and-now."

"Sojourner?"

"My daughter."

We all go silent. Wondering not so much at what he said but that such a taciturn man could talk like that. Must have been slipping off without us knowing it to the Baptists over on Fourth Street. It wasn't helping us one bit to get our farm stock back either, but not something you could easily ignore.

"Spartacus. How you know this . . ."

Look closely at her, maybe for the first time, been half afraid of her, eye contact might somehow clabber the spirit or even provoke attack. Not sure what to call her, *animal* the kindest thing come to mind, but in case she *was* his daughter, thought I'd better take some care not to injure his feelings any-more than they already have been tonight, and the long skein of the nights of his difficult life. No more difficult though, it looks like to me, than the lives of most of us, we all have had some mighty arduous rows to hoe, have spent our share of hours picking in the short cotton. Anyway, I look at her. What troubled me most was her eyes. Not an inkling of human passion in them that I could recognize, fixed on Cowboy, looking for some sign, a command, escape, totally separate from the society of the room but dedicated to the man who was its center.

". . . how do you know this *girl* is your daughter?"

He's disturbed, no doubt about that, but certain. Looks to the girl, to Cowboy, then to me. "Only thing make me sure she isn't my woman the fact I know many, many years have gone by since I was to meet her back in Mississippi over at the four corners in the thunderstorm and the high water. And my woman talk a lot more than this child does. It's her spitting image, though, sitting right here before us. And then there's that purple scattering of marks beneath her eye."

Tears in his eyes, no question he believes it, everybody else around the table hard pressed to doubt him. None of this, like I said before, getting us any closer to our livestock.

The whiskey jug is passed around the table again, even I have to take a little taste. Cowboy leans way back, straining the lashings on the bent-willow chair, clasps his hands behind his head, a big grin shows off the gold tooth with the star cut in it.

"Well, what you gonna do now, brothers and sisters? What any of us gonna do?"

The wind outside, wonder how long it will be before the drovers realize the Segundo and the horse wrangler are missing, before they figure out where they're at. I expect anytime to hear them hollering and starting to shoot, come to tree the town. "Mose, how long before they get that herd back together?"

"It's about dawn now, they should have it pretty well rounded up shortly after sunrise."

"We got to get word to them we got their men, their people."

"And how we do that without we get kidnapped ourselves—or shot."

Niles, who sometime in the last few minutes seems to have sunk down on the tabletop asleep, rises from his slumber rubbing his eyes. "Who said shot?"

"Mose did."

"Shot who?"

"Nobody, but how to keep from getting it."

"Aha!" Rubs one eye, then his nose. "Didn't we once have some Colombian coffee and refined cane sugar around this establishment?"

"Niles, how we going to let those cowboys know we want to trade their boss and wrangler for our animals?"

"Where's Mrs. Burley, she up yet? If we had some grits we could have grits and eggs before we do anything. If we had some eggs. Then Mose and I wander on down to the south shore of the river and call over to those rascals on the other side to negotiate. The intervening waters will assure our safety."

In no time at all the room was full of smoke from the cow-dung fire, Hiram and Mrs. Burley fried up a pan full of corn-meal mush, and Niles and Mose were on their way to the Solomon. The rest of us stayed at the hotel, too tired to go anywhere, too agitated to do more than fitful dozing. I was troubled. The story Spartacus told, Cowboy not acting like a captive but like a man been freed, and that poor dumb girl beside him—the only one of us at peace enough to sleep—curled in the spot of sun making its way into the gloomy sod interior through the small single window frame.

It must have been a hundred and ten outside, the damp, stuffy air of the hotel, the stale cigar smoke, close quarters of three or four whiskey drinkers nodding in and out of thick, dreamy sleep, sweat gone cold in the clothing. Could pick out the cowboy, smell him near me, still see him naked by the campfire, desire best for a woman alone not to dwell on, loud shouting and laughter confusing my stuporous mind. It was them, hear them coming clear from the corner of Seventh Street and Jackson.

We stand in heavy, dense sun on the public square to watch them ride up Third past Z. T. Fletcher's place, everybody in town out by this time, shielding the eyes squinting into the severe light, wind chasing dust devils swirling from beneath the hooves of the horse and the two mules, three riders shimmering in the rising heat, dogs and children nipping at their heels. A sensation in my toes and the soles of my feet, pure joy shivering up my legs and backbone like to blow the top of my head clean off. Everywhere I look are Africans, Niles, Mose, a man called Big Mouth Henry, all of us holding on to this windswept townsite, Nicodemus, a thousand miles from Kentucky and Tennessee, a scant few generations from Africa to here. Getting on. Not a god damned thing to guide us but mother wit, whatever companionship we find, and the hard occurrence of the plains.

It's puzzling the way things sort out sometimes. Spartacus and I kept the girl while Cowboy and Big Mouth Henry returned to his boys to round up our farm animals. The herd moved on north the next day, going to Montana. What wasn't expected was that Spartacus would go with them. Clear the man had come completely unhinged, wouldn't back off the story that that wild girl was his daughter, woke me up in the middle of the night to give me the freight company wagon and team, the deed to his claim, and to ask if I could get the rig back to Stockton, collect his pay, and hold it for him. He'd wandered too far too long to lose this trace.

And that's how it came that I started to hauling freight twixt Stockton and Nicodemus. Got his money under my mattress to this day, haven't seen hair nor hide of the nigger since.

Once a Band of Rustlers

Brother | Like the Ole Woman before him, he'd realized the eastern margin of the prairie was getting crowded. Knew it even before they'd flushed Will out of the den in the creek bank above the Ninnescah and he and Prissy Blackstrup had started the complex task of teaching him to be human. Could see the fear and blood lust in the eyes of the people he kept on trying to preach to, improvising, recalling inchoate and jumbled snatches, inventing from whole cloth passages of scripture from the Bible he'd tossed into the river, desperate, wanting to save someone's soul, whose or from what he was no longer sure of.

Only thing had kept him going was Prissy. She was the one tamed Will, got him interested in maybe being civilized after all. Brother moved into the old dugout down by the creek. He watched her, watched the wind blow her hair, her dress against her body, her mouth full of wooden pins, as she hung out the wash on the line, watched her move as she chopped and bundled sugarcane, as they worked the mill together. Watched in the big house kitchen or parlor as she went through her drills with Will, overwhelmed by mounting lust but more than that: a longing, something to grasp, to fill the expanding emptiness eating away at his essence, something akin to love. But the closer they became, the more hostile old man Blackstrup grew, the fellowship of that first-night gully-washer, when Brother had showed up bewildered and soaked to the soul, collapsing into open animosity and religious zeal. She never talked about her father again after that evening when she followed Brother out in the rain to the molasses shed, although an understanding shepherd might consider what she had said then enough. She grew sullen and distrustful, the open vulnerability, the innocent aura of her gaze gone obdurate and cold. She devoted all her energy to Will.

Brother would leave him with her when he went out to try to hold his circuit together. The love feast now was cold leftovers, long-winded and pointless stories instead of fiery sermons, his classes' religious passions giving way to perplexed politeness or outright desertion to the Baptists. A contamination, like wet stockings on a long dark winter ride, overspread his spirit, overflowed onto the land itself, could see it in the turned sod, the blight of volunteer elm saplings and red cedar sprouting along the draws, interrupting the line of the horizon, working their way west, creeping farther out onto the plains. Eastern preachers coming in to supply the pulpits of whitewashed churches, joining booster clubs to hobnob with bankers and mercantilers when the speculation towns are secured. Could see his conviction fail sudden as his conversion had been: Christ was not the son of God, immaculate savior who died in our stead, but the son of woman, conceived in sweat, spittle, semen, and lust, roaming over a dusty flatland, an eroded badland, till overwhelmed by the odds.

He'd known it even before the day he returned to the Blackstrup place, a hot, windy, dry early spring morning, the sky a blue-brown sun-saturated shroud, led his lame pony along the river to the house, and found nobody home. The wagon gone, humid bottomland air shifting now and again from side to side over the cracked soil. The mule shed door creaked and banged, flies buzzed fitful clusters across the yard from the barn.

His bones hurt, clothes clung like scum on pond water, mucus thick on palate and tongue. He heard something beneath the clatter of grasshopper wings and the heat. A whimper, a moan. Cause for alarm if it weren't for the giddy excitement called up through the loins and nostrils. He hitched the pony to the porch and cautiously approached the outbuildings, the moaning now a rhythmic chant, a confusion of danger and desire, his hand on his pistol butt for want of a better place, squinting against the glare into the heavy dark beyond the open mule-shed door. Asses and elbows, trousers bunched around Will's knees, bare bottom pumping, a sheen of perspiration, green-headed horseflies, and Prissy's long, muscular thighs, covered with downy hair, her horny feet, hooked heel in curled-back toes, squeezing his buttocks, fingers and hands working down the groove of his lower back, her dress gathered about the breasts, lower lip clenched, eyes rolled back, a pulsing, expended sigh.

Brother watched. They settled into themselves. Anger, envy, his balls beginning to ache, pride. After the store-bought clothes, the sheeted bed, home-cooked victuals, after all the alphabet games, the signs, the muttered phrases, tricks any clever dog could pull off—no doubt about it now, Will had come over to the human side. Prissy had rescued him, made him a man.

Will's head snaps around when he hears Brother's pistol drop back into its holster, eyes constricted against the harsh outside light, ears flattened, lowered down now, peering askance back up over his shoulder like an egg-sucking hound. Prissy's legs slither from his rump, her eyes still closed, oblivious, her body blotched red and damp. The languor riven by sudden awareness, she bolts upright, heaving Will to the hay, stares straight at afternoon sun flaring around the edges of the silhouette in the door. The tangled dress slowly uncrumples over one breast, the pubic mound parted, glistening, black tightly curled hair, startling inner lips swollen, moist and viscous, dim, dust-filled mule-shed air.

Brother didn't take his eyes off her, conflicting passions staked him to the spot, Will cowering in the straw. She made no attempt to cover herself, her eyes a frightening brew, lewdness, shame, release, and rage boiling over to tears. Her belly quivered and contracted, convulsive sobs exploding from her, then screams, then shapes of words: *I'm wicked, an evil bitch to bring godly men low to knot and wallow. Papa, you, and now I've lain with the devil child. Kill me please, your pistol, the double shovel, consume this loathing, misery, this queasy desire in the fires of hell.*

She bolted from the barn. Brother stood, looking down at the toes of his scuffed and dusty boots, once again a failure to his flock.

He'd gone to Blackstrups Mill looking for Prissy that night. To try to explain it wasn't her fault, it wasn't Will's fault, not even the fault of her father. To explain to her he loved her. He could hear angry voices before he topped the rise coming into town and saw the torchlight flicker on the clapboard facades of the saloon and the general store. Rode through the milling women and children, dogs and chickens at the outskirts of the mob, then recognized Blackstrup, face gone bleary, seething indignation, and a few scrawny men dragging a woman to a flour barrel below a hangman's noose dangling from the awning over the tavern door. Brother didn't stop to think, his confusion clarified, he knew that woman, the buckskin dress, the woman who'd found Will and Sojourner. He drew his pistol, fired into the air, spurred his lame pony hobbling through the street, lurched upon the boardwalk, knocking people down, fired again, then whirled to face Blackstrup.

"Let her go!"

"You'd free the devil woman, preacher?"

Bangs the revolver barrel right between the eyes. "I'd free your eternal soul."

Something hit him in the back of the head, the gun discharged. The town went silent. Brother would not open his eyes. A sobering despair, whatever he did was wrong. He listened for some clue what the world would be when he was finally forced to look upon it again. Nothing. The ringing pain in his head, the slow heave of the horse's breathing, the smell of gunsmoke, the weight of the Colt .45 in his hand, the totality of the universe. He opened his eyes.

Blackstrup still stood, an astonished paleness in his face. A trickle of blood down the forehead from the new part in his hair across the middle of the scalp. The townspeople in the street still stood. The woman was nowhere to be seen.

Brother had known it even before the Annual Conference of the Church called him up for trial. Everybody wanting to shit through the same hole. The knock-down-drag-out that broke loose at the end of the proceedings was the result more of concentrated idleness than deeply felt religious enthusiasm among the rabble factions throwing tables and chairs and stomping horse manure all over the meeting hall. In fact the clodhoppers who'd seemed to be offering him the hardiest theological support during the questioning were the ones—once he and Will had been slung through the open window onto the compost heap of the adjoining livery and had made their way into the street—they were the ones taking social umbrage at a man who'd claim any kin at all to a coyote, set aside the notion of consort with the Devil, and would have, if they had had some tar and feathers, tarred and feathered them both and run them out of town on a rail. If they'd of had a rail.

He had to go from here, scandalized, defrocked, lucky to escape Blackstrups Mill, lucky to escape the Annual Conference with his life, a piddly freight hanging from his weary bones. He and Will ride west along the Kaw. Autumn heat soon to give way to winter. No place to go but away from these thickly settled, quickly domesticated parts, to Abilene, then cut across the Smoky Hills to the Great Bend Prairie, up the Arkansas River to Dodge City, then down the Santa Fe Trail across the sand hills and high plains to the Old Cimarron cutoff, Stevens County, maybe home, where the Ole Woman had staked her claim.

The African sat in a chair making soap, her face ashy and weather-worn but still a supple determination in the way she carried herself despite loneliness and labor, pounding sticky green yucca roots on a board with a hammer, and told Brother how the Ole Woman had died. "You missed her by two years this coming winter. She'd been doing poorly, didn't seem anything out of the ordinary, I went off to Liberal for supplies and, when I come back, found her in the barn, looked like she was napping with the goats. Hated to disturb her, first good rest in years, since her youngest and my little Sojourner disappeared crossing the Ninnescah, lying there in the straw between the two nannies, her knees tucked up, balled fists pressed to her eyes, the first—then, I saw, the last—long sleep of her troubled life."

Brother watched her, the gnarled fingers of her hands, shoving pulp from the board into a dishpan to soak. As if the story had nothing to do with him. Finally leaned back and pointed over to Will, sniffing around the dugout door. "You know who this is with me?"

"Now I been living out on these quiet plains many a year, the last two all by my lonesome. How you expect me to know who that is? Specially one so sullen as he appears, sulking about the place like a mean-people's cur."

Brother motioned with his hand. Will looked over at them, Brother signed again, he slowly approached, Brother took him by the arm, pushed up his sleeve, then his own, to show the African the two jayhawk tattoos. She squinted, bent over close, sat back, an uncertain smile, not sure what to make of it, knew she was expected to make something of it, chuckled to herself, then abruptly grew silent. Brother leaned in as if to touch her shoulder. "This is my little brother, Will."

She's still not sure what this means. "Will. Now let's see, which one was he. The Ole Woman had so many she couldn't keep track herself, much less . . . but wasn't Will . . ."

"That's right. He was the one lost, he and little Sojourner. I found him—both of them—"

"Sojourner?"

"Yes. But she escaped."

"Escaped? The slavers had them?"

"They were raised by coyotes."

She looks blankly, then quick anger. "You should know better than to trifle with an old woman!"

"I'm not trifling, ma'am. Sojourner is alive, the last I knew." Watches her look at both of them, then get up to place the pan of yucca soap on a bench behind her. "Will knows who you are, recognizes you. You saw the way he's sniffing around. Looking for Sojourner."

"Well, she ain't here."

"He smells her in you."

"It's a cruel thing you tell me. All these years to convince myself they was dead. What am I to do or think now?" Stands, arms hugging her own shoulders, eyes on Will but rapt in awe, memory, near to tears perhaps, perhaps just dubious and confused. Finally extends the back of her hand, he takes it in both of his, licks, and presses it to his cheek. She blinks away whatever thoughts, weakly smiles. "Don't that beat all."

The land was his, theirs, a vast sweep of buffalo grass above the south fork of the Cimarron, unpopulated, good for nothing but yucca and sage and animals that like to graze. The horse people, who'd once chased the buffalo, who'd closed down the road ranch at Sand Wells and forced the abandonment of the Cimarron cutoff of the Santa Fe Trail, had been badly beaten at Adobe Walls, and the buffalo were gone. The Ole Woman and the African had been the only ones here for years, getting by as best they could, planting watermelons and cucumbers, raising goats, trapping, trading with the few rene-gade horse people who still wandered through now and then, travelers along the main branch of the trail, and the cattle drovers come up early summers from the south.

"This was your mother's land, Will."

Will was getting good at repetition, making efforts at his own two- and three-word constructions. "My mother. Our mother."

"But what are we going to do with it? Raise soapweed and sing at the moon?"

They're on the high ground overlooking the flat valley of gray-green buffalo grass, the low sky to the south shows dust along the horizon. Will points. "Look, cows. They push them to eat."

"All the way from Texas to Dodge City, load them on trains for Kansas City and the East. People eat lots of beef."

Will furrows his brow. "How far is the Texas?"

"A long haul, Will."

He watches, the herd now in sight, the singing of the lead man in the wind, sniffs the air for the first signs. "Cows taste better not tired, not walk a long way, plenty good grass to eat."

"That's right."

"Our good grasses have for cows to eat. Not have to walk from Texas."

Brother chuckles. "That's right." Stands there watching, the valley now full of cattle. "My God. That's right! Will, what we need is a herd of cows, we'll by God start us up a ranch."

They grabbed each other, danced and wriggled on the hill in the dust drifting up over them from the longhorns moving by to the cattle pens and the railhead. Will rolled over on his back, then jumped up, hopped in one spot. "And then I wear fancy chaps, put on good-smellum, and get me a woman."

It was an exciting notion Will come up with. I really had had no idea what I was going to do. Coming west to find the Ole Woman was an act of desperation, and then to find her already two years dead. I couldn't even mourn. The family devastated, my brothers and sisters scattered, some went to Denver, others went wrong, hadn't seen or heard of any of them since I left, like the family in me had died all that time ago when Will and Sojourner bounced from the wagon box crossing the Ninnescah. I was all mourned out. All I could do was point dumbly to Will, as if that somehow explained it, maybe even gave excuse. He'd come back to me like a grotesque haunt, a twisted remnant of family, a physical manifestation of failure and guilt, my wild double wrecking havoc on the domesticated world around us, his coyote family, the woman who helped me find him, Prissy Blackstrup, the Church. How much ruin could we spread?

Where were we going to find the wherewithal to get a ranch started? It wasn't like in Texas, where longhorns ran wild like pests that needed to be controlled, wasn't even like that in Texas anymore. There was still plenty of land out here, but where was a broken-down circuit rider with nothing to show for his years as yoke horse for the Lord but a bad case of harness gall going to acquire a herd?

We did what we could. Planted forty acres of watermelon, thirteen of cucumbers, shipped thirty-two hundred pounds of seed to Kansas City one year, sold yucca for four dollars a ton

green, six dollars baled. All the time I'm thinking about livestock. All the time civilization creeping in around us. Speculators formed a town company, located and platted the townsite
nearby the spread, organized the county, printed brochures
and sent them east, all for a cost of about fifteen hundred dollars, started selling off the lots. Inside a year, made half a mil-
lion dollars out of nothing but hope and promise, neither of
which with much basis in reality. All that money, banker can't
be far behind, and maybe that's where my experience in the
service of the Lord come in handy. Assuming bankers don't
spend too much time perusing the minutes of the Annual Conference of the Church. When the bank opened up in the town
of Moon Center, I decided it was time for me to go negotiate
myself a loan.

"Good morning, Mr. James. I appreciate you taking the
time to talk with me this fine day the Lord has sent us. And I
would like to say what a godsend your institution is for our
booming community."

"Thank you. What can I do for you?"

"As you know, I have served the Lord many years, the dark
times when these prairies were in the iron grip of Satan's savages."

"I didn't know that."

"Ah, well. Civilization and the circuit rider have gone hand
in hand. Spent my youth in the saddle bringing God's word to
the fringes of his flock. One day, and a stormy one it was, the
Lord spoke to me in the thunder, appeared in a flash of lightning like unto a cyclone churning down from the heavens, a
portent of what the future would hold for his chosen people.
And do you know what the Lord said, Mr. James?"

R. O. James leaned forward on his hogshead desk, a walnut one ordered from St. Louis not due in for a month or so, a couple of planks across two sawhorses served as counter, some of the walls not plastered yet, hammering and sawing all up and down the dusty ruts used as a street outside the window. He knew, had heard tell of, the Ole Woman and the African, lived out in these parts long before any other settlers arrived, and remembered stories of the two hombres claimed to be the Ole Woman's sons, but not quite sure what to make of me now standing in the flesh before him. The more money you get, it seems, the less God manifests himself in rhetoric and dramatic gesture, in the enthusiasm of the congregation, the more in purposeful deliberation of contingencies by upstanding forward-thinking individuals, but he still seemed to bear an uneasy respect for the faith of his fathers.

"No. What did the Lord say?"

"Cows."

"The Lord said cows?"

"Yes."

"That's all?"

"He has swept the plains clean of the buffalo and the heathen who follow them so that Christian men would have room to graze and fatten their livestock. As Christians replace the savage, so cows will replace the buffalo, all part of God's plan. Meat to fuel their expanding domination of this land kept virgin for this moment, give God's idlers something to do riding herd. Why run animals all the way from Texas when we could fatten them up right here in Stevens County. And, more important, bring cash money into the coffers of good Christian bankers. Like yourself."

"God said all that to you?"

"My family's been out here for years, we got all this common grazing land, grass going to waste since the buffalo's gone."

"What about the settlers?"

"Always be a few of them, but what would you rather be? The staker of small grubbers coaxing out a living hoeing fenced-in watermelon patches and gathering up cucumbers, trying to grow eastern crops, like their ancestors, on land like no other they've ever seen, or the financial adviser and backer of the cattle kingdom, proud Christian soldiers riding unhindered across the grasslands the way God made them, under God's blue heaven, on noble steeds, driving hundreds of thousands of beef cows to market."

Rubs his chin with thumb and first finger, then shoos a fly circling his nose. "Well . . ."

"And you know what else the Lord said?"

"He said more?"

"Yes, he did."

"I thought so."

"He said barbed wire."

"Well, the farmers got to try to keep the livestock from trampling their crops."

"No, Mr. James, that's not what the Lord, in his infinite omniscience, meant. He said barbed wire and windmills."

"All God's gifts to the homesteader."

"Ah, the Lord's more subtle than that, wondrous ways his mysteries to perform, it's the stockman going to profit from these inventions, use the barbed wire to keep his cows in, not out. Cheap, reliable fencing and the windmill to bring in water so you don't need to be driving them over wide ranges of expansive and expensive space, burning off weight, building up gristle, looking for a drink. Breeding, that's the key. Control. Improvement of the stock will produce more meat per mouthful of hay, super cows, easy keepers, bring nothing in but big money."

Move in close to the banker's face.

"And you can be in on it from the get-go. Why waste assets on these small-time dreamers—nesters, hoemen, and speculators—pick up and leave the minute the boom goes bust, manufactured from nothing more substantial than the flimsy paper and smudged ink of a sham booster's boxcar journalism, why invest in a vain hope, like every other yokel with a townsite and lots to sell, waiting for some eastern robber baron to run a railroad through these parts? Why base your economy on something controlled by outsiders when we can control what *they* need? No sir. My years in the saddle serving the Lord taught me the works and the will of the Almighty are plain to see before the eyes of him who takes the time and the trouble to look. If God would have meant for us to live off the iron horse, he'd have laid tracks on the seventh day instead of resting. Put the money you've collected into an industry suited to this country, that thrives on distances and mobility, the green grass God *did* raise up here for our beef cows—for us—to grow fat on."

I withdraw to the edge of the room, dust off, and sit down on a nail keg. I can see James is thinking about it, the way he's cogitating over the cigar he's pulled from a red wooden box, and when he finally lifts it up to offer me one I know the ranch is ours.

The Neutral Strip of the Public Lands, the eastern border, the western edge of the Louisiana Purchase, fixed at 100 degrees longitude by the Treaty of 1819 with Spain, the western border set at 103 degrees by the Compromise of 1850, the southern border at 36 degrees 30 minutes: No Man's Land, the panhandle—haven and hideout for every good-for-nothing low-down scoundrel, horse thief, murderer, and cattle rustler preying off the pickings for two hundred miles around—the northern boundary butted right up against our ranch. So it's the first place we go looking to when we find the fences cut and fifty head of our best breeding stock gone.

Ordinarily we wouldn't go to the trouble. A few cows, the sick and lame, the stragglers picked off the fringe of the herd is no big problem, doesn't matter if it's coyotes, a band of outlaw nomads, or rustlers, just part of the cost of doing business, kind of like a tax you pay for the privilege of skimming most of the cream off the top, and business had been good.

We had three ranges set up. The ones at Barney Bow and at Sand Wells didn't have any permanent buildings, just a chuck wagon and a sod house for the foreman and to store the supplies shipped from Lakin or Hartland, free range like it had been for years, buffalo grass and grama grass. The headquarters of the operation was at Pinnacle Peak, the old homestead, with the African in charge. That's where we set up our breeding, had our fenced-in pens and pastures with a windmill in each, brought in bulls from England and Scotland. Will claimed we had cows bred with right legs shorter than the left to graze clockwise on the hills, cows with the left legs shorter than right to go counterclockwise, short front for uphill and short rear for down. Turning the cattle business into a science instead of a haphazard chase across the wild. We planned to fence in the other spreads, too, but it took time to get the wire and posts and windmills from Illinois, demand was great and the shipping difficult.

Will took to ranching like a dung beetle to a fresh-dropped cow pie. First thing he had to do was get him a horse. Whenever we needed riding stock we'd go into No Man's Land, down to a place called Wild Horse Lake, a wetlands where mustangs come to drink, where you could drive a stallion and his harem off and keep them running for three or four weeks anytime you needed to. But the one stallion everybody was after nobody was ever able to catch: a big white stud maybe eighteen hands high, seemed to know the minute a bunch of wranglers left the bunkhouse coming south, would round up his mares and head into the Beaver Breaks where a man's lucky to get his own horse through without he has to dismount and walk, and nobody wanted to waste breath even on telling windies how they chased him along the north fork of the Canadian. The Pacing White Stallion, or Pegasus, as people called him, cause they swore he either ran faster than any horse ever had before or else he could fly. And of course this was the horse Will wanted.

He finally convinced me he had a plan, too. He was talking pretty good by now, been living out in the bunkhouse with the boys, picking up such skills as cigarette rolling and tobacco chewing, yarn spinning, even known to take a drink now and again. Learning language would hardly pass east of the short-grass prairie, but was softened some by the African, who seemed to take a liking to him, sense a connection between him and Sojourner, spent a lot of time trying to train out the wildness. Anyway, he had a plan, and it involved hiking on foot down to Wild Horse Lake, just the two of us, setting up camp at the water, and waiting for the stallion to come to us. It was early spring, a month to kill before the roundup scheduled to start, things going well on the spread, called it the Perpetual Motion Ranch, set up to run smooth with or without me, the African as good at operating it as I was, so I went along with him. A good chance to do a little hunting and fishing.

Every night Will would go out and sit by the water and sing. The frogs would join in, then the coyotes. Looked like something we'd never be able to break him of. Told me he was telling his friends to let the stallion know he was here waiting for him, wanted to ride him, if he thought he was horse enough to take him on. A trick, he said, he learned in the bunkhouse, how to bait a man casting aspersions on his virility. I had to laugh, a wild child learned his language from a defrocked preacher, a pack of itinerant cowboys, and the African, who spent all those lonesome years on this wind-swept flatlands reading the complete works of Shakespeare and a Bible she'd traded some traveler a pound of fatback for. Sure can talk that talk. And now he's trying it out on a horse. Next thing, he'll be insulting the stallion's mother.

But I didn't mind. I was enjoying the rest. Give me time to think about things: Prissy. Wondering if Will missed her. It didn't seem to be in his vocabulary, in his way of looking at the world, he didn't seem to have a past or a future to worry over—but maybe I missed her enough for the both of us.

Anyway, I'll be damned if one early evening the Pacing White Stallion didn't show up at our camp. Must have been the electricity that laden the heavy air, knew all day it was a weather breeder, I'd already decided we needed to move our gear the half mile from the lake to an old shack over on the meadow the mowers use when they come down to bring in a crop of hay. Could see the thunderheads building up all along the horizon since midafternoon. Will and I'd just picked up our rucksacks to go when we heard him, a snort and whicker seemed as much visual as aural, a dense yellow green glowing in the leaves and grass, suffuse, like the light shifting across the surface of the water, the gusty wind, the deep rumbling core of thunder all around. I looked up, uncertain what I'd heard, saw Will stockstill, except for a slight rocking to and fro, the trembling of his mouth, followed the intense gaze to the opposite shore of the lake. The stallion tossed his head and mane and pawed the earth.

Will emits something more vibration than sound, starts stalking the horse, moving slowly, one careful step at a time at first, around the lake to where the White Stallion stands his ground, unsure, it looks like, whether to flip or fly. He's sniffing, trying to find some sign of fear, doesn't find it, takes two steps back. Will's eyes hard on his, he rears up, slashing the air with his front hooves, Will keeps on coming, the horse moves two more steps back. Looks like Will's saying something to him, upper lip and nose quivering: you're an insult to the noble Spanish steeds who overspread this prairie, I've ridden broomsticks tougher than you are. Finally, right up in the stallion's face: go ahead, dink, cut and run.

The wind quickens. Leaves and branches of sumac, willow, and scrub locust twenty-five rods beyond begin to flail and thrash, a sudden front passing through, a shower of large cold raindrops, and hailstones rattle around us. A bolt of blue lightning, a thunderclap explodes the underbrush, scatters debris swirling in dusty gray-green air like frenzied flocks of birds, trees thrash and spiral, snap twisting into the sky. Cyclone!

The stallion starts at all this, looks over his shoulder, Will, louring, lurking for this moment of inattention, leaps, grabs the exposed throat, and swings up on his back. The stallion panics, whirls, slinging clods, tufts of grass, to face the vortex. A roaring wasn't there before, broken twigs and limbs revolving high above them. Whips his tail back and forth, a few mincing steps, begins to spin and buck. Takes off. Floats, slowly turning above the troubled water of Wild Horse Lake, Will, knees locked about the barrel chest, arms hugging the neck, lets out a spirited *yippee-ti-yay*.

They sail over my head and disappear into low boiling blue-black clouds.

A strange elation at the spectacular demise of my brother, ecstasy at the center of power greater than ourselves. Grief and cold guilt would surely clutch me later, but now a numb belief the consequences of such a display must be benign. The roaring gone, wind calm, and sun suddenly breaking through clean, golden green, contained and refracted from a billion beads of water and of ice. The other side of danger, an exuberant, awful certainty: the world, a complex contraption, operates not to slake human desire but from immaculate necessity, and our small consciousness a wondrous but transitory and superfluous attribute of its unspinning. I remember once attempting to preach a sermon to that effect anyway back in Tonganoxie. The congregation took it into their heads to run me out of town on a rail.

I adjusted the rucksack on my shoulders and started off to search for Will. My spirits beginning to darken and crumble by the time I'd gone a quarter mile, hopeless, and then I heard singing, saw the white horse prancing along the rise above me through twisted and matted-down johnsongrass and sunflowers, Will sitting back puffing on a cigarette he must've rolled with his left hand in full flight. You could tell from the look in the stallion's eyes he was his: *anybody take me on a ride like that, somebody I'm sticking with*.

"Brother, I think I'll call him Widow Maker."

Like I was saying, you lose a few cows to rustlers hardly worth the effort to get up a posse and ride down into No Man's Land looking for them. But when they go to tearing down your fences and cutting out fifty head of your best breeding stock at a time, and they're doing this on a regular basis, especially after last winter's blizzard froze so damn many cows to death, you know more going on than a pack of hustling ne'er-do-wells greasing their chops as best they can. Somebody building themselves a herd going to be rivaling your depleted bunch, filling up the cattle pens at Dodge City and Abilene, driving the prices down on the international market.

Will was mad. Had Widow Maker saddled and ready to go at dawn, rousing everybody, prancing back and forth in front of the bunkhouse, shouting and kicking the door, already sent out riders to Sand Wells and Barney Bow to tell the boys to meet us at Goff Creek, we going after those sons of mangy bitches, nothing lower in the eyes of a coyote than a thieving house dog, they didn't know the herd they stole was Will's. And they're not going to be hard to find, as many cows as they got now stir up a dust cloud we can spot thirty miles off.

It was going on ten in the morning time we all met up at the creek just south of the line in the Public Lands, and Will was right about spotting the herd. From the highland above the channel you could see the dust clinging to the southwestern edge of the plains.

"Those bastards headed for Hell's Gate Gulch."

"Just what I thought. It's the Devil's Cavalry."

"What the hell's the Devil's Cavalry?"

"A band of the meanest lower-than-a-snake's-belly varmints ever born of woman, hear tell they set up a ranch there, headquarters for their life of crime."

Will has to rein Widow Maker in. "They just made their first and last mistake."

We circle around, keeping to the lowlands, are able to reach the open end of the box canyon at Hell's Gate Gulch before them. Sure looks like someone's camp but hardly the lair of the Devil's Cavalry. Two tents either side a campfire, a frying pan or two, coffeepot and a silver grinder, some underwear hanging from a sisal rope strung between two saplings, but no question about it, lots of cows grazing in the area wearing the brands of any number of Texas outfits, soon to be joined by the stock from the Perpetual Motion Ranch. It looks like the camp of the cowboys who ride herd on the stolen cattle, not the headquarters, shouldn't be any trouble at all to get our stock back, worry about where the ringleaders are later.

We decide to let them enter, get some idea how many we're up against, wait till after dark to close in. Will and the foreman of the Barney Bow spread take half the men to one side of the entrance, and the rest of us hide out on the other. Close to sundown when we hear one of them singing a couple of miles off. Four riders come winding down the trail through the prickly pears, rocks, and the brush along the little dry creek runs the length of the canyon floor. This is gonna be a barrel shoot.

We all crouch low as we can get, holding our breath. Suddenly Will jumps up, looks to me like he wants to scamper down from the stand of scrub where he and his men are hiding. I can tell, even in the dusky light across the canyon, he's very excited about something, I should have known better than to let him out of my sight. The foreman drags him down from behind, pulls him beneath a chinaberry tree. One of the riders looks around but doesn't see them, stands still on the path, the smallest of the four, very dark, riding bareback, rises up like he's sniffing at the air, cocks his head, listening first one way, then the other, turning the horse full circle on the trail. Finally settles back down and starts off, stops again to look back where Will was, then catches up with the other three.

The foreman is up on the rock again, waving, I don't know what to make of it, runs across the canyon floor toward me, rifle in one hand, holding on to his hat with the other. I don't see Will anywhere.

"What's going on over there?"

"That damn wild-ass brother of yours went plumb loco."

"Where is he now?"

"Gone."

"Gone where?"

"Hornswoggled if I know. He'd been sitting up there staring at the sun going down like he does, all of a sudden started sniffing the air like a bluetick hound caught the scent of a bitch in heat over in the next county, even before we heard the singing. Soon as he saw the riders on the trail he sprang up in the open, all I could do to wrestle him to the ground till they'd passed, kicking and butting like a bull got into a patch of jimsonweed. When I turned him loose he hightailed it all fours out through the tall grass along the rim of the canyon." Holds up the right hand to show a clear set of teeth marks between the thumb and first finger. "I always told you that boy not tame enough to be trusted."

It's true, he had. I'm sitting there wondering what to do next when the first hair-raising howl permeates the thickening dark, caught and held echoing close around us between the canyon walls.

"What in tarnation was that?"

Everybody hunched lower to the ground. Then a second voice, higher pitched, drawn out longer, forlorn and expectant all at the same time, years of progress and civilization drop away and there's nothing but a primal and vast wilderness every direction you look, a rising blood-red moon. The duet swells again, minor harmony, like an oldtime Baptist hymn gone pagan, drifts about our ears. Then every coyote and feral canine from every streambed and hollow for miles around joins in the heathen cry. I listen terrified, near to tears, not for lost innocence, that's what we are now, lost and innocent. For an unfettering, some terrible freedom from what we are destined, condemned to be. When I turn, my men are gone.

I take it all in for a while, even soothed finally by the singing, no need to trouble my mind with the implications of the second voice, time would no doubt make all things plain. I move slowly along the canyon wall toward the campsite, the howls, yip-yip yowls, welling up from the box end beneath and separate from, yet of a whole with, the general chorus resounding all around, a turmoil of darkness, then words, stumbling in the brush.

"Where the hell did she go?"

"Goddam, somebody light a lantern."

"What the hell's that out there with her?"

The Devil's Cavalry. I'm right in the middle of them, the only thing I seem to know how to do in extreme circumstances: raise my pistol and fire. The night echoes back silent, the coyotes and dogs, crickets and frogs, the trickle of wind in the creek, it seems to be an opening for a speech, the scripture lesson or benediction, but damn if I'm not at a loss for something appropriate to say. So I squeeze off another round.

Somebody moves. Crashes through the willows right in front of me, a wiry guy, headfirst into my gut, exposed the way it is, my arm still holding the Colt aloft, the pistol goes flying, I go flying, doubled and all the breath knocked loose, cursing as best I can. Never have been a very good man in a fight, my attacker up waiting for me and, if I don't get to my feet, ready to eat me alive where I lie. Just then a growl would curdle the bowels of Beelzebub himself, can't see much, but hear a thump, the crack of flesh on flesh over bone, a moan, another pop, shadows thrashing in shadows is all I can make out, then *whomp,* a man hits the ground beside me, holding his mouth, spitting something so dark and gelatinous can only be blood.

"The bastard's knocked out my god damn gold tooth."

The first moonlight breaking over the ridge of the canyon reveals Will standing there with a gun in his hand: mine, I assume. I'm the only one knows he's never held a firearm in all his life. I look to the man flopped over beside me. "Well, now we know for sure there's gold in them thar hills."

Someone appears, sudden and silent, behind Will, the smallest of the rustlers, looks like we've had it, but instead of jumping him, it just now clearly dawns on me—the curve and swell under flannel shirt and dungaree—*she*, it's her! Sidles up to him, he turns, they jump and circle, then rub noses. Little Sojourner.

She sees the man squatted on the ground leaned over daubing his mouth with a bandanna, whimpers, and goes to him. A call from across the creek. "Cannonball, where the fuck you at?"

I take the pistol from Will. "Better come on over and join the party." Motion with the barrel of the Colt to the man on the ground I reckon must be Cannonball.

"Come on, Big Mouth. They got us dead to rights."

Wait in silence, still nothing comes to mind to say, a comment on the weather or the price of beef in Dodge City, the possibility of the Texas Itch spreading north. I can't keep my eyes off Sojourner, sure it's her, and neither can Will. Both of us a little confused and nervous, and so is she, can't decide between Will and Cannonball, finally a big man comes from the creek, hands up, even though by this time the Colt is hanging at my side and he could more than likely just walked up and borrowed it from me. The moon completely visible above the canyon, the night creatures returned to their usual mayhem, I can't figure out what the Sam Patch is going on.

"Evening, sir. My name is Henry. Big Mouth Henry."

"Glad to make your acquaintance. Who's the rest of your crew?"

Points without lowering his hands below his head. "That there is Cannonball and Coyote."

"Where's the Devil's Cavalry?"

"Sir?"

"The pack of outlaws said to live in this canyon."

Looks around him, at Cannonball sitting dejected on the ground holding his mouth, Sojourner, and Will. "Then that must be us. Cause we're the onliest ones living here, I'm pretty sure of that. If you don't count the scorpions, tarantulas, and the rattlesnakes."

"You rustling all these cows?"

"Now, don't exaggerate. Rounding up mavericks. It's true we might overlook a brand or two, but—"

"You cut down my fencing to get to my herd."

Cannonball looks up. "*Your* fence?" Stands up. "That was yours? Now don't that frost your balls. I thought nesters the only ones put up barbed wire. Figured we was cutting you a favor taking down that infernal stuff. What's a self-respecting cattleman doing putting up fence?"

"Scientific management. The times are changing."

Looks at me awhile, shrugs, then sits back down. "I should hope to kiss a pig they are."

Big Mouth Henry steps in, still reaching for the sky. "And that's why we find ourselves in such dire straits. Some of the best cowhands ever come up the trail, and ever since we delivered an unruly pack of long yearlings and scab-ends to the Big Bellies up north in Montana we can't get no honest job of work. What with Cannonball and Coyote carrying on the way—" Notices Will and Sojourner cuddled up together. "What the Sam Patch *is* going on here? He the one doing all that caterwauling?"

I holster the pistol, getting mighty heavy in my hand, and sit on a pithy log. "Well, this reminds me of a sermon I preached once back in Oskaloosa. It'd be a shame to hang some of the best cowpunchers ever was. Especially ones been so kind to my kid brother's litter mate."

"Huh?"

"Looks like most of my crew run off when I needed them. How'd you fellers like to work for us at the Perpetual Motion Ranch?"

Big Mouth Henry finally lowers his hands, looks over at Cannonball. Cannonball looks up at me, then the others. "I reckon, brothers and sisters, it would beat the end of a rope."

Big Mouth Henry slaps his hands together, more to get the circulation going again than anything else. "This calls for a cup of Coyote's coffee."

I get up with the rest of them to go to the campsite, feeling heavy and wore out, still not sure what the meaning is of all this. "Hold on a dogbone minute. Wasn't there four of you come into this canyon?"

"Oh, yeah. Spartacus took off at the first howl. Probably halfway back to Mississippi by now."

The Real Wild West

Coyote Dropping He had left Buffalo Bill at Fort Yates in North Dakota, had intended to go home. Wanted to see the old campsites, the tipis along the river, smell smoke from the seven sacred woods, plenty of yap root, sego lilies, and bitter onion to eat. Been gone a long time, a confusion of what he knew and what he'd learned hovering in the mind, the specter of Autumn Tallgrass, the scent and touch of her skin, golden-red braids greased with deer fat, the young child, the burned nose, in the clearing along the river, the girl wielding a butcher knife wanting to sleep with him, the woman he had left not once but twice, to travel the earth alone. Resentment he hadn't realized he bore, the futility of trying to control events, the excitement of the unknown world erupted into the known, a newness, he understood now, really an oldness invading the prairie like the ancestors before, Europe, which he had now seen, which he now knew he, everybody, would not survive. Winter visions. An old man alone on the high northern plains.

He was Cody's friend, brother from the hunt with Duke Alexis, an important member of the cast in the early theatrical productions, Buffalo Bill had said, and then in the Wild West troupe. Able to talk to all the others joined up with the show— Red Shirt, Cut Meat, Poor Dog, Little Bull, and their people, who knew much less of the great world beyond their own council fires, beyond the prairies, than Coyote Dropping did— and to interpret for them what they saw.

But he had been afraid.

The sacred buffalo, one of the few left alive in this world, twisted and thrashed about, bawled out, hanging in a sling from a giant crane. The rest of the herd on the crowded New York City dock butted and kicked at the brusk, shouting handlers trying to load them on board the *State of Nebraska*. A band of curious instruments made strange and noisy music. What could Coyote Dropping say?

They had come east on the iron horse into the rising sun, through humid forests and hills. The towns became cities, took on fantastic shapes, colors, and sizes, smoking, stinking, clamorous places of tall red-brick houses sprawled along big muddy rivers, peopled by strangers in strange dress speaking strange tongues. And the things they would eat! Men and boys handing out bags of potatoes, onions, cabbages, carrots, turnips, kohlrabi, and collard greens on street corners, sides of beef and pork, lambs, chickens, ducks and turkeys, rabbits, squirrels hanging behind large glass panes, iced trays of fish, mussels, clams, oysters, and eels. Streets full of men, women, children, horses, dogs, donkeys, and oxen, carts and wagons rumbling about, going somewhere, doing something. But you rarely saw what it was. What could there be for so many to do: they didn't hunt, make their own clothing, they didn't even farm the way they tried to do out on the plains. Had always been a puzzlement out there what they were up to, but here it was a mystery of fearsome power. These towns, the farther east you came, took on a permanence, became part of the landscape, the landscape itself, no longer the transitory slap-dash of the grasslands, liable to blow away—more often than not *did* blow away, the first big storm come along—or just abandoned for no apparent reason, to be worn down by wind and sun. These eastern cities looked eternal as the woods and prairies, the buildings embedded in time, the narrow streets durable as the canyons disgorging mountain rivers out onto the plains, as the trails through the passes of the Dakota Black Hills. Once you were inside them, contained by some ominous, exotic magic, it was the trees and creeks, the sorrels and grasses struggling up in the cracks between brick and cobblestone, seemed out of place.

They stood now by the enormous fireboat and watched. The buffalo bellowed one last time and succumbed in dumb terror, hung in the sling like limp breechcloth on a scrub-oak limb, nose and hind hooves bumping in irregular rhythm with the screeching machines, resigned to whatever indignities lay ahead. They were next.

Even those who had been with the Wild West before on tour through the major eastern cities, had seen things make the folk back on the reservations click their tongues and shake their heads, chuckle at the stories these travelers can tell once they see a little of the world, even those been to Canada grew weak at the thought of crawling into this monstrous iron boat, steaming and trembling in the oily green river, to head over the great waters to Europe, to sail out into the cloud-shrouded, foggy, and unimaginable void. They had all heard the stories the old folks told, no matter where they came from, what people, what hunting grounds they traveled, what river they wintered on in the old days, whether they wore eagle feathers or buffalo horns, fought on foot or horseback, it was always the same: don't you go on that big boat, it'll kill you, specially now the magic's weak, the medicine lost its kick, don't do it, not worth however many pounds of tobacco, quarters of beef, kegs of gunpowder, or government dollars they give out. Might as well be deer pellets and cow pies, all the good it'll do you. One of us tries to cross the big salt ocean in for big trouble. You know that much water bound to be bad for you, even if you could drink it and cook with it, look at the misery brought us from across it. Your flesh going to waste away, rot, corrode, ever day a little less, like a snowbank in springtime, like buffalo meat after the professional hunter's slaughter, until that shriveled hide of yours all that's left and even it going to slide from the bones, drop to the ground like the rind of an old dead cottonwood, and your exposed skeleton rattle loose in the breeze the rest of the days of the world. Never find burial till the end of time. It is so.

But they had all come along. What else to do, hang around the reservation, sneak off to the seamy towns after firewater, starve visionless beside a dusty cavalry outpost. Some didn't have a choice, kidnapped or rounded up by the government and sent, get the troublemakers out of the country where they couldn't stir up discontent. Some came for the money, adventure, the same as the cowboys no longer had anything to do, now the drives had dwindled, the range fenced in with barbed wire, bought up by foreign gentlemen or parceled out to settlers trying to hang on by their fingernails. Seemed like the only wild west left was Buffalo Bill's.

Coyote Dropping had come for understanding. To see the land the invaders had come from, where their ancestors had sent them forth to overswarm the earth. If he could see this great world, smell its soil, bring himself to eat its food, walk among the people there, talk with them, maybe he could bring it all together, bend the sacred hoop around, bind it, make it whole again, coax the tree to blossom.

By the time they loaded him into the dark narrow hold of the fireboat, he was beginning to despair of his quest. Not even out on the big water yet and had already seen enough confusion and inexplicable chaos take a lifetime of meditation to sort. And then the boat began to move.

They were given loosely woven nets, for sleeping, the crew had said. Coyote Dropping huddled in a corner against a bulwark holding the thing up to examine it in the feeble light.

"Good thing it's so hot down here, this holey weave not make much of a blanket."

"No wonder these people so mean, sleeping on something hard as this make anybody cantankerous."

Then the ship sent forth a voice, a powerful, polytonal whistle rising from the innards through the entire body, vibrating the decks beneath their feet, a quaking fear of whatever unknown lay ahead. The first stomach contents splashed along the wall.

Coyote Dropping spread his netting, they'd called it a hammock, on the steel floor and lay down. The others had their families, their clans and brotherhoods, leaders and sages with them. He was alone. No one to help in his interpretations. But also no one to hinder. The air foul, thick with salt, oil, and vomit, moans and pleas for relief, cries of nightmare despair mixed with the snores of those exhausted enough or terrified enough to flee into sleep. Then the plaintive death songs of those convinced they were going to die. Then a roaring beyond the bulwarks, a wind at once reassuring, like prairie wind, and terrifying, out of place and lost. The deck began to tilt, rise, and fall, the ship shudder and jolt, the ocean to pound and thunder, they all slid and banged against each other, the walls, back and forth, the floor becoming the wall sometimes, the fireboat on the verge of rolling over. They were right, the old folk, right, all of us doomed, our skeletons, a loose knot of bones rattling through this liquid universe forever seeking a scoop of dry dirt to be buried in.

Coyote Dropping decided, if he was going to die, might as well go looking for it, no need to cower down here in the heave and stench of this dank belly like a cottontail waiting to be dug out of a moldy log. Found his way through terror, the confused maze of pitching and yawing passages, the pivotal directions of the world destroyed, the sickness among the cowboys too, death songs along every corridor, less melodious but just as sincere, wrought up in the howling all around. Made it out into the open gale. More water than air, debris strewn over the deck, a few people bundled in corners inside the lounges, and the crew. A vast saltwater prairie as far as he could see into the turmoil, billowing and churning hills, wind surges on the surface ripples and ridges, foam flung back like gusts through grass. Instead of sickness, his life's spirit seeping from him, instead of death, a joy of recognition: the common expanse of the world. The crew going about their tasks along the ropes strung from rail to bulkhead, ducking the waves crashing over them when the boat bobbed and dipped. He watched them, the studied way they moved, the look of concentration and ecstasy, a contrivance, an accommodation to the uncertain flux and wild confusion about them akin to dance.

He found their dining room. Soup, bread, sausages, and cheese, the more he ate the better he felt. He could fight off this corrosive ailment supposed to melt away his flesh, stayed topside the entire three days the storm raged, practiced the gait of the sailors, their stance and swagger, slept on a couch in one of the lounges, rocked to sleep like a baby wrapped in a cradleboard tied to a sycamore branch. When the seas began to calm, the food became more lavish, others from steerage came up to join him at the table, seemed to have discovered powerful medicine to overcome this ancient curse, their spirits returning from the other world, the meat replenished on their bones.

The second European tour left New York two years later for the Exposition Universelle in Paris. Coyote Dropping could now guide those new to show business on the road, held in some respect as fancy dancer and leader at Adobe Walls. Could tell them how the food overcame the legendary sickness, tell of the wondrous things they'd see—trains that travel through underground burrows and dens, rock buildings as old as the mountains, ceremonies celebrated in large houses on platforms before thousands of spectators dressed in amazing costumes sitting in plush chairs—show them the pictures taken in buckskins, moccasins, and feathers sold in all the cities, tell how Prime Minister Gladstone called in camp, the Prince and Princess of Wales and their three daughters came to rehearsal, how Buckingham Palace requested a special showing for Grand Duke Michael of Russia, the Crown Prince of Austria, Graf Ludwig von Baden, the King and Queen of Belgium, the kings of Saxony, Denmark, and Greece. He could tell them how Queen Victoria of England herself came to greet the players, and Red Shirt did not bow. Looked her straight in the eye and delivered greetings from his people.

But the new ones, especially the young ones, didn't want to hear it. They grumbled about the treatment, shipped east like cattle in railroad cars, crowded and cold at night, hot in the day, forced into the innards of the fireboat, where the air is stale and the light dim. They told stories of their own how many of the people returned from the last tour lower than the belly of a prairie rattler, confused, despondent, and ill. They talked of the reservations, the two-year drought, the reduced annuities, outrage and anger, how so many leaders were taking the government path, Running Antelope now a Congregationalist, Gall an Episcopalian, his brother-in-law, Gray Eagle, gone over to the other side, trying to get Sitting Bull, the only shaman left, to farm. But excited conversations too about Mighty Porcupine, who went to visit Wovoka and learned about the dance.

Coyote Dropping, without family or other political ties, had to sit at the margin of the counsels given between decks, himself the outsider, had to watch and listen to the malcontents and figure who he should approach. Didn't take long to notice White Horse. He had been set upon by agents and beaten, drug behind a North Dakota railroad station, shipped east with the Wild West: a resourceful man, quick reflexes, a ready laugh, but serious. Coyote Dropping decided it would be good to have him on his side. Waited until two or three days out, night, the ship slowly lolling on moderate seas, the languid throbbing engines, most people asleep, hanging in the hammocks this time, White Horse pacing the gangway like a caged puma, finally sat on the deck, legs folded, hands lying limp on the knees, staring intensely at the many layers of thick gray paint on the wall.

Coyote Dropping slipped to the floor beside him. The stare did not change. They remained silent, the ship groaned and creaked. Coyote Dropping stuffed his pipe, lit it, blew smoke in what he arbitrarily chose to be the four directions, handed it to White Horse. White Horse savored a long pull, handed the pipe back. Coyote Dropping cleaned it and returned it to his pouch. They sat.

"Who is Wovoka?"

"The cutter. The prophet. One of the fish eaters from the high plateau between the mountains in the place the dogfaces call Nevada. A dreamer. Had a vision on a day when the sun died, fell asleep beneath a haying wagon and was taken up to the other world on the sacred mountain of his people. Saw all the ancestors, happy and young, vigorous in the old occupations. There was buffalo and elk and prairie chicken, and these ancestors taught Wovoka to dance."

"I am always interested in dance."

Turns for the first time. And smiles. "You will like this one, Fancy Dancer. This dance will bring the rain, call the buffalo, the pronghorn, elk, and deer back to the plains. The ancestors will follow. Hordes sweeping down like snowflakes before the north wind in winter. This dance will make you invisible to your enemy."

"Ha! Quite a dance. What makes you think it will work?"

A dull thud, a slow shudder passes along the hull of the ship. "We do not know for sure. And do not care. Where is there hope for us on earth? We have been forgotten. We snatch at this hope because it is the only one we have."

"You know what we are up against."

"We are mocked in our misery, we have no newspapers or other voice to speak for us. We have no redress. Those who eat three times a day and see their children well and happy around them don't understand what a starving person feels. Weak with hunger and maddened by despair, we hold our dying children and feel their little bodies tremble as their spirits depart and leave a dead weight in our hands."

Coyote Dropping stayed close in Paris, pulled on feathered costumes to accompany him and the chiefs on their publicity rounds with Buffalo Bill, rode up the steel tower high above the river and the spiderwebbed pattern of streets, had their picture taken, and Coyote Dropping talked to the newspapermen. Not for Buffalo Bill but for himself and for White Horse. Wheedled information from them, stories about ghost dances broken up back home, the jittery fear of men in power. Told stories himself, of hunger and anger among the troupe, food reduced to save money, the people paraded around like the buffalo and camels, the newborn babies displayed in the sideshow like freaks.

He talked with Buffalo Bill. He could see, he thought, a longing in his eyes not unlike that in White Horse's and, he supposed, in his own, a yearning for the simplicity of an open sky and a wide expanse of grass, things by no means simple yet, compared to this Europe, this civilization, a thing of almost childlike certainty. Buffalo Bill would slip away from the dukes and duchesses, princes and newspapermen, when he could, to the separate mess tent and the tipis. Sometimes he brought a little firewater. Whatever else you could say about these Europeans, they did understand and commune with the spirit of the grape, of barley, wheat, and corn. Buffalo Bill ignored his own regulations to recapture with his prairie brothers some semblance of the life they all now mocked two shows a day before thousands of spectators as strange to him, though he sometimes may have forgotten it, as they were to Coyote Dropping and to White Horse.

"Cody, it is not right, we ride in cars like the animals. The horses eat better than we do. Why do you not help us?"

Takes the bottle. "I can't, when you get right down to it. I'm as much captive of this menagerie as you. Trying to run my ranch back home, if it wasn't for my sister the whole shebang would be in ruins. I'd sooner be hunting along the Powder River or bringing in the hay from the north meadow, but folks fool enough to give out money for this nonsense, I'd be a bigger fool not to take it. What else to do? The buffalo is gone, and I'm no more than a clown, a trained circus animal doing clever tricks for my supper. Same as you."

"Yes, Cody. But a big difference."

"What's that?"

"Your supper much tastier to eat."

Buffalo Bill holds up his pointer finger, White Horse reaches out and yanks it, releasing Buffalo Bill's ripping, humid fart, billowing and settling among the earthy odors of straw and buffalo dung.

They would laugh. Sometimes, in the cool blue-green Paris moon, they would stand, lock arms, and dance. From a distance perhaps, in that light, surrounded by the low buildings and spires of the city, to passersby not knowing what was going on, they could have looked like ghosts.

Then White Horse disappeared.

They had traveled from Paris to Barcelona. A poor city, a cold December, the troupe disheartened, meager gates, homesickness, more rumors of scandal and unrest on the plains. Drought, the annuities cut back again, the government trying to starve us out, force us off whatever little land we have left. The Dawes Act to divide it up, everybody getting a little patch, the rest sold off to settlers, people squabbling about what to do. Some said take what you can get while something is being offered, but Short Bull, Kicking Bear, and Big Foot still resist, Hump sent his men with their war clubs through the windows of the meetinghouses to break the councils up, and Torn Belly's people have taken up the dance. The messiah and the ancestors, who we always see dancing in the ghostly curtains of light in the northern sky, will bring back everything that has been lost.

Stories had begun to be published in newspapers back home about the mistreatment of the people in the Wild West. Sickness spread among the troupe from the squalid run-down Barcelona tenements, the docks: influenza and smallpox, the hacking and whooping coughs from the tents and tipis all through the night. The old folks were right, we should have never crossed the salty ocean, doom settling like dirty rain.

Buffalo Bill decided to pack up and leave, but before they could get out the city was put under quarantine.

Coyote Dropping and White Horse had performed the funeral dances for the babies, the old, then those struck down in their prime, far from the prairie, carried off in the carnal wagons by foreigners to be turned alone into a cold, strange winter soil. Ten death songs, plus Christian hymns for three members of the crew, then finally the death of the Master of Ceremonies of the show.

Buffalo Bill had chased after one government official or health authority, one ambassador after another, and was able to convince the bureaucracy, not without considerable outlay of what capital they had, to let the Wild West slip through the quarantine. He broke into the grounds shouting, healthy and sick alike, up and at em, strike the show, let's get her down to the harbor and onto the ship before some petty, corrupt son of a bitch of a potentate or other changes his mind.

After they had disembarked at Naples, Coyote Dropping had walked around the camp to check on everybody. White Horse was gone. No one knew where he was. Not sure they had seen him get on the ship at Barcelona. Lost. Off somewhere to die alone. Or show up in a day or two just wishing he was dead after trying to drink all the grape in Italy. No one knew.

They moved north through Rome, Florence, Pisa, Bologna, Milano, into Germany. He didn't show. Coyote Dropping gave up all hope. Like many before him, White Horse had vanished, absorbed into the world, large, complex, everywhere dense and multidirectional, without trace.

They bedded down in Strasbourg for the winter. A dark low ceiling crowded over the tents, smoke from vents and chimneys

fell to the ground and slid along the narrow streets, a malevo-
lent spirit settled like thick fog after the long months of constant movement. Unstructured idleness freed the troubled
mind to fester and precipitate heavy on the soul. Sit silently
wrapped in blankets around the sputtering fire chewing on the
stories from the reservation, the postponed mourning for those
who had died in Spain, for those dying at home, sit there
scratching signs with a broken-off stick in the foreign dirt that
contains no solace, the cold damp sky sucking vitality through
the skin. The nights much longer than those at home, the
coughs and sneezes, the restless shuffling, snorts, and grumbles
of the horses and the buffalo in their pens.

Buffalo Bill finds Coyote Dropping sitting on a stack of hay,
large snowflakes spiraling through breathless air and melting
everywhere but the loose strands of hair about their heads. He
takes out his pipe, lights it, lets smoke slip between his lips
to the four directions—after they've discussed and verified
just where they think they lie—offers it to Coyote Dropping.
Smoke in silence, church bells ringing from the city, someone
in the crew exercising the stock. Buffalo Bill taps the bowl of
the pipe on the muddy heel of his boot, takes out a barlow, and
scrapes it clean.

"We're in a little trouble, Coyote Dropping."

"Some of us more than others."

"Our friend White Horse has shown up."

"What! Where?"

"Last place I ever expected him, I'll tell you that. Washington, D.C."

"Across the water?"

"I don't know how the hell he did it. Got on the wrong boat
in Barcelona, I guess. What the trouble is, he seems to be

talking to anybody who'll listen about how bad we been treating everybody."

"It has been a hard season."

"For all of us. You know how these newspapermen are, they'll print anything, not taking too much trouble to check the veracity of it."

"Hmmph."

"You know, I always have suspected it was you taught White Horse that about newspapermen."

"White Horse's people and mine are ancient enemies, wouldn't even tell each other where to find a buffalo chip for a fire in a snowstorm before you people came along. Any talking we do now—how do you say it—laid to your doorstep, so step on it."

"Something like that. Anyway, you're the one *hablas* American the best, and I could sure use your help now. Seems the newspapers not the only ones listening to White Horse. Politicians like to talk too, and we want you to come with us back to Washington to set the story straight."

The sky grown deeper violet-gray, snow thicker, a crystal covering on Buffalo Bill's goatee, Coyote Dropping's blanket. "When do we leave?"

The world is saturated with power. Manifestations of it everywhere—crow, bear, thunder and lightning—and humans can weasel their way into possession of some of this power, conjure and trick the forces of the universe, the human share of it contained and parceled out in words—slippery congelations, both the words and the power. Travel in Europe and finally the trip to Washington with Buffalo Bill reveal how large a gulp a human group can seize, how concrete, how permanent it can seem to be. A few comments groused in Rome or Stuttgart eventually compel a body of men in Washington to require Buffalo Bill to travel eleven days across the ocean—hundreds of steamships large as villages, in fact villages themselves, loaded with food, barber shops, general stores, and taverns, ply the seas constantly—to answer their pestering questions. All very puzzling, enough to make you wonder, to question the life you'd thought so obvious for so many years. Curiosity has made you suspect something beyond the mountains and forests that bound the plains, but imagination has been insufficient to fathom just what it turns out to be. And then the notion of other places beyond the margins of this, as incomprehensible to the inhabitants here as they are to you, and you to them. Yet all peopled by the same animal. Buffalo Bill, White Horse, the Cossacks from beyond the eastern mountains of Europe, the buffalo people you learn now come from Africa, their offspring walking the streets of Barcelona and Paris, New York and St. Louis, fighting like demons out on the plains, the English and French and Spanish and Germans. All the same beneath the uncanny costumes, twisted tongues, comic eyes, weird noses, and oddly hued skin. Some of them remind you of an uncle, a sister, and not just in the way they hold their shoulders and toss their heads when telling a story, or prop one leg over the other sitting on a stool, sometimes the very structure of the bones of their faces. Very subtle, this great world, and the magic that bonds it together.

Powers were in flux when they got back from Europe. R. V. Belt, Acting Commissioner of somebody else's Affairs, and a confusing flurry of other people around Coyote Dropping wanting to know the strangest things, what he ate, who he talked to, where he slept, and even with whom. Hard to follow all of it, his language making great leaps to comprehend, confounded by what the interpreters were telling him it all meant and patched together with the whispered tales filtering in from the West: Sitting Bull has broken the peace pipe he smoked when he returned from his flight to Canada, calling for the peoples of the prairie to drive the intruders out, the last great effort to regain the land, the ghost dance calling the lost herds of buffalo and elk, all the deceased ancestors home.

Late afternoon, after a long and perplexing inquisition about dancing, two government men took Coyote Dropping into a room off a long corridor, small and stuffy, a pungent oily odor he could not identify, dark even before they closed the door, leaving him, he thought, alone. His eyes adjusted to the piddling light seeping in around sill and jamb, long sticks with bristles and rags on the ends, buckets, a growing sense of confinement, panic, then a sudden flare in the far corner. Buffalo Bill lighting up a cigar.

"Howdy, Coyote Dropping."

Smoke in the four directions, Coyote Dropping more at ease but wary, acknowledged his presence with a nod, took the cigar, drew and held a mouthful, passed it back, waited for Buffalo Bill to continue. He was content to savor the tobacco in silence. The atmosphere oppressive, narrow, and noticeably warm. Finally he snuffed the cigar on the heel of his intricately tooled and stitched boot, cleared his throat.

"Things are not only serious, but they're getting tense."

"I told the truth as best I know it, Cody."

"I don't mean that. No need to worry on that account. I mean out west. Seems there's a plot afoot to get Sitting

Bull, everybody in this town worried he's going to lead an uprising."

"What with? A dance step and a few shirts supposed to stop bullets?"

"You and I know it doesn't make sense, but when did things have to make sense for politicians on either side. Little war scare keep people's minds off other things going on."

A long pause. "Why are we lurking in this choking room?"

"General Nelson A. Miles has called me back into service. I'm now a brigadier general."

Coyote Dropping salutes, Buffalo Bill proffers his first finger, Coyote Dropping reaches, then thinks better of the pull in such a small tight space. "And such generals always meet in closets."

Smiles, farts anyway. "He wants me to arrest Sitting Bull."

"Ah-h-h!" Looks around for something. "Our old friend and show-business buddy."

"Yeah. We had quite a time together up in Canada, didn't we." Contemplates the dead cigar still held in the tips of his fingers. "Many people are out to bring him in, one way or another, be a feather in their cap, they think, good for the career, and all hell will break loose if anything happens to him. We've got to get to him first, convince him to come in on his own."

"What do you mean, *we*?"

"I want you to come with me."

They took the train to Chicago, riding in separate coaches. Buffalo Bill the plainsman, surrounded by newspapermen in the smoking car, vast amounts of tobacco and spirits. Buffalo Bill the showman, whatever else he might be, whatever else he might know, he understood the power of the word. Coyote Dropping rode in silence, alone.

The most dangerous assignment of my whole career, Buffalo Bill had said, and what good is danger if it can't be shared with good friends. Stopped off in Wisconsin to pick up White Beaver Powell, John Keith, the manager of his North Platte ranch, and Pony Bob Haskin. In Bismarck, North Dakota, they met behind the railroad station, where Buffalo Bill had mules, horses, and two wagons full of supplies waiting, started out in the middle of the night for Fort Yates. Bitter cold, brilliant stars spangled across the sky, a moderate but relentless north wind caught the breath of mules and men, slung it swirling white out into the darkness. Buffalo Bill prattled on endlessly about whatever came to mind. Coyote Dropping had never seen him like this, or had forgotten the last time, the hunt with Duke Alexis. The dull veil shadowing his eyes in the Wild West arena as he shattered glass balls Coyote Dropping hurled into artificial light, the gaze of distracted concentration in a trained animal's eyes as he jumped through hoops to get at the lump of sugar such bizarre behavior produced, the boredom of precisely timed routine had all fallen away, been washed clean by the tears the sharp wind stimulated, the precise sparkle of the midnight heavens.

Coyote Dropping come alive too, back on the native prairie, the awful freedom of empty distance, all attention called out, away from this mortal husk making its way through an unpredictable scrabble of dirt, rock, wind, rain, and fire. But he was troubled by the mission they were embarked upon, the brooding during the long train ride in the cold uncomfortable coach, the monotonous clacking of iron wheels over iron rails not totally dispelled. Everything had changed. He'd been gone performing distorted imitations for a lusty, foreign audience, the so-called civilized long-ears pounding their hands, stomping their feet, shouting and whistling at every simulated act of violent blood-letting cruelty. He knew nothing first hand of what was happening out here, this potent dance sweeping the northern plains—people circling and hollering out plaintive songs, billowing dust visible thirty miles away, stomp and sing until they fall into an exhausted tranquility, lie for hours motionless on the ground—he had never seen a ghost shirt, held a ghost stick in his hand. Which side was he on, out to save Sitting Bull or to betray him? All structure gone from the world, powers set loose to buffet and baffle him, what medicine is there for this, his choice not to form or direct but to resist or to be swept along.

Buffalo Bill stopped the wagons a mile from the fort. "Got to prepare for my grand entrance, boys." Put on his crimson shirt, the buckskin jacket with the fringed sleeves, his silk stockings and patent leather shoes. "Coyote Dropping, you take a horse and all the firearms. Wait for me on the road to Sitting Bull's village. I'll be along sometime tomorrow morning."

Coyote Dropping huddled close to a small fire in the ravine where they were to meet, coyotes yapping on all sides, alone. The land around him as it had always been, haunted, restless spirits blown about in the wind, buffalo, red-tailed hawk, the ancestors who came, generations past numbering ago, groveling out of the western mountains, eating grubs and roots, onto the plains to live on horseback, to follow the buffalo, exalted striders, calling to their extension into the quickened now, to their living selves, to him, to hold on, not to submit easily to grovel again.

The next morning he heard Buffalo Bill's determined singing, a wagon banging and clattering over the frozen ruts of the river road. He tied his horse on behind, loaded the firearms, and climbed up beside him.

"Coyote Dropping. Did you have a pleasant night?"

"Miserable."

"You missed quite a shindig. Looks like Agent McLaughlin and Lieutenant Colonel Drum resent me being dispatched over their heads in this delicate matter. Invited me in for a drink, a road-shortener—a friendly gesture, I thought, under the circumstances. But as the whiskey kept flowing and my drinking companions kept relieving each other in regular shifts, it became apparent my generous hosts had something else in mind. Some sort of delaying tactic. But you know me, nothing I like better than a challenge, and I'd stake a month's pay any day on a scout against an officer in a drinking contest. My compadres' reputations on the line. Time dawn rose in the windows, only one left above the table was me."

Coyote Dropping looks at him closely, the gray grimace at the banging of the axle, the sudden clenching of the brow. "You're a good man, Cody."

"I got a wagon full of beads, knives, axes, calico, tobacco, and especially horehound candy, a hundred dollars' worth of stuff for every pound of the old Bull's weight. We'll get him."

"Where are John, Pony Bob, and White Beaver?"

Buffalo Bill clicks his tongue, gives the mules their head. "Feeling a little under the weather, a touch of the flu, I think. Headed back east on the train. It made a better show if I started out alone, unarmed, to persuade Sitting Bull, the man who killed Custer, one old enemy and friend to another, to return to the fort."

They ride on, close on the seat, hunched against the cold, Buffalo Bill become subdued and quiet, a pained sadness, the spirituous residue in his eyes, staring out beyond the team at the road meandering over the flat countryside.

"A lot going on that don't bode good. The folks at the Agency believe in order to live in the modern world you got to become like them, and in order to do that, Sitting Bull's, Big Foot's, Hump's people, everybody who's got another way of thinking, got to be crushed, then remolded into Europeans. A bunch of chuckleheads in the government smell blood and are out to get it. Force the only answer to whatever question comes up."

"You fear for Sitting Bull?"

Long silence. "That I do. Him, and all the rest of us too."

They hardly spoke for the rest of the day, huddled separately around the fire at night. The next morning, the frozen mist held low to the ground, a winter prairie like hundreds they had both seen, but somehow remote and refined, an essence held out but no longer theirs. Midmorning, the north wind had blown the sky clear, a cold accretion of light on the hills, stained with dust and crystal ice beyond the horizon. Noontime, pulling a long rise out of the valley from Oak Creek Crossing, they saw a horseman. Buffalo Bill reined in the mules, the man came forward and saluted.

"General Cody, sir!"

Buffalo Bill sticks out his finger to be pulled. "Louis Primeau. I don't recall requesting scouts on this mission."

Primeau circles around in front of the wagon to get his back to the wind. "Glad I ran into you, Cody. I've been at Sitting Bull's cabin. He's decided to come in. Started north this morning on the Grand River road."

Buffalo Bill, eyes watering from wind and sun he has to face into, glances at Coyote Dropping, back at the scout. "What led him to do a thing like that, I wonder."

Primeau's horse nosing the ground, mane and tail ruffled, coated with dust. "Hard to tell. We better get on back to Fort Yates in case there's trouble."

"What sort of trouble you expecting?"

The nigh-wheeler snorts, rattles its harness, Primeau's horse jumps and prances. "I couldn't say. I'm sure McLaughlin'll be happy to parley with you when we return."

Primeau leaps three long strides past the wagon, then slows to a trot. Buffalo Bill looks at Coyote Dropping, finally shrugs, snaps the reins, and swings the team around to follow. "Just as well. I'd like as not ended up telling the old fart to break for Canada."

The telegram from President Harrison rescinding Buffalo Bill's orders was waiting for them when they returned to Fort Yates, and Sitting Bull was nowhere in sight, nor was he expected. Buffalo Bill slipped into a quiet rage. He had been tricked.

"Goddam bastards, railroad companies and the army want to demonstrate how fast they can muster troops, ship em by rail like damn cattle to slaughter, all the way from California, show off their new toys. Not the first time they've jerked the country around. And damn sure won't be the last. I'm going to kick the pee-wadding out of Primeau next time I catch up with him. Don't have time for this foolishness. We got a Wild West to mount, come on."

Coyote Dropping rubs his chin. "No, Cody. I think my show-business days are through. Time I got back to home."

Buffalo Bill hesitates, then steps toward him, takes both shoulders in his hands. "You sure?"

"Yep."

Blinks a few times. "Good luck, then." Wrinkles his nose. "We all going to need it."

Buffalo Bill finally smiles, holds out his index finger. Coyote Dropping gives it a tug.

Coyote Dropping kept telling himself he was on his way home. News had filtered in before he left Fort Yates that Short Bull and Kicking Bear had broken for Cluny Table, the stronghold high above the Cheyenne River valley where they could hold off anybody's army, dance, and await the ancestors' return come spring. He rode now through the bitter-cold evening, wandering more than traveling, stopping to talk to whomever he met, how many days, convincing himself there was a home there somewhere to the south, warmer winds, plenty of jerked venison, prairie artichokes, even buffalo, Autumn Tallgrass's tipi tucked in beneath some earthy riverbank in the late-afternoon sun. His horse led the way. A freezing mist concealed the waxing moon of popping trees.

Around midnight he heard singing. Muffled, tangled in the sumac channeled between the hills along Cherry Creek. A death song. He clung to the back of his pony, exhausted, hungry, and cold, not sure if it was his song, inside his skull, till he found the feeble firelight, the several people shivering around the embers. They paid no attention. He slid from the horse, approached the camp, and settled to warm himself.

"Hau."

They do not look up, he is a foreigner. Travel-worn, some without blankets, the woman lying closest to the fire a head wound clotted with coagulated blood. After a brief pause, they continue the song.

Coyote Dropping gets his pouch from the horse, offers hardtack and bacon. They eat in silence. He stuffs his pipe, picks up a coal and lights it, blows smoke in the four directions, passes it to the man who appears to be the oldest. After it has made the rounds he gives out the rest of the tobacco. They begin to sing again.

The old man walks out into the bushes to piss. Throws a few sticks on the fire, then settles next to Coyote Dropping.

"The metal-breasts have killed Sitting Bull."

"Ah-h-h!"

"The long-ears are afraid of the dance, the police hauled him out of his cabin before the sun was up, we surrounded them, there was much confusion, pleading, and insults. Sitting Bull said he would not go another step. Bad blood on both sides. Many words, then gunshots, and in the melee the pony soldiers showed up and began firing the Hotchkiss cannons everywhere."

The dance. Creates power, but for whom?

"Sitting Bull's old gray horse, the one Cody gave him for the Wild West, was saddled to take him to jail." Coyote Dropping looks up at the old man. He is staring out into the darkness. "When the first shots rang out, the outburst that killed Sitting Bull, Old Gray took a bow."

Heard this all before, it has happened before, to the folk. He is on the way home. Like chasing last year's wind. "What will you do now, Old Man?"

"We are going to our friends and relatives in Big Foot's camp on the Cheyenne."

Home. It had happened there so fast, the dissolution, Adobe Walls, Hard Stick Canyon, swept along, no time to see, savor it, too caught up to think, to understand. This time an outsider, an observer, can watch it as it occurs. "Old Man, I will travel with you."

When Coyote Dropping arrived with Sitting Bull's people in the camp at the mouth of Cherry Creek, Big Foot was already ill, all the settlers along the river had fled in panic, newspapers spreading wild stories of uprising and blood. People were hungry, they were traveling to Fort Bennett to pick up their annuities, but many counseled it was too dangerous to go on. Hump had gone over to the other side, scouting now for Bear Coat Miles, the army out to get Big Foot just as they had Sitting Bull, why else would Colonel Summer be coming downstream toward them, another patrol making its way upstream behind.

After contentious discussion they decided to turn back to their cabins on the grassy delta where Deep Creek joins the Cheyenne. Sod roofs bristling dead sunflower stalks and pigweed below sharp gray ridges, rough-grooved river bluffs, gullies of dark rusty plum brush. Sitting Bull's people fled in the night. Coyote Dropping stayed. He had come to watch.

Big Foot could not rise from his bed in the morning. Red Beard Dunn, a farmer with a large herd of cattle nearby, came to talk: Colonel Summer had orders to take Big Foot to Fort Bennett, planned to attack at night, take all the men to an island in the eastern sea from which there was no escape.

The council advised they should flee south toward Pine Ridge Reservation, along Deep Creek, and when Summer followed they were convinced Red Beard spoke the truth.

Coyote Dropping rode with them to see. The sky cleared, a strong bone-chill wind rattled down the badlands, the crumbling wall just before the White River. They camped, Big Foot coughing up blood. The wind rose higher in the night, a wild roaring dawn, tipis blown down, alkali dust billowed and swirled, low clouds driven across the gray and red rumpled land. It looked as if the earth itself were falling away.

Then the wind died. It began to warm. A traveler brought word Short Bull and Kicking Bear had given up, were coming in from the stronghold on Cluny Table to the Agency, and General Forsyth's soldiers were waiting for Big Foot's band at Wounded Knee Creek. Yellow Bird, the medicine man, heard an owl call three times as the sun went down.

Big Foot too sick to resist any longer, the people worn out and dispirited from this hopeless flight across the winter prairie, they would meet the soldiers at Wounded Knee.

They arrived at sundown, set up camp along a sheer-sided ravine running from the western ridge to the creek, the cavalry a hundred yards to the north. The army erected five Sibley tents in the open space between: one on the west for the interpreter scouts, one with a stove for Big Foot and the regimental surgeon to tend to him, and the eastern three for those who had no shelter. Coyote Dropping settled in the middle one.

He sat before the flap and watched the full moon rise. The 7th Cavalry, Yellow Hair Custer's old command, arrived from Pine Ridge. The storekeeper Mousseau brought a keg of whiskey, the officers toasted Big Foot's capture. Slowly the orange light faded within the canvas tents and the buffalo-hide tipis in the two camps. A mild night for sleeping.

Coyote Dropping awoke, well rested, a sense of relief after the wild dash over the winter-struck land, the morning sun already filling the tent with a heavy warm aroma of canvas, children laughing and women talking, campfire smoke, coffee, and bacon on the air. A winter day outside, liquid sunshine, gentle currents like summer river water in a pool carved below a northern bluff, an April blossom the middle of December, a temporary seam, an intense honey sweetness, fragile transitoriness, muscles gone slack as the will. Big Foot's weak, wracking cough from the next tent, a storm out there a day beyond the northern horizon, the January blizzard Yellow Bird's owl foretold.

Coyote Dropping strolled through camp. The soldiers lining up, joking, at ease, but an ease resting on taut expectations. He'd seen these men before, not even men, boys, faces like theirs on the corners and stoops, drinking meaningless quantities of spirit water, hopeless, cramped taverns smelling of sour bitter beer, gambling, fighting in the foul back streets, the overcrowded, smoky, stench-filled, brutal hovels of the desperate eastern cities he'd traveled to with Buffalo Bill. What did they know of all this: newspapers and cheap word books, lurid pictures on the covers of murder-crazed savages.

All Big Foot's men were being gathered in the open space between the two camps. Coyote Dropping watched.

General Forsyth greeted them, reassured them, joked, told them they should give up their guns.

"Ah-h-h!"

The stillness of the air became a tension. Smoke rising straight into the sky from the kitchen chimney of Mousseau's store. The men counseled with Big Foot, sitting, barely conscious, between Iron Eyes and Horned Cloud in front of his tent. He spoke, not a whisper, a rasping gurgle.

"Give them the bad ones."

Forsyth is angry, the two rifles brought forward clearly used by children for toys. "Where are your firearms?"

"We gave them up on the Cheyenne, your warrior-brother Summer burned them."

"That's a lie! I saw guns when you surrendered."

The men standing about, milling now, their blankets held tight around what's concealed beneath. Coyote Dropping has come to watch, shifts uneasily in front of the Sibley tent, hand held to shield out the morning sun. Forsyth approaches Big Foot, bends down over him. "I will search your camp."

The soldiers begin rummaging through tipis, pulling women and children from blankets, unwrapping bedrolls, unloading wagons, scattering cooking pots. The sullen men watch, grumble, curse beneath their breath. Yellow Bird walks among them, whispers, the young men bunch together on the eastern margins, Yellow Bird, to the west, raises his arms, the white muslin shirt, painted blue across the back, a yellow line along the side and the spotted eagle, the ghost shirt clearly visible when he drops the blanket from his shoulders to pray. *The ghost shirt stitched tight enough, strong enough, brothers and sisters, to shed all harm!*

Begins to dance a slow circle, chanting, vigorous, quick steps forward, back, then to the side, swoops down to the earth and throws handfuls of dust into the air, the piercing whistle of his eagle bone. Dances through the gathering ground, dust hanging in slanted light, till he comes to the young men on the other side.

"Ahau! I have lived long enough!"

The air like cold wind running before a thunderstorm. "Hau! Hau!"

Two sergeants surround Yellow Bird, tell him to sit, the soldiers deployed to the south and west of the gathering ground, beyond the ravine above the camp, tense, knuckles tight on the stocks and grips of their Sharps rifles. Yellow Bird spins away, silent, a few voiceless incantations. Then sits.

Coyote Dropping, his head beginning to hurt from squinting, sees the search party return, stack old rusty Winchesters before Big Foot's tent. Forsyth had seen good rifles yesterday, orders them all to remove their blankets, he will have the weapons. Yellow Bird leaps to his feet, begins chanting, someone else—who is that, pumping his Winchester over his head?—Black Coyote, deaf as a lodgepole, *it's mine, gave much money for it, I will not give it up!* Somebody else singing now, *Father, give us back our arrows! The soldiers' bullets like dust slung out over the plains, will scatter and drift!*

Black Coyote, always a troublemaker, stops to tear a large strip of paper from a brown bag, trying to roll a cigarette, rifle slung in the crook of his arm, his hunched back turned. The two sergeants jump him, twist, and grapple. The Winchester fires.

A sudden sharp explosion of dust and smoke. Screams. Big Foot struggles to sit up, struck in the head, knocked down next to Iron Eyes and Horned Cloud, Coyote Dropping leaps to his feet, through obscured light toward him, a blow from behind, soft and complete. He is back down on his knees, incredulous, a sphere of receding discharge and outcry, warm thick liquid filling up his shirt, his body a dance beyond control.

Once again it is all happening beyond the grasp of consciousness.

Come spring the Agency sends survivors to Europe with Buffalo Bill's Wild West.

The Last Roundup

Cannonball They call me Snaggle T now. Ever since I got my gold tooth knocked out in the fracas down at Hell's Gate Gulch. And I'm here to tell you, sisters and brothers, things ain't been the same since. A gold tooth not the only thing I lost. My woman's gone, no more longhorn herds to drive, the whole damn land divided up, fenced in, and parceled out, can't pitch a bedroll on the ground without some Easterner or English gentleman's hired hand kicks you in the ass, tells you to move on, posted, no pissing in the bushes.

I tried to get along. I saw the old days dead as a bent branding iron, me and Big Mouth Henry and Sojourner went to work for Brother, the African, and Ninnescah Will on the Perpetual Motion Ranch. Thought we'd at least give it a try, beat the hell out of a plank bed in the hoosegow for cattle rustling. It just didn't work out.

The first time Sojourner laid eyes on Will I knew there was gonna be some damn trouble. I couldn't do nothing but stand there like a wet dog and watch. She kind of squatted down, sniffing and whimpering, wagging her hind quarters like— only one way to put it, brothers and sisters—like a bitch in heat. He sees her and they're all over each other, panting and licking, it got downright embarrassing to look at.

Then there was the ranch work. Don't get me wrong, I can do my share, done a damn sight more than that many a drive, and I did kinda take a liking to Will, had to hand it to him, he ran a mean outfit. It's just that we were all used to being our own boss, knew honest-to-God freedom out on the trail. Now we're dragged about in the noose and kicked about by the spurs of this upstart son of a coyote. We're slaves, no better than cowardly slaves.

I hightailed it out of there. Drifted up toward Denver, met a man worked for the railroad, said there was where the future lay, looking for some good men. So here I am, brothers and sisters, all prettied up in my Pullman car porter's uniform, coast to coast across this great land of ours. What better life, on the road, seeing the sights and hobnobbing with the movers and shakers, the men whose shit don't stink. I've shined J. P. Morgan's shoes and lit the cigar of John D. Rockefeller. Good tip from both of them, too.

I'll admit not quite so exciting as bringing down a longhorn in the coastal brush or a stampede through persimmon along the Canadian. But you get by as best you can.

Now I have heard the stories of Will's demise. Like I told you, I didn't stick around long, so I can't be certain, but I don't believe a word of it. There are those who tell it was smoking that killed him, lots of people preach how unhealthy it is, and that gets my hackles up. You got to remember I got my start raising up tobacco, and I can tell you there's not a more beautiful crop on God's earth, to this day I can still smell it, damp and warm, curing in the barn, a whole world in that aroma. But maybe there is something to what people say. I knew a fellow used to run cows from south Texas, had a little spread north of Brownsville, smoked a sack of Bull Durham a day, and mighty proud of it. Folks always telling him it would kill him, and by God, after seventy-five years of it, he up and died.

And no question about it, Will did smoke. But not Bull Durham, had his own mixture of Kentucky homespun, sulfur, and a pinch of black gunpowder. When matches was short, he'd light up his cigarette with a streak of lightning.

Which reminds me of another story I heard the other day, some Englishman and his daughter, returning from an inspection of property he'd just bought in Stevens County, told me Will had been struck down in an electrical storm. A damn lie! You'll never get me to swallow that one. I know for a fact that a few years back on a bet Will threw a surcingle around a bolt of lightning and rode the son of a bitch all the way over Pike's Peak.

Then there's those try to get you to believe it was liquor killed Will. Now he was a little bad to drink, you can't deny that. I understand he's raised on whiskey and onions before the coyotes carried him off. After he was found and halfway civilized he discovered his natural taste for it hadn't atrophied all those years as a child of nature in the wild, but the store-bought stuff, and even the product of some of the best private stills in all the Oklahoma District, had lost its kick. Got to introducing nitroglycerin into his toddies. That worked for a spell, but then he had to go to wolf bait, from that to number nine fish hooks, the only way he could get an idea from his booze.

But they say that's what proved to be his undoing: over the years the fish hooks rusted out his interior. Another damn lie, sisters and brothers! No doubt concocted by the Women's Christian Temperance Union.

Autumn Tallgrass | I don't know about Ninnescah Will. After I was run off the river, the night Black Woolly disappeared and Brother rescued me from the lynch mob in Blackstrups Mill, I went back to the folk, found Coyote Dropping again. Things fall apart. The battle at Adobe Walls, the slaughter in Hard Stick Canyon, surrender and confinement on Cache Creek, the hunt. Nothing left but to get by as best you can.

Coyote Dropping joined up with Buffalo Bill, became a big man, traveled in the East, sailed across the ocean, knew the Queen of England, the Duke of Russia, and the President of the United States. People said I might as well find me some strapping youngster, too young to know the shame and despair of ruin, set up a tipi along the creek, and show him how it's done. Coyote Dropping not coming home.

Then the story of the massacre at Wounded Knee Creek. I traveled to that desolate place to see for myself. Talked to anyone I could find. It was certain, Coyote Dropping was dead.

Springtime. The land still parched brittle and brown. I decided to return. A crazy idea, but the world is crazy, see if I could find the riverbank where we were camped when I was first brought to the folk, the very spot I first saw Coyote Dropping dance, the clearing where we danced.

Carried off again. This time by my own will, possessed by some spirit guiding me—the same one rode with me from Texas, initiated me to womanhood—clinging to the sweating back of a horse, just like then, I had to have a vision of the sky. Hot. South wind booming across the world, a shimmering, dusty haze, and I see it, the same curve of horizon. Over the embankment, the same magpies rising from the sycamore and cottonwood, sandbars, voices. Campfire smoke. I dismount, push my way through the same underbrush to the same clearing, and there he stood: Brother, surveying the river with Black Woolly and Ninnescah Will. This was the land the Ole Woman had claimed.

Whatever life I have left lies with the folk scattered in cabins and huts along Cache Creek. Teach the language that will keep the ancestors alive, and the one that will keep us alive. And maybe that young strapping boy in his canvas tent.

I don't know what happened to Ninnescah Will.

I did hear it told, though, he was done in by coyotes. Him and his horse. His own kith and kin killed them both, devoured their carcasses. Blamed him. Turned on him for bringing civilization to the plains.

The African I know what happened to the boy, all right. He the reason I left out of there. Who'd have ever thought I'd end up going back to Mississippi. After all those years of delicious solitude, right back in the ass of it. Jim Crow.

When Brother sold off his half of the place to the English gentleman, I couldn't run my spread by myself anymore, not as young and spry as I once was. The Englishman putting pressure on me to sell, diverting the creek water, his cows tramping through my truck garden. Then I lost Sojourner. The only one of my five children I had any idea of where she's at, even though she didn't consider me anymore her mother than she did the barnyard dog. In fact, looked like she was closer to the dog than to me. What else could I do.

Then that good-for-nothing cowboy, the one I call Snaggle T, the one I blame for Sojourner being so wild—know the coyotes taught her better manners than she showed after traveling with him—then he told me about Spartacus. Good Lord Almighty, I hadn't thought about that man in years. Like the prairie sun had burned ever last vestige of my Mississippi life right on out of me, melted me down, and cast me into the mold of the plains, the notion of me and a man in Mississippi as fabulous as King Solomon and the Queen of Sheba.

Snaggle T told me how Spartacus traveled all this way through misery and fever looking after me, and how he found Sojourner. Told me how crushed he was that she paid him no mind. His hard journey, his past life in Mississippi meant no more to her than the urine sprayed on a limestone corner post by some passing hound-dog stray. And how he come so damn close to finding me but turned back, his spirit broke in No Man's Land, only miles away. Well. It moved me. Guess a sign I'm getting old, the past come back all of a sudden vivid like that, push the present moment right on out. Specially when that moment as sorrowful as it was.

But all the tangled knot of memories couldn't prepare me for the shock—that's the only way I can put it—the shock of seeing Mississippi again. The air was muggy, good Lord Almighty, like to choke me to death, the heavy sultry smell of mud enough to put you to your knees, but at the same time like some magic incense conjuring up a powerful life once lived, a world long ago gone. I climb off that packet steamer at the landing and see all those black folks, the dockhands, the men working in the warehouses, the draymen and porters, swear I'd fallen asleep and the boat sailed plumb to Africa. I'd forgotten what it was like being among my own people. Among people of any kind, come to think on it.

My soul was a jumble. I asked the way to where Spartacus's sister and brother-in-law lived, lucky I remembered his old master's name, even after all these years. Found a woman cooking in the kitchen of an inn close to the river knew exactly who I was talking about, told me all there was to know about Spartacus.

"Yes indeed, the man left out of here during the exodus fever years ago, and after everybody figure him for dead he straggles home again, not too many months back, telling all sorts of wild tales about life on the open range. Still staying with his sis, and if you don't mind waiting around a bit till I finish up here, I'm heading that way myself, take you right to the front door. You know, that Spartacus never was the same ever since his woman and all the children disappeared way back in slavery times. Not that times have changed all that damn much now. A crying shame to see a good man pine away like that, don't know what made him so damn sure in the first place those children his, comely house nigger like she was. But they say that's where he's been all these years, out in Kansas looking for that woman. I always said he'd have more luck at

278

the bottom of the creek run past the four corners where they were to meet. That's where she's at—that is, unless she and ever one of those five kids been washed all the way to New Orleans. Come a hell of a rainstorm that night, I know it drowned them all. Shame to see a good man waste away longing for that woman."

"I'm that woman."

She stops, wipes her hands on her apron, looking at all the fine new clothing I'd bought in St. Louis. Like she's not only just seen a ghost but one that's a damn liar too. "Good Lawsy. It goes to show you. There's just no way of telling what peculiar twists this old world is going to take."

When I come near that old weatherboard cabin I was numb with fright, the chickens in the bare yard scattered from me, even the hogs squealed and banged against the sides of the pens among the shagbark hickory trees the other side of the house. I smelled tobacco, yams, collard greens, and pork. It was Sunday afternoon. Then I heard a booming deep laugh. It was Brother-in-law, I knew it, knew him, though I'd never laid eyes on the man in all my born days, hadn't even much thought of Mississippi in over thirty years, but it all came back in that laughter Spartacus had told me about when we'd cuddle in the old mildewy wagon sheet and leaves in the hollowed-out log lean-to in the woods where we used to run off and meet. Dumbstruck. Confused. Afraid to take those last few steps around the corner of this strange dwelling, face-to-face with a past I'd forgotten I'd had, refused to think about, even if I'd of had the time and energy out on the grasslands. The man's been pining all this time, and I don't even remember what he looked like when he was young and strong. Yet here I am, compelled by circumstance and maybe even a desire I carried hidden all these years, who was it and what was it I thought about during those stifling prairie nights when the wind moaned so loud I couldn't sleep, and the emptiness of my bed extended clear on out to the dark horizon. Here I am standing right in the middle of a Mississippi yard dressed in my store-bought clothes, coming home to meet the folks.

The first one I saw was a big man, hair white as cotton bolls ready for picking around his shiny pate, black as Mississippi bottomland, a starched white collar and tie still on, and protruding from his cuffs two large cold iron hooks. They all grew quiet when they saw me appear in the middle of their Sunday afternoon, the woman beside him looked familiar, and then, at the edge, remote and motionless in an old rocking chair, I saw Spartacus. And he saw me.

For a moment it was hard to tell who was going to break and run first, me or him. He stood up and looked for the back door, I glanced around at the front. Him standing there wondering, it appeared to me, just who the hell he'd been chasing after for what seemed to be all his life, and me realizing that this was it, one way or the other, no place left to go. Then Brother-in-law and Sis both boomed out laughing at the same time, gathered us up in a communal embrace: *the Lord does truly move in mischievous ways his connivance to perform.*

When I talked to them later, after dinner, around the old table, wisps of coffee-cup vapor in the warm room walled with grainy worn boards catching shadow and light from the kerosene lamp, because they asked about my travels and the danger, I didn't know how to frighten them, with what sudden word to move them so they could see, like me, the wind, the rising of that moon that made the danger turn. It wasn't in the raging and the roar. Soundlessly it overcame the witnesses, surrounded by a stillness that contained the entire prairie, drifted about the horse, his ears laid back against his head, the rider. How could I make them—make him, Spartacus—see how Sojourner died.

Like I said, we never got along as mother and daughter. It was Will she was drawn to, and he to her, although that didn't keep him from sniffing around every other female come into the vicinity, including the daughter of the Englishman who came out wanting to buy ranchland, so I knew it was a mistake to be talking about marriage. What did either of them know about it, or any of us, me or Brother, when you get right down to it. But there was no denying the two of them were closer than unrelated people ought to be, and it was finally decided, for no other good reason than to try and avoid the shame and the scandal of their carrying on—I mean you never knew what you might come upon those two doing any time of day or night, anyplace on the spread; the barn, the creek, the kitchen, or in the outhouse—it was agreed Ninnescah Will and Sojourner ought to be man and wife.

Sojourner was wild and unruly, the handler of horses on the high plains and all the other animals too. One time we were all out fishing and she reached in under the bank and noodled out a hundred-and-fifty-pound mud cat, jumped on that monster's back, and rode it down the Cimarron halfway to No Man's Land. But the main thing she wanted to ride was Will's horse, Widow Maker. And he wouldn't let her, said it was too dangerous, and that made her all the more set upon doing it. Finally he gave in, said she could try after they were married.

It was some ceremony. The preacher came out from town, Will wearing a large Stetson with a Mexican beadwork band, a white silk shirt, and a red satin vest, his coat covered with delicate quilling, had on California breeches, lavender with inch-square checks, his polished hand-stitched high-heel boots, and golden spurs. Instead of a best man Will had Widow Maker by his side, and Sojourner had the barnyard hound as maid of honor. I'm pretty sure this affair not doing much to calm the scandal amongst the town folks and neighbors.

It was right at sundown. A hot dry wind blowing so hard from the south you couldn't hear a word of what anybody said, kicking up dust and dried cow manure, so the reverend cut his remarks short and got right to the point. After they'd been pronounced wed, instead of kissing the groom, Sojourner bolted from the corral, where the whole thing took place, disappeared into the house, and before anyone could even say what the hell that girl up to, was out again, wearing a big sombrero, woolen shirt, and cowskin vest pulled over her wedding attire, high-heeled boots ever bit the match of Will's in elaborate needlework, and spurs.

"Ee-yow!"

Heads straight for Widow Maker, still standing in the reception line by the platter of fresh-fried bear sign set up downwind of the granary, leaps on his back before anybody could do anything to stop her. The wind blowing to beat the band, dust turning the enormous rippling moon fire red at the horizon. But a chamber of silence seems to loom about the horse and rider in the very middle of the corral, an ominous stillness embedded in turbulence all around. Widow Maker's ears lie back flat against his head. Then he springs like a young cat surprised by a hog snake, ten feet straight up into the sky, lands on all fours, snorts, looks over his shoulder, an aston-ished double-take, Sojourner still there. Snorts again and shakes his head, charges the fence, clears it by three and a half hands, and gallops for the open road.

The wind collapses around us, like water after the dam bursts. We all jump on horses, into wagons, take out on foot in pursuit. Give chase all the way to Moon Center, where Widow Maker seems to decide straight running isn't going to catch it, skids to a halt between the boardwalks fronting the saloon on one side and the post office and general store on the other, and breaks into a complicated exposition of bucking. Sojourner hanging right in there with him, but damn if it didn't look like, in her haste to get at that stallion, she'd forgotten to take the steel spring bustle from up under her wedding dress. She com-mences to bounce, harder and higher, hanging on now to the end of the mane with her fingertips. Widow Maker spins, col-lects himself for one last mincing step, syncopated to throw Sojourner off her timing, and a final buck, a loud, frightening *boing*, and she is launched, it looks like, clear above the rooftop of the tavern into the face of the moon.

We all rushed to where Sojourner lay. Will dropped down beside her, nudged her chin with his nose, licked her cheek, whimpered and whined, threw back his head and let out a bone-chilling howl, yip-yip yowls whipped from his mouth by the wind out across the land like bounding tumbleweeds. The mournful cry of coyotes rose up all around Moon Center, com-memorating the death of one of their own.

Will finally stood and walked away, down the dusty street, out onto the dark plains, the lone grasslands, the flat solid platform of the world.

Crawled into a prairie-dog hole and died of solemncholy.

Brother | Most people in these parts thought they were beasts. Had to hand it to them, though, Sojourner knew her horses and Will his cows. We ran the most successful ranch in the state, maybe even the entire country. They had to give Will that. Probably envy got them started talking. Once they were sure he was dead.

He never did fit in with other folk. What do you expect with a life like the one he had, we'd done our best to teach him, but ever since I rescued him from that creek bank he'd been kind of a loner. Not really close to anybody but me and Sojourner in the end, talked very little to me and didn't have to to her. Couldn't sit around the stove at the general store and spin yarns, and while his mind worked in ways other humans could hardly grasp, you couldn't really call him quick-witted, sharp-tongued with a storehouse of windies to get him through the difficult church socials and barn dances. His behavior around women left a lot to be desired. Or should I say tried to leave nothing to be desired, damn near got himself killed any number of times and came close to ruining the deal to sell the ranch. So I suppose it was to be expected that after he died people would start telling lies about him.

Said he was mean, nasty-tempered. Even went so far as to call him a killer. Said after the hands taught him to use a gun he got downright dangerous to be around. Never knew when he'd draw on you, spring out at you like a cat hiding behind a hay bale, use the can of tomatoes in your hand for target practice, the eyelashes of your horse, the cigarette dangling from your mouth. Said he shot Pigmeat Malone in his sleep for snoring on a drive to the railhead. Said he killed Ris Risbone too. The man always was a clown, had a great repertoire of jokes, some two dozen in all, would laugh and slap his knee anytime he pulled one, and one day he caught Will asleep in the shade of the chuck wagon, his head between the wheels. Ris snuck up and rattled the trace chains, yelling *Whoa! Whoa!* Will thought the team was throwing a runaway, jumped up, and banged his head on the bottom of the wagon box. Ris just stood there laughing and slapping his knee. A few weeks later, after they'd delivered the herd to Dodge City and Will and the boys had gone down to the White Elephant to cut the alkali dust from their throats, right after Will had dropped the fish-hooks into his whiskey, the place so crowded you didn't need a stool to sit down, Ris Risbone sticks his head in at the window and yells: *Fire!*

And Will did.

People will tell you any damn thing.

Will did have a lot to be mean-spirited about. In that respect you could see he was some kin to the Ole Woman and, I guess you'd have to say, to me. The range was getting too crowded, too many hoemen, bankers, lawyers, railroad people, and preachers. Ranching being turned into something it never was and, if you ask me, never should have been: the cattle industry instead of the cattle kingdom. People wanting to make a living replaced by people out to make a killing. Fences, breeding, damn bull has to have a pedigree before he ever gets a shot at a cow, and before you know it his owner has to have one too. Too many Easterners and foreigners, aristocracy's second sons, moving in. And what makes it all the worse to bear, we have to admit that we were the ones responsible for it, the innovators so successful it drew all these money-grabbing investors out here where they'd never dreamed of setting foot before, their heads full of dime novels and their pockets full of change. Just like what happened to the towns and cities, and to the churches, on the eastern plains. That's what stuck in Will's craw, I think. Sure as hell what stuck in mine. And the other night, about the time I'd finished reading the *Cattleman's Gazette* and was fixing to blow out the kerosene lamp, I thought I heard a tornado churning across the south pasture. Headed out for the cellar, halfway down the stairs before I realized it was nothing but the Ole Woman turning over in her grave.

I remember once, shortly before Will died, I happened upon him and Sojourner. A long summer evening, out on the highland a couple miles from the river, I was approaching from downwind, they didn't hear or smell me coming. Lying on the ground, Will on his back, Sojourner cuddled up beside him. Naked. Could tell by the way they snuggled and fondled they'd just finished coupling. Like the wild animals they still were, yet different. I stood there watching them. They sniffed, chortled, woofed, and wooed, the grass, the summer drought, the low sun, a burning gold scrim of dust. Could imagine the prairie looked then just like it had before the first Asians ventured out onto it: all of us, the Asians, the Africans, the Ole Woman, Will, Sojourner, all of us reaped and winnowed on this enormous thrashing floor, broken loose from history it seemed, annihilated, made over, the troubles, suffering, the absolute beauty of it stronger than any bonds to anything that came before. It isn't blood that makes us all brothers and sisters, it's the distances, bluestem and grama grass, prickly pear, wind and thunderstorm, grasshopper, coyote, antelope, turkey vulture, and the red-tailed hawk.

But then I looked closer. In the lengthening shadows, the long straight lines of fence post and barbed wire. Then, carried on warm summer air, a windmill creaking, clanking from the river bottoms, and the baleful whistle of a train.

I don't care what stories you've heard, I'll tell you what happened to Will. It was when I decided to sell the place. I had wanted to keep it at first, continue the work the Ole Woman started. Despite the big blizzard of '81—killed most of our cows, the beginning of the end to look back on it—despite the drought didn't seem like would ever be broken, despite the people sniffing around looking for petroleum oozing out of the ground. I'd always had it in my head that I'd settle here, raise a family, that this land would be ours forever. When I thought of it, it would be Prissy Blackstrup who came to mind as wife and mother, the way she taught Will back then, the time we'd spent together. She'd never left my imagination from that first day in the rain-soaked dugout, still feel her thigh pressed against mine, she'd haunted me from that last day, still see her and Will together in the barn, still hear her curse me when she fled. I even made a trip back east to Blackstrups Mill to try to find her. Her old man was dead. She'd left and gone to Wichita. Married a preacher, the star of a splendid church built downtown, dressed in fine silk dresses, a fringed carriage with rubber tires. I stood across the street Sunday morning and watched her greet the worshipers after the service, her husband's droning sermon, the powers that be of the town, bankers and merchants, and the wives and children, saw the prideful, lust-filled glance of the pastor by her side. I wanted her to be happy but still read that constant sadness I'd seen the first time in her eyes when she came to me in the molasses shed. Maybe it was just mine reflected back.

I put the Perpetual Motion Ranch up for sale. Didn't make any sense trying to keep it, worth a lot more on the market than we'd ever make cutting hay and raising cows, and if there were fools enough to pay that much money for it, I'd be a fool not to take it. I didn't tell Will what I was up to. When he saw the first prospective buyer coming along the lane, a Boston man decked out in his brand-new mail-order cowboy outfit, he just laughed himself to death.